22.95

BLOODY MARY

ALSO BY J. A. KONRATH:

Whiskey Sour

A Jacqueline "Jack" Daniels Mystery

BLOODY MARY

J. A. KONRATH

HYPERION NEW YORK

The Lt. Jacqueline "Jack" Daniels mystery series is not sponsored by, endorsed by, or related to Jack Daniel's Properties, Inc., makers of Jack Daniel's Tennessee Whiskey.

ISBN: 1-4013-0089-8

Hyperion books are available for special promotions and premiums. For details contact Michael Rentas, Assistant Director, Inventory Operations, Hyperion, 77 West 66th Street, 11th floor, New York, New York 10023, or call 212-456-0133.

FIRST EDITION

10 9 8 7 6 5 4 3 2 1

This book is for Laura Konrath, whom I'm honored, blessed, and tickled pink to call Mom.

I love you.

ACKNOWLEDGMENTS

So many people to thank . . .

To fellow writers Raymond Benson, Jay Bonansinga, Doug Borton, David Ellis, Eric Garcia, Rick Hautala, Libby Fischer Hellmann, Warren B. Murphy, Ridley Pearson, James Rollins, Steven Spruill, Andrew Vachss, F. Paul Wilson, David Wiltse, and especially Robert W. Walker, for their words, encouragement, and inspiration.

To my advance readers: Marc Buhmann, Jim Coursey, Laura Konrath, and authors Barry Eisler and Rob Kantner, for their comments, opinions, and assistance in making this book better.

To my family, friends, and those who went the extra mile: Robin Agnew, Lorri Amsden, Chris Bowman, Bonnie Claeson, Latham Conger III, Tom & Melanie Meyers Cushman, George Dailey, Moni Draper, Judy Duhl, Mariel Evens, Dick File, Holly Frakes, Maggie Griffin, Joe Guglielmelli, Maryelizabeth Hart, Jim Huang, Steve Jensen, Jen Johnson, Steve Jurczyk, Edmund and Jeannie Kaufman, Chris Konrath, John Konrath, Talon Konrath, Steve Lukac, Sheldon MacArthur, Otto Penzler, Barbara Peters, Sue Petersen, Terri Smith, Dave Strang,

Jim & Gloria Tillez, Chris Wolak, and the many others who have helped out on this journey.

To Officer Jim Doherty for police questions, Jeffrey Evens for law questions, and Mike Konrath, whom I hope one day will embalm me, but not in the manner described in this book. Any technical mistakes in this book are mine, not theirs.

To the publishing folks: Michael Bourrett, Jane Comins, Jane Dystel, Miriam Goderich, Jessica Goldman, Eileen Hutton, Navorn Johnson, Elisa Lee, David Lott, Karin Maake, Joni Rendon, and Leslie Wells, who continues to be the world's best editor.

And of course, to my rock, Maria. Every day with you is a day worth living.

BLOODY MARY

1½ oz. vodka

4 oz. tomato juice

1 tsp. Worcestershire sauce

Several drops of Tabasco sauce

Shake well over ice and strain into an old-fashioned glass.

Add a celery stalk.

PROLOGUE

"It would be so easy to kill you while you sleep."

He rolls onto his side and faces his wife, tangling his fingers in her hair. Her face is shrouded in a dried blue mask; an antiaging beauty product that has begun to peel. The moonlight peeking through the bedroom curtains makes her look already dead.

He wonders if other people look at their partners at night, peacefully dozing, and imagine killing them.

"I have a knife." He brushes his fingertips along her hairline. "I keep it under the bed."

Her lips part and she snores softly.

So ugly, especially for a model. All capped teeth and streaked hair.

He wedges his hand between the mattress and box spring and pulls out the knife. It has a large wooden handle, disproportionate to the thin, finely honed blade. A fillet knife.

He places it against his wife's neck, gently.

His vision blurs. The pain in his head ignites, a screw twisting into his temple. It tightens with every heartbeat.

Too many headaches in too many days. He should, will, tell the doctor. The six aspirin he took an hour ago haven't helped.

Only one thing helps when the pain gets this bad.

He caresses her chin with the edge of the knife, shaving off some of the mask. Sweat rolls down his forehead and stings his eyes.

"I can cut your throat, reach in and rip out your voice before you even have a chance to scream."

She twitches, her head tilting away. Her neck is smooth, flawless. He clenches his jaw hard enough to crush granite, teeth grinding teeth.

"Or maybe I should go through the eye. Just a quick poke, right into the brain."

He raises the blade up, trying to control the trembling in his hand. The blade wavers over her lid, creeping closer.

"All you have to do is open your eyes, so you can see it coming."

She snores.

"Come on, honey." He nudges her shoulder. "Open your eyes."

He bites down on his tongue, the inside of his mouth hot and salty. His brain is a tiny clawed demon trying to dig its way out.

"Open your goddamn eyes!"

She shifts toward him, mumbling. Her arm falls over his bare chest.

"Another headache, honey?"

"Yeah."

He places the knife behind her head, at the base of her skull. He imagines jabbing it in, the tip poking through the front of her throat.

Wouldn't she be surprised?

"Poor baby," she says into his armpit. She rubs his cheek, her fingers cool against his burning ear.

He gives her a little prod with the knife, just under her hairline. Her head jerks away.

"Ow! Honey, cut your nails."

"It's not my nails, dear. It's a knife."

She snores her response.

He nudges her again. "I said, *It's a knife.* You hear me?"

"Did you take some aspirin, baby?"

"Six."

"They'll work soon. You should see a doctor."

She hooks a leg over his stomach. He feels himself become aroused, unsure if it's her touch that's causing it, or the thought of peeling off her face.

Or perhaps both.

He smiles in the darkness, knuckles white on the knife handle, ready to finally give in to the nightly temptation. But as he readies the blade, he notes that the pain in his head has begun to subside. Gradually, the sharp throbbing melts away into a dull ache.

Bearable.

For now.

"I'll kill you tomorrow." He kisses her on the scalp.

The knife goes back under the mattress. He holds her tight and she makes a happy sighing sound.

When he finally falls asleep, it's to the image of cutting her open and bathing his face with her blood.

CHAPTER 1

"Dammit."

My fan had died. It didn't surprise me. The fan had ten years on me, and I came into the world during the Eisenhower years. It belonged in a museum, not an office.

Today was the first day of July, and hot enough to cook burgers on the sidewalk, though you probably wouldn't want to eat them afterward. My blouse clung to me, my nylons felt like sweatpants, and I'd developed a fatal case of the frizzies.

The 26th Police District of Chicago, where I slowly roasted, was temporarily without air-conditioning due to a problem with the condensers, whatever the hell they were. We were promised it would be fixed by December.

I hit the base of the fan with my stapler. Though I was the highest ranking female cop in the Violent Crimes Unit, I tended to be useless mechanically. My handyperson skills maxed out at changing a lightbulb. And even then, I had to read the instructions. The fan seemed to sense this, slowly wagging its blades at me like dusty tongues.

My partner, Detective First Class Herb Benedict, walked into my office, sucking on a soda cup the size of a small garbage can. It didn't seem to be helping him cool off. Herb weighed about two hundred and sixty pounds, and had more pores on his face than I had on my whole body. Benedict's suit looked like it had been soaked in Lake Michigan and put on wet.

He waddled up and placed a moist palm on my desk, leaving a streak. I noticed droplets in his gray mustache; sweat or diet cola. His basset hound jowls glistened as if greased.

"Morning, Jack."

My birth name was Jacqueline, but when I married my ex-husband, Alan Daniels, no one could resist shortening it to Jack.

"Morning, Herb. Here to help me fix my fan?"

"Nope. I'm here to share my breakfast."

Herb set a brown paper sack on my desk.

"Donuts? Bagels? Cholesterol McMuffins?"

"Not even close."

Benedict removed a plastic bag containing, of all things, rice cakes.

"That's it?" I asked. "Where's the chocolate? Where's the canned cheese?"

"I'm watching my weight. In fact, I joined a health club."

"You're kidding."

"You know the one that advertises on TV all the time?"

"The one where you get to work out with all of those Olympic body-builders for only thirty bucks a month?"

"That's the one. Except I've got the Premier Membership, not the normal one."

"What's the difference?"

He named a monetary figure, and I whistled at the amount.

"But with it, I get full access to the racquetball and squash courts."

"You don't play racquetball or squash."

"Plus, my membership card is colored gold instead of blue."

I leaned back in my chair, interlacing my fingers behind my head. "Well, that's different. I'd pay extra for that. How is the place?"

"I haven't worked out there yet. Everyone that goes is in such good shape, I thought I should lose a few pounds before I start."

"I don't think they'd care, Herb. And if they do, just impress them by flashing your gold card."

"You're not being very supportive here, Jack."

"Sorry." I picked up a file to fan myself. "It's the heat."

"You need to get in shape. I've got guest passes. They've got Pilates at the club. I'm thinking of taking a class after work."

Herb smiled, biting into a rice cake. His smile faded as he chewed.

"Damn. These things taste like Styrofoam."

The phone rang.

"Jack? Phil Blasky. There's, um, a bit of a situation here at County."

County meant the Cook County Morgue. Phil was the Chief Medical Examiner.

"I know this is going to sound like a paperwork problem . . ." He paused, sucking in some air through his teeth. ". . . but I've checked and double-checked."

"What's wrong, Phil?"

"We have an extra body. Well, actually, some extra body parts."

Phil explained. I told him we'd stop by, and then shared the information with Herb.

"Could be some kind of prank. County are a strange bunch."

"Maybe. Phil doesn't think so."

"Did he say what the extra parts were?"

"Arms."

Benedict thought this over.

"Maybe someone is simply lending him a hand."

I stood up and pinched the center of my blouse, fanning in some air. "We'll take your car."

Herb recently bought a sporty new Camaro Z28, an expensive reminder of his refusal to age gracefully. Silly as he looked behind the wheel, the car had great air-conditioning, whereas my 1988 Nova did not.

We left my office and made our way downstairs and outside. It was like stepping into a toaster. Though it couldn't have been much hotter than the district building, the blistering sun amplified everything. A bank across the street flashed the current temp on its sidewalk sign. *One hundred and one.* And the sign was in the shade.

Herb pressed a gizmo on his key chain and his car beeped and started on its own. It was red, naturally, and so heavily waxed that the glare coming off it hurt my eyes. I climbed in the passenger side and angled both vents on my face while Herb babied the Camaro out of its parking space.

"Zero to sixty in five point two seconds."

"Have you taken it up to sixty yet?"

"I'm still breaking it in."

He put on a pair of Ray-Bans and pulled onto Addison. I closed my eyes and luxuriated in the cool air. We were at County all too soon.

Cook County Morgue was located on Harrison in Chicago's medical district, near Rush-Presbyterian Hospital. It rose two stories, all dirty white stone and tinted windows. Herb pulled around back into a circular driveway, and parked next to the curb.

"I hate coming here." Herb frowned, his mustache drooping like a walrus. "I can never get the smell out of my clothes."

Years ago, when my mother walked a beat, cops would smear whiskey on their upper lip to combat the stench of the morgue.

Sanitation had improved since then; cooler temps, better ventilation, greater attention to hygiene. But the smell still stuck with you.

I made do with some cherry lip balm, a small dab under each nostril. I passed the tube to Herb.

"Cherry? Don't you have menthol?"

"It's a hundred degrees out. I wasn't worried about windburn."

He sniffed the balm, then handed it back without applying any.

"It smells too good. I'd eat it."

The heat hit me like a blow dryer when I got out of the car.

A cop walked over and eyed the Camaro—there were always cops around County. He was young and tan and didn't give me a second glance, preferring to talk to Herb.

"Five speed?"

"Six. Three hundred ten horses."

The uniform whistled, running his finger along some pinstriping.

"What's under the hood, five point seven?"

Herb nodded. "Want to see?"

I left the boys with their toy and walked into the entrance, to the right of the automatic double doors.

The lobby, if you could call it that, consisted of a counter, a door, and a glass partition. Behind the counter was a solitary black man in hospital scrubs.

"Phil Blasky?"

He shot his thumb at the door. "In the fridge."

I signed in, received a plastic badge, and entered the main room.

Death overpowered the cherry, so strong I could taste it in the back of my mouth. It had a sickly-sour smell, like rotting carnations.

To the right, a mortician in an ill-fitting suit hefted a body off a table and onto a rolling cot. When he finished, he pulled off his latex gloves and shot them, rubber-band-style, into a garbage can.

Next to him, resting on a stainless steel scale built into the floor, was a naked male corpse, grossly obese, with burns covering most of his torso. The LCD screen on the wall blinked *450 lbs.* He smelled like bacon.

I held my breath and pulled open the heavy aluminum door, which led into the cooler.

The stench worsened in here. Bleach and blood and urine and meat gone bad.

Cook County Morgue was the largest in the Midwest. Indigents, unclaimed bodies, accident victims, suicides, and cases of foul play all came through these doors. It held about three hundred bodies.

Just my luck, they were running at capacity.

To my left, corpses lay stacked on wire shelves warehouse-style, five high and thirty wide. Stretching across the main floor was a traffic jam of tables and carts, all occupied. Some of the dead were covered with black plastic bags. Some weren't.

Unlike movie depictions of morgues, these bodies didn't lie down in peaceful, supine positions. Many of them had kept the poses they died in; arms and legs jutting out, curled up on their sides, necks at funny angles. They also didn't look like a Hollywood conception of a corpse. A real dead person had very little color. Regardless of race, the skin always seemed to fade into a light blue, and the eyes were dull and cloudy, like dusty snow globes.

The temperature hovered at fifty degrees, fans blowing around the frigid, foul air. It chilled my sweat in a most unpleasant way.

To the right, in an adjacent room, an autopsy was being performed. I focused on the figure holding the bone saw, didn't recognize him, and continued to look around.

I found Phil Blasky near the back of the room, and walked up to him carefully; the floors were sticky with various fluids, and all of them clashed with my Gucci pumps.

"Phil."

"Jack."

Phil was leaning over a steel table, squinting at something. I stood next to him, trying not to gape at the nude body of a toddler, half wrapped in a black plastic bag, lying next to him. The child was so rigid and pale, he appeared to be made out of wax.

"I went through every stiff in the place a second time. No one is missing arms."

I glanced down at the table. The arms were severed at the shoulder, laid out with their fingertips touching, the elbows bending in a big *M.* They belonged to a female, Caucasian, with fake pink nails. A pair of black handcuffs connected them at the wrists. There was very little blood, but the jagged edges to the wounds suggested they didn't come off easily.

"I suspect an axe." Phil poked at the wound with a gloved finger. "See the mark along the humerus, here? It took two swings to sever the appendage."

"It doesn't look humorous to me." Benedict had snuck up behind us.

"Funny," Phil said. "Never heard that one before, working with dead bodies for twenty years. Next will you make some kind of *gimme a hand* joke?"

"I did that one already," Herb said. "How about: *It appears the suspect has been disarmed?*"

"She was always such a cut-up?"

"Would you like a shoulder to cry on?"

"Can I go out on a limb here?"

"At least she'll get severance pay?"

Phil cocked an eyebrow at Herb.

"Severance?" Herb said. "Sever?"

I tuned out their act and got a closer look at the arms. Snapping on a latex glove, I pushed back the cold, hard fingers and peered at the handcuffs. They were Smith and Wesson model number 100.

"Those are police issue." Benedict poked at them with a pencil. "I've got a set just like them."

So did every other cop in our district, and probably in Chicago. They were also sold at sporting goods stores, sex shops, and Army/Navy surplus outlets, plus a zillion places over the Internet. Impossible to trace. But maybe we'd get lucky and the owner had etched his name and address on the . . .

I inhaled sharply.

This couldn't be right.

On the cuffs, next to the keyhole, were two small initials painted in red nail polish. I tugged out my .38, holstered under my blazer, and looked at the butt. It had the same two red letters.

JD.

"Herb." I kept my voice steady. "Those handcuffs are mine."

CHAPTER 2

I treated the morgue like a crime scene, calling in the CSU, cordoning off the area, gathering a list of employees to question.

No one had seen anything.

The Crime Scene Unit, consisting of Officer Dan Rogers—tall, blond, goatee—on samples and Officer Scott Hajek—short and compact, blue eyes hidden behind glasses—on photographs. They were young, but knew their stuff.

Rogers scanned the arms with an ALS, and they glowed flawlessly pale under the high-intensity light.

"Not a thing." Rogers scratched at his beard.

Unusual. Under Alternate Light Source, even the tiniest bit of foreign matter glowed like a hot coal. Particles, hair, dirt, bone fragments, blood, semen, bruises, bite marks—they all fluoresced.

Dan bent down, his nose to one of the wrists.

"They've been washed. Smells like bleach."

"Are you sure? The whole morgue smells like bleach."

Rogers, in a move characteristic of his thoroughness, touched the tip of his tongue to the arm.

"Tastes like bleach too. Probably diluted with water, or it would have mottled the skin."

"Get a sample to burn. And go brush your teeth."

Rogers dug into his breast pocket for some cinnamon gum. After popping three pieces, he moved the soft blue light closer to the fingers on the right hand.

"I have a slight indentation on the index finger. Looks like she usually wore a ring."

Hajek brushed past me, zooming in on the fingers. He snapped a close-up.

"I missed the taste test." He playfully shoved Rogers. "Can I get one with you sucking on the fingers?"

Rogers showed him a finger of a different kind. Hajek's shutter clicked.

"When you're done scraping the fingernails, I need one of the fakes."

"Finished already, Lieut."

Rogers snapped off a pink press-on nail, bagged it, and handed it to me. Then he used a scalpel to take skin samples from each arm, putting them into glass tubes.

"Nothing on the handcuffs?"

"Wiped clean. I can take them back and fume them to make sure."

"Do it. You'll need these."

I took the cuff keys from my ring, where they'd been attached for the last year. Rogers undid the handcuffs and placed them in an evidence bag. Then he brought the ALS around.

"No abrasions on the wrist."

Hajek moved in, shooting a few frames.

"Thanks, guys," I said. "If you can get the pictures on my desk tomorrow, along with the prints."

"I'm on it."

Rogers dug into his bag, removing fingerprint ink and two sets of cards. I left him to his work and went off in search of Herb.

Benedict stood in the lobby, talking to one of the attendants. Herb's hand cradled a snack-size potato chip bag, half full. The other half was in his mouth.

He must have noticed the question on my face when I approached, because he said, "They're fat-free."

"Herb—it's a morgue."

"My Pilates instructor told me to eat small snacks several times a day to keep my metabolism up."

He offered the bag.

"Try one. They're baked. One-third less sodium too."

I politely declined. "Get anything?"

"They run three eight-hour shifts, twenty-four hours. I questioned the four attendants here, and no one saw anything. Full list of employees is in my pocket."

"Won't help."

The thin black man standing next to Herb offered his hand. I took it.

"And why won't it help, Mr. . . . ?"

"Graves. Carl Graves. All them bodies come here in bags. Cops and EMTs wrap them up before dropping them off. Be real easy to put some extra parts in a bag, wheel it in, then sneak them out. No one would see a thing."

"How many bodies are dropped off every day?"

"Depends. Sometimes, five or six. Sometimes, a few dozen."

"Who has access to the morgue?"

"Cops, docs, morticians. Some days fifty people sign in."

"How many employees?"

"Around twenty, with the ME's staff."

I frowned. If the arms had been here for a few days before being discovered, we could be dealing with several hundred suspects.

"Thanks, Mr. Graves." I handed him my card. "If you hear anything, let us know."

Graves nodded, walked off.

"Anything with the arms?" Herb asked, lips flecked with bits of greasy potato.

"Nothing, other than the fact that they're my handcuffs."

"Should I read you your rights?"

"Not yet. First you have to trick me into confessing."

"Gotcha. So . . . was the rest of the body hard to dispose of?"

"Yeah. I'll never get those stains out of my carpet."

My cell rang, saving me from further interrogation.

"Daniels."

"Ms. Daniels? This is Dr. Evan Kingsbury at St. Mary's Hospital in Miami. Mary Streng was just admitted into the Emergency Room. You're listed on her insurance as a contact."

My heart dropped into my stomach.

"She's my mother. What happened?"

"She's sedated. I know you're in Chicago, but is it possible for you to get here? She needs you right now."

CHAPTER 3

I hadn't realized how fragile my mother had become until I saw her in that hospital bed, an IV cruelly jabbed into her pale, thin arm. She couldn't weigh more than a hundred pounds, eyes that were once bright and active now sunken and sparkless.

This couldn't be the woman who raised me, the tough-but-loving beat cop who played both mother and father in my upbringing. The woman who taught me how to read and how to shoot. The woman with such inner strength that I modeled my life on hers.

"The doctors are overreacting, Jacqueline. I'll be fine." She offered a weak smile in a voice that wasn't hers.

"Your hip is broken, Mom. You almost died."

"Didn't come close."

I held her hand, feeling the fragile bones under the skin. My veneer started to crack.

"If Mr. Griffin hadn't made the police break down your door, you'd still be lying on the bathroom floor."

"Nonsense. I would have gotten out of there soon enough."

"Mom . . . you were there for four days." The horror of it stuck in my throat. I'd called her yesterday—our twice weekly call—and when she hadn't answered, I assumed she was out with Mr. Griffin or one of the other elderly men she occasionally saw.

"I had water from the bathtub. I could have lasted another week or two."

"Aw, Mom . . ."

The tears came. My mother patted the back of my hand with her free one.

"Oh, Jacqueline. Don't be upset. This is what happens when you get old."

"I should have been there."

"Nonsense. You live a thousand miles away. This is my dumb fault for slipping in the shower."

"I called you yesterday. When you didn't pick up, I should have . . ."

My mother shushed me, softly.

"Sweetheart, you know you can't play the what-if game, especially in our profession. This isn't the first time this has happened."

She couldn't have hurt me more if she'd tried.

"How many times, Mom?"

"Jacqueline—"

"How many times?"

"Three or four."

I didn't need to hear that. "But you never hurt yourself, right?"

"I may have had a cast on my elbow for a while."

I fought not to yell. "And you never told me?"

"I'm not your responsibility."

"Yes . . . you are."

She sighed, her face so sad.

"Jacqueline, when your father died, you were the only family I had left. You were also the only family that I ever needed. I would never, ever allow myself to become a burden to you."

I sniffled, found my center.

"Well, get used to it. As soon as you're released, you're moving in with me."

"Absolutely not."

"Yes, you are."

"No, I'm not."

"Please, Mom."

"No. I have a very active social life. How could I get intimate with a gentleman when my daughter is in the other room?"

Reluctantly, I played my trump card.

"I spoke with your doctors. They don't feel that you're able to take care of yourself."

Mom's face hardened.

"What? That's ridiculous."

"They'll only release you from the hospital into my custody."

"Was it that Dr. Kingsbury? Smarmy little bastard, talking to me like I'm a three-year-old."

"You don't have a choice, Mom."

"I always have a choice."

"It's either me, or assisted living."

I watched my words sink in. My mother's biggest, and only, fear was going into a nursing home. Before meeting my father, she worked briefly as an activity director in a continuing care facility, and swore that she'd jump in front of a bus before ever checking into one of the "death hotels," as she called them.

"No way in hell."

"Mom, I can invoke power of attorney."

"My mind is sound."

I made myself keep going, even though I hated this.

"I have friends in the courts, Mom."

My mom turned away, shaking her head.

"You wouldn't do that to me."

"Look at me, Mom. How far do you think I would go to protect you?"

Mom continued to stare at the wall. Tears streaked down her cheeks.

"Bullying an old lady. Is that how I raised you, Jacqueline?"

"No, Mom. You raised me to care. Just like you said: You're the only family I've ever had. You took care of me for eighteen years." I squeezed her hand. "It's my turn to take care of you."

Mom pulled her hand away.

"I'd like to be alone."

"Please. Don't be like this."

She pressed the button to page the nurse.

"Mom . . . please."

A white-clothed figure poked her head into the room.

"How are we doing, Mrs. Streng?"

"I'm very tired. I'd like to take a nap."

The nurse looked at me, sympathetic.

I stood up, briefly fussed with the get-well flower arrangement I'd brought, and then turned to leave.

"Nurse," Mom's voice cracked. "Please make sure I don't have any visitors for the next few days."

"Perhaps you'll feel differently tomorrow, Mrs. Streng."

"No. I'm sure I won't."

The tears came again. I took a deep breath and stopped my chest from quivering.

"I love you, Mom."

For the first time ever, she didn't respond with "I love you too."

The nurse put her hand on my shoulder, giving me a gentle push.

I took one more look at my mother, and walked out of her room.

CHAPTER 4

Mom lived in Dade City, a pleasant town that seemed out of place in Florida. Rather than tourist-crammed beaches and mega theme parks, Dade boasted gently rolling hills, actual woods, and so many antique malls you couldn't spit without hitting one.

The night had arrived, hot and thick like a soggy blanket, but I kept the windows down. The rental had decent air-conditioning, but I didn't feel I deserved it.

I'd been to her place twice before, and always missed the turn onto her street. Tonight was no exception. I pressed through three lefts and found it on the second pass.

Her condo had a matching numbered space in the parking lot. Overnight bag slung over my shoulder, her keys in my hand, I was just about to enter the lobby when I stopped, mid-step.

Was I doing the right thing?

A quick image of Mom facedown in the bathtub spurred me on.

The Highlands were retirement condos, regardless of what the brochures promised. No one under fifty-five lived here. A full-time staff kept the pool clean, ran errands for the tenants, and tended the prerequisite eighteen-hole golf course. They also had EMT training, a necessity since the elderly often acted, well, *elderly.* But even though they were available twenty-four hours a day, they didn't routinely check on their residents.

I took the elevator to the fifth floor, and found a painfully thin old man in a bright Hawaiian shirt crouched before my mother's open door, fiddling with a screwdriver.

"Hello?"

He peered at me through thick glasses; first the upper half, then tilting his head up so he could squint through the bifocals. The man had a bald head so speckled with age spots it was a dead ringer for a sparrow's egg.

"Mmm? Oh, hello."

The man stood, with much creaking of bones. Fully erect, he wasn't much taller than when he'd been squatting; his back curved like a question mark. He smiled, flashing bright white dentures, and offered his hand.

"You must be Jacqueline. Sal Griffin. I'm a friend of your mother's."

I forced down my smile. Mom often told me stories of her trysts with Mr. Griffin, and usually described him as "insatiable," "unrelenting," and "He's a machine; his pelvis is spring-loaded." I'd always pictured him as a distinguished, Sean Connery type. Instead, standing before me was a bald Don Knotts.

"Nice to meet you, Mr. Griffin."

"The police made a bit of a mess." He motioned to the door. "I'm putting in a new jamb."

"Don't they have people here that can fix it?"

"Sure. But I wanted to make sure it was done right. Excuse me, where are my manners? Let me take that for you."

Mr. Griffin reached for my carry-on. I thought about protesting, fearful he might hurt himself lifting it, but then let him play the gentleman. He led me into the condo, flipping on lights as he walked.

The place was clean, tidy, well-kept. I resisted the immediate urge to check the fridge and the cupboards to make sure Mom was eating right.

"I spoke with your mother a little while ago. She mentioned you might be coming."

He set my bag down on the dining room table.

"How long ago? I've tried to call a few times since leaving the hospital, but she has a Do Not Disturb on the line."

"Oh, about five minutes. She called me. I've never heard her so upset before."

"We had a . . . disagreement."

He frowned, nodding.

"Proud woman, your mother. When I had the police break in, earlier today, her first words to me were to get the hell out of her bathroom, because she didn't want me to see her like that."

I smirked. "That sounds like Mom."

"I'm sorry she was there for so long. I just got back into town this morning. If I'd have even considered . . ."

"Thank you for coming to her rescue, Mr. Griffin. I'm the one who should be feeling guilty. She's fallen before."

"I know. Eight or nine times. I installed the safety bar in her shower."

I tried to keep the surprise out of my voice. "Eight or nine? She told me four."

"I'm not surprised. You'd have just . . ."

His voice trailed off. We both knew what was unsaid. If I'd known she'd been falling a lot, I'd have forced her to move in with me earlier.

"Well, I appreciate all you've done for her. Thank you."

Mr. Griffin shrugged. "Beautiful woman, your mother. Nice to finally meet you. She talks about you incessantly."

"It must be irritating."

"Not at all. I'd love to hear your version of how you got that guy who killed all those women, the Gingerbread Man. The way your mom tells it, that private investigator fella, the one who was the hero in the TV movie, he really didn't do a damn thing."

"True."

"And you're much prettier than that fat actress they got to play you."

"Thank you, again."

"Though I will admit, that scene in the sewer, where you grabbed that fella's leg and begged for him to save you . . ." Mr. Griffin chuckled. "That was pretty funny."

I frowned. That wasn't how it happened, but I figured I got off easy. In the original screenplay, the writer had me wet my pants in that scene. I had to threaten legal action to get that taken out.

"I'm sorry, I didn't mean to offend you."

"It's fine."

Mr. Griffin grinned. "It's hard, having your pride trampled on."

Then he winked at me. Clever old coot. I was about to explain the difference between having a bruised ego and having a broken hip, when a beeping sound interrupted us.

"My phone. Pardon me."

He removed a cell from his baggy shorts.

"Hello? . . . Hi, how are you feeling, Mary? . . . Yes, she's here right now. . . . Hmm. I see. Would you like to talk to her? Perhaps you should tell her that yourself. I wouldn't feel comfortable . . . Yes. Okay. I understand. I'll talk to you tomorrow."

He folded up the phone and put it away, his wrinkled face pained.

"Just tell me."

"Your mother said that she'd prefer it if you didn't stay at her place."

I think I flinched.

"She's just angry right now, Jacqueline. Angry and hurt. I'll talk to her."

"She was stuck on the bathroom floor, in pain, for four days—"

"I know."

"—lying in her own mess—"

"I know."

"She could have died, Mr. Griffin. I can't let that happen to my mother again."

Mr. Griffin put a hand on my shoulder, patted.

"You have to understand something about getting old, Jacqueline. We can't hold on to our health. It's impossible. But we try like mad to hold on to our dignity."

My eyes teared up, but I refused to cry.

"I just want my mom to be safe. Dignity doesn't matter."

"But it does, Jacqueline. Once dignity is gone, the will to live isn't far behind."

I walked away, heading for my overnight bag.

"Fine. I'll stay at a hotel."

"You can, but your mother was quite clear. She refuses to speak to you until you stop bullying her. I'm sorry."

I clenched my teeth and my fists, wanting to scream. Instead of picking up my carry-on, I walked past it and headed for the bathroom. Seeing where it happened, seeing the mess, would help steel my resolve.

The bathroom was spotless.

"I cleaned it up earlier." Mr. Griffin put his hand on my shoulder again. "She'll come around. Just give her time. Asking for help just isn't your mother's way."

I spun, ready for a fight.

"Neither of you seem to think she needs help."

Now it was his turn to look sad.

"Oh, she does. Yes, she does."

"So you agree with me?"

He nodded.

"Why does that make me feel even worse?"

Mr. Griffin, with the spring-loaded pelvis, hugged me, and I hugged him back, and we spent a moment trying to understand the unfairness of it all.

"Should I get a motel room?" I asked. "Try to force her hand?"

"She doesn't want you here right now, Jacqueline. It's best if you go home. I'll talk to her. This will all work out."

I nodded, but deep down I knew differently.

The three-hour plane ride back to Chicago seemed to take a million years.

CHAPTER 5

I made it home a little after three in the morning. I live in Wrigleyville, in an apartment on Addison and Racine. It's a loud neighborhood, the streets always full of Cubs fans and barhopping kids, many of whom like to spend their evenings directly under my window, shouting at one another. As a consolation, the rent is too high.

Exhaustion hammered at me like the tide, but sleep and I weren't close friends. On good nights, I could get two hours of REM before stress woke me up.

Tonight wouldn't be a good night.

I blame my job, since it's easier than blaming myself. I've been to several general pracs, but haven't broken down and seen a shrink yet. The latest wonder drug, Ambien, worked for me, but with consequences—the next morning I swam in an unending groggy haze that severely impaired my ability to serve and protect. So I only took it as a last resort. Besides, insomnia gave me an edge; less sleep equaled more productivity. Plus, my boyfriend found baggy eyes sexy.

There was a message from him on the machine. I let it play as I undressed.

"Hi, Jack. The conference is going well. Accountants are actually a fun bunch, once you get a few drinks in them. Naw, I'm kidding—we become even more boring. I just had a two-hour argument with some guy about accruals. I'll be back in Chicago tomorrow night, so tell your other suitors you're mine for the evening. I have an important question to run by you. Miss you. Love you. Hope you're keeping the city safe. Bye-bye."

I smirked. I met Latham Conger, head accountant at Oldendorff and Associates, ten months ago, through a dating service that Herb had conned me into joining. Latham was pleasant, attractive, attentive, employed, and heterosexual. Which, for a forty-something woman in Chicago, was like winning the lottery. He also loved me, and wasn't put off that I didn't return the sentiment yet.

I liked Latham, a lot. And I might love him someday. But my heart muscle atrophied when Alan left me, and I haven't been able to get it up to speed since.

I pulled on an old T-shirt and climbed into bed. Latham's cologne clung to the pillows, and I hugged one to my chest, thinking about his phone call.

I have an important question to run by you.

What could that mean?

As if I didn't have enough on my mind.

Rest, as expected, defied me. I tossed. I turned. I did deep breathing and relaxation exercises that brought me close to sleep, and perhaps actually into sleep for short periods of time, but I always jerked myself awake after a few minutes.

I felt immense relief when my alarm went off and it was time to go to work.

After showering and changing into a yellow blouse, a tan jacket, and matching slacks, I did a quick makeup job with extra attention to eye concealer and headed for work.

Eight in the morning, and already the temp hovered in the nineties. Chicago, a city that didn't smell good on average days, reeked in heat like this.

I had to pass an alley on the way to my car, and the smell from the garbage cans hit me like a punch.

Kitty-corner to the 26th District, a gourmet coffee place had set up shop. I got a Columbian dark roast, black, for myself, and almost ordered a double chocolate hazelnut cappuccino for Herb until I remembered his diet. He also got a dark roast.

Caffeine in hand, I entered my building and was surprised to find it cool. In fact, it was downright chilly.

Violent Crimes Division was on the third floor. Herb sat in his office, hand in a box of fat-free chocolate cookies. He brightened when he saw me.

"Jack? Why aren't you in Florida? Is your mom okay?"

Rather than get into it, I nodded a yes and handed him his cup.

"Coffee, thank God. I'm freezing."

"I see they fixed the air-conditioning."

"They did, but the temperature regulator isn't working. They can't shut it off."

"Feels good."

"Give it ten minutes, and you'll start seeing your breath. I tried opening a window, but I can't handle the Dumpster smell. This is just what I needed." Herb took a sip, then made a face. "What's this?"

"It's coffee. That's what it tastes like without cream and sugar."

"It's supposed to be this bitter?"

"Yeah."

Herb dug through his desk and pulled out a fistful of little pink packets.

"Well, I'm glad your mother's okay, and it's good that you're back. Index got a match on the prints."

As Herb added carcinogens to his brew, I leafed through the reports on his desk.

The arms belonged to Davi McCormick of 3800 North Lake Shore Drive. Arrested once for solicitation, but clean for the last five years. Mug shots were known to be unflattering, but hers looked good enough to print. Davi was an attractive woman, much more so than the average prostitute.

I read her case details and it made sense. At the time of her arrest, she'd been working for Madame Pardieu, a high-class escort service that charged up to a grand a night. That would account for the nice neighborhood.

"Does she look familiar?" Herb asked. His jowls were stuffed with fat-free cookies, giving him a chipmunkish appearance.

"Yeah, she does."

"You've probably seen her a few dozen times. When we got her name I cross-reffed with Missing Persons, and found a report from yesterday, called in by her agent. She's Sure-a-Tex Girl."

Sure-a-Tex was a brand of tampon marketed to the younger crowd. Sure-a-Tex Girl, wearing a not very subtle red cape, flew to the rescue of women who started their period in extreme situations, such as mountain climbing or white-water rafting. The product came in a variety of designer colors, including neon green and hot pink.

"Did you contact the agent?"

"He'll be here any minute." Herb took a sip of coffee and searched his desk for more saccharine.

Phil Blasky's postmortem report was the shortest I'd ever read, due to the amount of material he had to work with. An elevated histamine level and platelet count indicated the victim had been bleeding prior to her arms being severed. Tests for several dozen drugs came back negative. Lipid levels normal. No evidence of heart disease, STDs, or pregnancy. Everything else about the arms was unspectacular.

Phil noted that the handcuffs were put on after death; axe marks indicated the swings came from the front, with the arms splayed out crucifixion-style.

Officer Dan Rogers knocked on my open door. I invited him in.

"Got the GC results from the burned skin samples." He handed me a file. "My tongue was correct. The arms were diluted with bleach."

"No trace of anything else?"

"Nope. Bleach will clean up just about anything. That's why it's used by HazMat teams. Hey, Lieut, you got any aspirin? I've got a headache that's making my eyes water."

I found a bottle in my desk and tossed it to him. He shook out five, and swallowed them dry.

"Thanks, Lieutenant. Call me if I can be any more help. I like CSU, but *Detective Rogers* has a nice ring to it too."

Rogers left. Herb made a grunting, satisfied sound, and tossed his empty cookie box into the garbage, on top of three other such cookie boxes.

"Herb, not that I want to question your dieting efforts, but how many boxes of those cookies have you eaten today?"

"Why?"

"Let's just say you could hibernate with all I've seen you eat in the last ten minutes."

"So what? They're fat-free."

"Chocolate syrup is fat-free too. Look at the calories."

He fished out the box he'd tossed and squinted at the nutrition panel. "Ah, hell. No wonder I've gained four pounds on this diet."

"You need to watch the carbohydrates, not the fat."

"Oh. These only have fifteen grams of carbs."

"Per serving. How many servings per box?"

"Ah, hell."

A knock. I turned to see Officer Fuller in the doorway. Fuller was an ex–pro football player, tall and wide, and he towered over his companion, a short, balding man wearing Armani and too much Obsession for Men.

"This is Marvin Pulitzer."

Marvin smiled, his caps unnaturally white, and offered his hand to me. I took it, and discovered he was palming something.

"Pulitzer Prizes Talent Agency. Very pleased to meet you, Miss . . . ?"

"Lieutenant. Jacqueline Daniels."

He held on to me a moment longer than necessary. When I got my hand back I saw he'd given me his card.

"You've got great bone structure, Lieutenant. Do you model?"

"I did *Vogue* a few issues back."

Pulitzer narrowed his eyes, then smiled again.

"Joking. I get it. Funny. But seriously, I just landed this new account. They're looking for distinguished, mature women. You should come in, take some test shots."

"What's the company?"

"Ever-Weave."

I confessed to never hearing of them.

"They sell protective undergarments. You know, adult-sized diapers."

Fuller chortled, deep and throaty. I dismissed him.

"Think it over. You wouldn't have to pose wearing the product. You just have to stand there, looking embarrassed."

No kidding.

"I don't think I'm quite ready to delve into the glamorous world of modeling, Mr. Pulitzer. Come in and have a seat."

Pulitzer and Herb exchanged greetings, and then he sat in a chair between us on the right side of the desk.

"So, where's Davi?"

Herb handed Pulitzer the mug shot.

"This is Davi McCormick?"

"Yeah. Oh, Christ, she's in trouble, isn't she? What did she do? Has she called a lawyer yet?"

Pulitzer pulled out a cell phone the size of a matchbook and flipped it open, dialing with his pinky.

"She doesn't need a lawyer, Mr. Pulitzer. The county medical examiner found Davi's severed arms in the morgue yesterday morning."

"Her . . . arms?"

Herb handed him another picture. Pulitzer lost all color.

"Oh shit! Those are Davi's? Shit! What the hell happened to her?"

"When was the last time you spoke with Davi?"

"Four days ago. We did lunch at Wildfire. Right after that I had to catch a flight to New York."

"What did you talk about during lunch?"

"The usual stuff. Upcoming gigs. Auditions."

"Did Davi seem nervous, or afraid?"

"No, everything was completely normal."

Herb and I took turns interrogating Pulitzer. We confirmed his trip, and asked several dozen questions about Davi, her friends and family, her state of mind, her life.

"She has no enemies. Not one. Which, in a competitive business like this, is amazing. She's just a nice girl."

"You called in a missing person's report yesterday."

"Yeah. She missed a shoot two days ago. Davi never missed a shoot. I called her. Even dropped by her place. She just disappeared. Jesus, who could have done something like that to her?"

Pulitzer had to take a time-out to reschedule his afternoon appointments. While he was on the phone, Herb and I conferred.

"Davi was a celebrity. She may have had stalkers."

"We'll call Sure-a-Tex."

I added it to my notes.

"We also need to call Davi's parents, check with her friends, and try to pinpoint her movements for the last week."

Pulitzer finished his call and asked where he could get some water. I pointed him to the washroom.

Herb took a sip of coffee, then reached for more sweetener. The pile of pink wrappers on his desk was almost as high as his cup.

"If it's someone who knew Davi, where do your handcuffs come in?"

"Coincidence? They could have fallen out of my pocket, someone picks them up and pawns them?"

"I don't buy it."

"It's thin. But the only people with access to my office are cleaning people and cops."

The maintenance staff was carefully screened during the hiring process, and cops were, well, cops. I didn't know anyone working out of the two-six with a grudge against me, and I especially didn't think I had any murderers on my squad. The process to become a police officer included psych profiles, mental evals, and endless personality tests and interviews. Wackos were supposedly weeded out early on.

"Maybe someone pinched them."

That seemed more likely. I didn't carry a purse, and most of my outfits had oversized pockets to hold all of my essentials, cuffs included. Even a mediocre thief could have gotten them from me without much effort.

"But why me?"

I used Herb's phone to call Fuller back into the office. He'd been particularly helpful on the Gingerbread Man case, and I needed an extra man.

"Officer, I'd like you to cross-reference my previous case files with the names from County's sign-in book. You know how to build a database?"

Fuller snorted.

"You think because I can bench three-fifty I can't work a spreadsheet?"

"You can bench three-fifty?" Herb asked. "I almost weigh three-fifty."

"It's not that hard. Just a combination of diet, exercise, and supplementing."

"Maybe that's why I'm not getting results. I'm not supplementing."

I thought of a hundred things to say, but managed to keep a lid on them.

Fuller walked next to Herb and leaned against his desk. The desk creaked. "I stack to boost my metabolism. Plus I use chromium, L-carnitine, CLA, and

I protein-load before working out. If you want, I could take you through my NFL routine sometime."

Herb beamed in a way that he usually reserved for chili dogs. "That'd be great! Can I get a list of those supplements you're taking?"

"Sure. See, an ECA stack is a combination of—"

"Officer Fuller," I interrupted, "we could really use that database."

"Gotcha, Lieut. I'll get right on it."

Fuller left. Herb gave me a frown.

"What's wrong, Jack?"

"I wanted to stop the conversation before the two of you started flexing."

"Too much guy talk, huh? Sorry, didn't mean to exclude you."

Herb said it without sarcasm, but the comment chafed. Being a woman in the CPD meant constant, unrelenting exclusion. It didn't matter that I was the number-one marksman in the district. It didn't matter that I had a black belt in tae kwon do. Herb wouldn't ever think to ask me about my workout routine. Unconscious sexism.

Or perhaps I was just being overly touchy because of the situation with my mom.

Pulitzer returned, looking a little better.

"I thought of something, but I don't know if it will help or not."

We waited.

"If Davi was doing anything illegal, it wouldn't matter now, right? Because she's gone? It's silly, but I still feel protective of her."

"Drugs?" I asked.

Pulitzer's shoulders slumped.

"Cocaine. Recreational, as far as I knew. It didn't affect her work."

"Do you know where she got her drugs?"

"No idea."

Again, we waited.

"I really have no idea. I want to help, but I'm not into that scene. I could put you in touch with some of my other models who might know, but I wouldn't want them getting into trouble."

Pulitzer reached up to rub the back of his neck, exposing a bandage beneath the cuff on his right wrist.

"How did you get that?" Herb asked, pointing it out.

"Hmm? Oh. Mr. Friskers."

"Mr. Friskers?"

"Davi's cat. I hate that damn thing. Mean as hell. I went over to Davi's apartment before I called the police. She gave me a set of keys. I figured, I don't know, maybe she had a heart attack, or fell and broke her leg so she couldn't get to the phone."

I felt Herb's eyes on me. I kept focus on Pulitzer.

"We'll need to check the apartment. The keys would save us some time."

Pulitzer dug into his pants and handed me a key ring.

"Be careful. That thing is like a little T. rex."

After assuring Pulitzer we wouldn't pursue any narcotics possession charges with his models, he gave us the names of three who used coke.

"Is there anything else? I wasn't able to reschedule my afternoon meeting. Big client. I want to help Davi, but I really can't miss this."

"Thank you, Mr. Pulitzer. We'll be in touch."

We shook hands.

"Please catch the guy that did this. Davi is—was—a real sweetheart."

After he left, I stood up and tried to stomp some blood back into my toes, which felt frostbitten.

"You up for a drive, Herb?"

"Hell, yes. My nose hairs have icicles hanging from them."

"We can only hope those are icicles."

Keys in hand, we headed for his car to check out Davi's apartment.

The summer heat felt wonderful for the first five minutes. Then Herb cranked the air-conditioning.

CHAPTER 6

It's a bad one.

He looks around his office, a knuckle jabbed against his temple, trying to will the pain away.

Does anyone notice? They must. His neck muscles are tight enough to strum, he's drenched in sweat, and he can't control the trembling.

He's never experienced pain this intense. Not even his injury hurt this much. It's as if his head is in a vise, being slowly tightened until his eyes are ready to pop out. The pills he took earlier aren't doing a damn thing.

Maybe his wife is right. He should see a doctor. But the idea terrifies him. What if the doctor finds something seriously wrong? What if he needs surgery? He'd rather deal with the pain than let some quack poke around in his brain.

"You okay?"

A coworker. Female. Plain-looking, heavy hips, short brown hair in a spiky Peter Pan style.

"Headache." He manages a sickly grin.

"Do you need some aspirin?"

He decides to kill her.

"Yeah, thanks."

She walks to her desk. He imagines her, kneeling on the floor in his plastic room. She's crying, of course. Maybe he's taken a belt to her first, to loosen her up. Leaving marks on this one will be okay. Since she works with him, he can't allow her body to be discovered.

"Tylenol?" she calls over the cubicle wall.

"Fine."

How should she die? Her haircut inspires him. He will draw his knife across her forehead, pull back the skin to expose the bone. Work a finger in there, then two and three.

Skin stretches. His hands are large, but he should be able to get his entire hand between her skull and her scalp.

"Like a warm, wet glove," he says, shivering.

"What's like a glove?"

She's holding out the Tylenol bottle, one eyebrow raised.

"I want to thank you for this."

"No problem. I used to get migraines. I would have killed somebody to take the pain away."

Me too.

"You know, Sally, we've worked in the same building for a few years now, and I don't know anything about you."

She smiles. Her front teeth are crooked. He can picture her mouth stretched open, screaming and bloody, as he practices some amateur dentistry with a ball-peen hammer.

"I'm married, with two kids, Amanda and Jenna. Amanda is eight and Jenna just turned five."

He forces a grin, his hopes shattered. Who would have guessed an ugly thing like her had a family? He doubts he'll be able to get her alone, and even if he manages, she'll be missed.

"How about you? Married?"

"Yes. No kids, though. My wife is a model, and she doesn't want to ruin her body. You know, hips spreading, stretch marks, saggy tits."

Ugly Sally's smile slips a degree.

"Yeah, well, it happens. But I think it's worth it."

"Look, I gotta get back to work. Thanks for the Tylenol."

"No problem. *TOSAP.*"

He inwardly cringes at the slogan. "Yeah. *TOSAP.*"

Ugly Sally waddles away, and he works the cap off the bottle and dry-swallows six Tylenol. The throbbing, which abated slightly during his murder-fantasies, comes back harder than ever.

He needs to kill somebody. As soon as possible.

The pain-relieving properties of murder were discovered by him at a young age, when he was in his third foster home. Ironically, he'd been removed from his previous home for being neglected—the couple who had taken him in had also taken in eight other children, for the monthly check from the government. They would blow it all on drugs and let the children go without food. Well-meaning Social Services had whisked him away from the neglect, and handed him over to a psychotic alcoholic instead.

After a particularly nasty beating with a car antenna, he and his younger foster brother were locked in a closet.

He'd really been hurting. But along with the pain was a sense of helplessness, of frustration.

He took that frustration out on his foster brother, in the dark, muffled confines of the closet. The more he hurt the smaller boy, the more his own pain went away.

His new foster father went to jail for the murder.

When the headaches began, he knew just how to deal with them.

After four clicks of the mouse, his monitor fills with eligibles.

He finds a girl, one who lives just a few blocks away. Address seems to be current. He calls, using his cell.

A woman answers, her voice deep and throaty.

Perfect.

CHAPTER 7

The doorman at Davi McCormick's apartment building wore a heavy wool blazer, dark red, complete with gold epaulets and matching buttons. In this heat he looked positively miserable.

"Last time I saw Ms. McCormick was Sunday evening, right before Murry took over. Murry works the six P.M. to two A.M. shift, and she left the building about fifteen minutes before that."

"Do you remember what she wore?"

"A black cocktail dress, heels, diamond-stud earrings. Her hair was up. As I held open the door I told her she looked beautiful and asked where she was going."

"What did she answer?"

"She said, *Big date. Real big.* And then laughed. Is she okay?"

Herb gave him the news, then got the phone numbers for Murry and the morning doorman. He called them during the elevator ride. Neither had seen Davi since Sunday.

Pulitzer's key got us inside. I could have fit three of my apartments inside of Davi's, with room left over to park my car.

"I'll take the bedroom," I told Herb.

Then we heard the scream.

I tugged my .38 from the holster strapped to my left armpit, senses heightened.

Movement, to the right. Both Herb and I swung our guns over.

A cat, wearing a large disposable diaper, bounded out from under the dining room table and into the hallway, screaming like a train whistle.

Herb exhaled. "I just had about four heart attacks."

"That must be Mr. Friskers."

"Either that or a small, furry toddler. Did you check out the diaper?"

"Yeah. Talk about pampering your pets."

I tucked my gun back under my blazer and fished a pair of latex gloves from my pocket.

"We've got an hour," I told Herb, indicating when the CSU would arrive.

Davi's bedroom was the bedroom of a typical young woman, albeit one with money. Her unmade bed had a stuffed animal infestation, over a dozen of them swarming on top of the pink comforter. A framed Nagel print hung on the far wall. The near wall was obscured by a collage of pictures, most of them Davi, snipped from magazines.

A large pile of clothing rested near the closet, and a makeup mirror—the kind movie stars have with bare lightbulbs surrounding the frame—hung above the dresser. Cosmetics rested on every flat surface in the room.

On the nightstand, next to the bed, a phone/answering machine combo blinked, indicating twelve messages. I scrolled through the caller ID numbers. Four of them read "blocked call," the last from 4:33 P.M. Sunday night.

I played the messages. All were from Pulitzer but one: a long-distance call from Davi's mother. The blocked calls didn't seem to correspond to any messages.

Davi's walk-in closet was so crammed full of clothing I could barely walk in. Some of it occupied hangers, but most of it rested in large heaps on the floor. Rummaging through the piles yielded nothing but an empty cat carrier.

A quick search of her drawers found more clothes, makeup, and a nickel bag of cocaine. I placed it in one of the evidence bags I always keep in my pocket. Then I pulled every drawer completely out and checked to see if anything was hidden behind them or taped under them. I'd been doing that ever since seeing a *Hill Street Blues* episode where a cop found a clue that way. Maybe someone somewhere saw the same episode.

No such luck today.

Under the bed I discovered two stray stuffed animals, a cat toy, and several years' worth of dust. Nothing hidden between the mattress and box spring. Nothing behind the Nagel print.

I returned to the phone and hit Redial, copying down the last number called and disconnecting before it went through. Then I copied down all of the numbers on the caller ID.

"Jack!"

I've been partners with Herb for over a decade, but had never heard such raw panic in his voice before. I rushed out of the bedroom, gun drawn.

Herb stood in the living room, stock-still. Tears ran down his cheeks.

Perched on Herb's head was Mr. Friskers, claws dug in tight.

"He leaped off the curtains. His claws are like fishhooks."

I took a step closer. Mr. Friskers hissed and arched his back.

Herb screamed.

"Get it off before he scalps me, Jack!"

"You can't pull him off?"

"His claws are stuck in my skull bone."

Only years of training and consummate professionalism prevented me from breaking down in hysterical laughter.

"You want me to call Animal Control?" I tried to say it straight, but a giggle escaped.

"No. I want you to shoot him."

"Herb . . ."

"Shoot the cat, Jack. Please. I'm begging you. It's not just the pain. There's gotta be several days' worth of cat mess in that diaper. The smell is making my eyes water."

I'd never owned a cat and had zero experience with the species. But I did recall an old TV commercial where the cat came running when it got fed. Couldn't hurt to try.

"I'll be right back."

"Don't leave me, Jack."

"I'm just going to get my camera."

"That's not even close to being funny."

I located the canned cat food in a cabinet. When I opened one of the tins, Herb screamed again. Mr. Friskers appeared in the kitchen a heartbeat later.

"You were just hungry, weren't you, kitty?"

The cat yowled at me. I set the can on the floor and watched him inhale the food.

Herb came through the doorway. His gun was out, pointing at Mr. Friskers.

"Herb, put that away."

"It's evil, Jack. It has to die."

Mr. Friskers looked at Herb, hissed, then bolted out of the room. Herb holstered his weapon.

"Am I bleeding?"

"A little." I handed him some paper towels. "Find anything?"

"Bank and credit card statements, phone bills, a few personal letters. You?"

"A few grams of cocaine."

"Give it to the cat. Maybe it will calm him down."

I gave Herb a fake smile. "Funny, for someone bleeding to death. Want to stop by the ER on the way back for your rabies shot?"

Herb narrowed his eyes, then looked past me, through the kitchen.

"The crime scene unit will be here soon."

"So?"

A yowl pierced the room, and Mr. Friskers shot past us and pounced his diaper-clad ass onto the counter. He sat there, hissing. His tail, which poked out through the center of the diaper, swished back and forth like a cobra.

"I'll try Animal Control." I took out my cell.

The news wasn't good.

"Sorry, Lieutenant. The heat wave has all of us doing triple time. Soonest we could pick it up is Monday."

"We might all be eaten by then."

"It's the best I can do. You can try the Humane Society."

I tried the Humane Society.

"Sorry, Officer. We couldn't come for at least a week. When the temperature gets this high, animals are hit hardest. We don't even have any room for another."

Herb nudged me.

"Tell them this cat is evil. If you shaved its head, you'd see a 666."

I relayed the info, but they weren't swayed. Herb suggested calling the Crocodile Hunter, but neither of us knew his number.

"We can't let him stay here, Jack."

I agreed. A cat could mess up a scene in a dozen ways. Not just by destroying evidence—it could get in the team's way, hurt someone, or even get hurt itself if it inhaled the wrong chemical.

"You want him?" I asked.

Herb frowned and tore off another paper towel to blot his scalp.

I reached a tentative hand out to stroke the cat, and he bared claws and took a swipe at me.

"Try offering him your head," Herb suggested. "He'll jump on and we can walk him out."

I left the kitchen and went into Davi's bedroom, returning a moment later with the cat carrier and some ski gloves.

Herb raised an eyebrow. "Should I start dialing 911 now?"

"No need to worry. Animals love me, because they can sense my pure heart."

Without hesitating, I grabbed Mr. Friskers around the body. He countered by screaming louder than humanly possible and locking his fangs onto my right index finger. The gloves protected me, and I managed to get him in the carrier without losing a digit.

"So now we throw him in Lake Michigan, right?"

"I'm sure one of Davi's friends will take him."

"And in the meantime?"

I let out a big, dramatic sigh.

"I guess I'll have to keep him for a few days."

"I don't think that's a good idea, Jack. I don't want the next murder I investigate to be yours."

"He's just scared and grumpy. You'd be grumpy too if you had the same diaper on for four days. Right, little guy?"

I poked my gloved finger into the cat carrier, and Mr. Friskers pounced on it, biting and scratching.

"Try showing him your pure heart," Herb suggested.

The cat screamed for the entire ride back to the office.

CHAPTER 8

"My place is just up the next block."

"This isn't a very nice neighborhood."

"On purpose. My wife would never think to look for me here."

He smiles at the girl. Eileen Hutton. Young, pretty, perfect body. She knew it, too, which is why this date cost a cool thousand bucks.

She won't get the chance to spend it.

They're driving south on Kedzie, property values dropping block by block. The flophouse where he takes his women is dilapidated, filthy, and came complete with a handful of winos lounging in front. When he parks in the adjacent alley, she doesn't want to get out of the car.

"What's wrong?" He grins. His head feels ready to burst, an incessant pounding that's making his vision blur. Sweat streaks down his face in rivers. Hopefully, she'll think it's just the heat.

"I don't feel comfortable here."

"Don't you trust me? I'm one of the good guys."

He unlocks the glove compartment, takes out a silver cigarette case. Lined up inside are six rolled joints. He lights one up, hands it to her.

"I married my wife for money, and believe me, she's got a lot. She won't put out, though. So I have to get it on the side, and I have to be discreet about it. You understand."

She puffs and nods.

Enjoy it, baby. It's your last.

No one gives them a glance as they walk into the building. The hallway smells like piss and worse. Lighting is at a minimum. She holds his arm until they get to his room.

His hand is trembling as he unlocks the door.

Almost there. Just a few more minutes.

They enter and she turns in a full circle, taking it all in. "Wow! What's your kink, man?"

The floors and walls are lined with clear plastic sheets. The only piece of furniture in the room is a bed, and that's also similarly covered.

"I like plastic."

"I can tell." She smiles in a way that she probably thinks is sexy. *Annoying bitch.* He's going to enjoy slicing her up.

"I want you to wear something for me."

"Let me guess. A plastic garbage bag?"

"No. These."

He reaches into his pocket and takes out a pair of earrings. Silver hoops, antique-looking.

"Those are pretty."

She removes the dangly gold ones she has on, shoves them into her little spaghetti strap designer purse. When she puts the first hoop in, he begins to pant. His expression must scare her, because she stops smiling.

"You know, I usually don't make dates on my own. I normally go through the escort service."

"Don't worry. You trust me, remember?"

She nods, but it's uncertain.

"These earrings look beautiful on you, Eileen."

"Thanks. Um, how did you get my number, anyway?"

"I have ways."

"Yeah. I guess you do."

"The bathroom is over there. I'd really like it if you came out wearing nothing but those earrings."

She gives him a half smile, hesitates, then trots off to the bathroom like a good little whore.

He undresses, folding his clothes neatly and putting them on the floor of the closet, next to the axe. His other instruments are laid out on a stained towel.

What to use, what to use?

He selects a garrote for the murder and a box cutter for the detail work. The garrote is something he picked up at work—a twenty-inch strand of piano wire, the ends twisted around wooden pegs. He hasn't tried it yet. Should be fun.

She comes out of the bathroom, strutting. Her confidence is back. Her naked body is flawless.

But it won't be for long.

"Well, you're a big one, aren't you? What do you want to do first, big boy?"

Severing her head is harder than he'd have guessed. He has to prop his knee up against her back for leverage, and then use a sawing motion with the garrote to get through the spine.

There's a lot of blood.

When he's finished, he goes to work with the utility knife.

He attends to her eagerly, like a starving man. The feeling is more than sexual. It's euphoric. Mind-altering.

Pain-relieving.

The moment he walked behind her and stretched the wire across her pretty little throat, the pain vanished. His vision cleared, his jaw unclenched, and a feeling of pure relief a thousand times better than any orgasm flooded through him.

He doesn't understand why. He doesn't care why. The throbbing is gone, replaced by a mad giggling fit as he works harder and faster with the utility knife.

It soon escalates into a mindless frenzy.

Afterward, he takes a shower. The water is tepid and smells like rust. He doesn't care.

The pain is gone.

How long it will stay gone is unknown to him. Sometimes it lasts for weeks. Sometimes, only a few hours.

He takes what he can get.

He scrubs his nails with a toothbrush and a lot of soap, cleaning out all of the gore and little bits. He notices similar bits in his mouth, spits something bloody onto the shower floor.

Must have really gotten crazy there.

Stepping out of the bathroom, he sees how crazy he's actually been.

It's a mess. Worse than he's ever done.

He sits on the bed, naked, in a Thinker pose, staring at the body. He doesn't even remember doing half of these things to her. And using only a one-inch blade and pure strength. Impressive.

"I am one scary son of a bitch," he says to himself.

Careful to avoid the blood pool, he pads over to the closet and quickly dresses. On his cell phone, he presses 3 on speed dial.

"I've got another one."

Chuckles on the other end. "Busy little bee, aren't you?"

"Come get her."

"I'm already out the door."

He stands in the corner. Staring at the mess. Memorizing it.

Twenty minutes later, there's a knock.

"Who the hell is it?"

"The password is *psycho.* Open up."

He grins, letting Derrick inside. The man is short, compact, with acne scars on his chubby cheeks and a lazy eye that always looks to the left.

Derrick views the room and whistles.

"Damn! This is some piece of work. I'm going to need a shovel to clean this up."

"So?" He hands Derrick fifty dollars. "Go buy a shovel."

"Be right back, tiger."

In half an hour, Derrick returns. He wheels in the cart, the body bag resting on top.

"I thought you went to get a shovel."

"It's in the bag."

Derrick gets to work, rolling up the body and the mess in the plastic tarps lining the floor.

"Boy, you really did a number on her," Derrick says. "Where's her heart?"

The killer belches, pounds his chest.

Derrick laughs. "Talk about having heartburn."

The joke is lost on him. He's becoming anxious. Now that the rage has passed, he has to make sure everything goes according to plan.

"How are you going to dispose of her?"

"This one I think I'll cremate. I can't risk one of my famous two-for-one specials. The casket would leak."

"I want these to be found at the morgue, same as before."

The killer hands him a plastic bag.

"Ears? That's a riot." Derrick brings the bag to his mouth and yells, "Hello! Can you hear me?"

Idiot. But beggars can't be choosers.

"Leave the earrings on. They're important."

"No problem. These will be easier to sneak in than those arms. Hell, I could keep them in my pocket."

"Her things are in the bathroom. Take what you want. There's a grand in her purse."

"Righto, chief."

The cleanup continues for another fifteen minutes. The body and bloody tarps are zipped up in the bag.

"I'll line the room with new plastic sometime next week."

"Sooner."

"Sooner? You got the itch again already?"

"Not yet. But it could come back."

Derrick didn't know about the headaches. He thought he was dealing with a run-of-the-mill sex killer.

"Damn. I'm glad I'm not a good-looking chick with you loose in this city."

That won't save you. When the time comes, I'll gut you as well.

They leave the room, Derrick pushing the cart, the killer walking alongside. A few liquor-stained eyes peek at them, then quickly turn away. Derrick's van is parked in the alley, behind the killer's car. He pushes the cart into the rear, spring-loaded legs collapsing as he eases it in.

"Hey, you think, maybe, next time you do one of these women . . ."

"You want to watch?"

Derrick's face lights up. "Yeah! I mean, I'm no stranger to this shit. I'm not as, uh, *extreme,* as you are. But I've done things."

You pimple-faced freak. I know about the things you've done. You make my *stomach turn.*

"We'll see. A tag-team match might be fun."

"A tag-team. Yeah, I like that."

He claps Derrick on the shoulder, forces a grin. He knows the hardest thing about getting away with murder is disposing of the body, and having a mortician under his thumb makes things a lot easier. Still, there's no way he'll ever let Derrick see him in action. He might have to get rid of him sooner than expected.

"Hey, I'll call you when I drop the ears off at County."

"Make sure you wash them, first. I don't want to leave trace."

"Got it. See you, man."

Derrick climbs into his van and pulls away. The killer takes a deep breath, sucking in foul alley air that reeks of garbage.

It doesn't bother him at all.

Nothing does.

CHAPTER 9

"That cat's driving me crazy."

Herb pushed away from the computer and shot Mr. Friskers a look. Mr. Friskers howled his reply.

"He probably wants to be let out of the carrier."

"I'd sooner let Manson out. What are you going to do with him, anyway?"

I rubbed my temples, trying to work out the tension. We'd gotten back to the station two hours ago, and the cat hadn't shut up for any longer than it took to catch his breath.

"I've called all of Davi's model friends, her ex-boyfriend, and her mom. No one wants the cat."

"What a surprise. He's such a lovable bundle of joy."

"I also called a few pet stores. Apparently the heat wave doesn't affect a cat's promiscuity—the stray population is the highest it's ever been, and no one is accepting any more cats."

Herb stroked his mustache, an indication he was lost in thought.

"Stray . . . that's not a bad idea. Just let the little monster free to prowl the city. That's what he's howling about anyway."

I considered it. On one hand, a cat that wore diapers probably wouldn't last too long on the street. On the other hand, Mr. Friskers was so damn mean he might do fine. I wouldn't even put it past him to join a gang and start robbing banks.

"Fine. We'll release the cat into the wild. You coming?"

"I'm staying. Kiss him good-bye for me."

I picked up the carrier, which caused Mr. Friskers to increase the pitch of his howling. A brief, chilly elevator ride later, we were in the back parking lot.

"Okay, my loud friend. This is where we go our separate ways." I unlatched the door on the cat carrier and opened it up. "Go. Be free."

Mr. Friskers stayed where he was.

"Go on. You got your wish."

The cat howled again, but didn't move.

Figuring he just needed a little help, I lifted up the cat carrier and tilted it forward. The cat spread out all four paws and clung to the sides, refusing to be dumped out.

I knelt down and peered into the carrier. "What's the problem, cat?"

He stared back, as if asking me the same question.

I thought about leaving him there. He'd get the hint eventually. Chances are he'd run off as soon as I was out of sight.

Then I thought about my mother.

Sometimes the ones who need help the most are the ones who refuse to accept it.

"Fine," I said, latching the carrier door. "You're stuck with me, then."

He yowled his reply.

Herb wasn't impressed to see his nemesis still hanging around.

"I thought you were going to let the cat out of the bag."

"I did. He wouldn't go."

"Did you try poking him with a stick?"

"No, I didn't. Maybe I should check a taser out of the armory and zap him a few times."

"Want me to go get it?"

"I'll save it as a last resort."

Herb took a bite out of a rice cake. He made a face, found a packet of saccharine in his pocket, and dumped it onto the remaining half.

"Want one?"

"Thanks, but I'm trying to cut back."

Herb took another bite, then added more sweetener. "At least the cat finally quieted down."

I looked into the carrier. Mr. Friskers had curled up into a little ball of fur.

"He's sleeping. Maybe we can get some work done."

"Those few minutes of silence were all I needed. I got a name to go with that last number Davi called. Cell phone, belongs to a man named Colin Andrews. Twenty-three, black, lives on 95th and Wabash."

"He's got a record?"

"A long one. He's a dealer."

"Davi's coke supplier?"

"All of his charges are for marijuana, but that'd be my assumption. And he was a guest of the city just a few weeks ago. Guess which district."

For the first time since the case began, I had that flutter feeling in my stomach that indicated we were getting close.

"You're kidding. Here?"

"The old two-six. For possession."

The ducks weren't perfect yet, but they were forming a row. If Colin Andrews had been in our building, he could have had an opportunity to pick up my handcuffs.

"Who booked him?"

"Hanson." Herb pressed a few computer keys. "She's gone for the day. Speaking of which, I need to leave early."

"Big plans?"

Herb gave me a grin that was positively wicked. I understood.

"Ah, those kind of plans. That requires leaving early?"

"In this instance, yes."

"Okay then, Romeo. We can get rolling on Andrews tomorrow."

"Good. You know"—Herb eyed the cat—"I drive by the Chicago River on the way home."

"Thanks for the offer. I think I'll let him live for the time being."

Herb said good night and left my office.

"Just me and you, Mr. Friskers."

At the mention of his name, the cat awoke and commenced howling.

I tried to ignore him, and attempted to finish up a report on a suicide from last week. After struggling through that, I went through my in-box and played pass-along with some current homicides that seemed open and shut.

My position in the Chicago Police Department allowed me more wiggle room than many of my contemporaries. As far as I knew, I was one of the only lieutenants in the Detective Division—the title had been mostly phased out around the time Homicide morphed into Violent Crimes. There are lieutenant inspectors, who are one silver bar below captain, but those are supervisory positions and I had no desire to give up investigative work. My rank allows me to skip morning roll call, operate in other districts without jurisdictional issues, give commands when needed, and pick and choose my cases.

It took over twenty years to gain this autonomy, and I enjoyed it. Which is probably why no one in the office knocked on my door to complain about the cat noise. Rank has its privileges.

In the midst of filing, my cell rang. Latham.

"Hi, Latham. Back in town?"

"I'm back, Jack. What are you wearing?"

I smiled. "A plaid flannel shirt and overalls."

"Stop it—I'm getting turned on. Might I request the honor of your presence tonight for dinner?"

"I'll have to check with my boyfriend first."

"Screw him."

"I was planning on it. Is six o'clock okay?"

"It's perfect. I was thinking someplace nice."

"Heels-and-a-dress nice?"

"Ooh, I like that even more than the overalls."

"Does this have anything to do with that important question you mentioned on my answering machine?"

"Maybe, maybe so. Are you beating the confession out of some criminal right now?"

"That's a cat. Long story. I'll tell you when you pick me up."

"Great. I'll be the guy knocking on your door with flowers. See you soon."

He hung up, leaving me sitting there with a dopey grin on my face. I was glad Latham was back home, and not just because I hadn't had sex in three weeks. Latham made me feel special. He was funny, considerate, attractive, successful, romantic, and in love with me. What wasn't to like?

Though, I had to admit, part of me kept waiting for the other shoe to drop. He had to have *something* wrong with him. But so far, the annoyances were only minor. Snoring. Back hair. Leaving the toilet seat up. A juvenile affection for bad horror movies and '80s pop songs.

He probably had wives in four other states. Or his mummified mother tied to a rocking chair in the attic.

Speaking of mothers . . .

I called Florida, but the Do Not Disturb was still on her room phone. I spoke with a nurse, and Mom's condition had improved, though she still seemed mad as hell. I asked the nurse to pass on an "I love you, Mom," and hung up, spirits dampened.

"I won't bend," I told Mr. Friskers. "She needs my help."

He howled, which I took to be agreement.

With only two hours to make myself gorgeous before my guy showed up, I decided to call it a day. On the way home, I stopped at a pet supply superstore and bought the essentials: litter box, litter, cat food, and a mouse toy stuffed with catnip. I asked an employee if they had muzzles for cats, but she looked so disgusted I'd even suggest such a thing that I left without getting an answer.

My apartment was where I'd left it, and it took two trips to bring everything up from my car. I kept the air-conditioning off to save money, which meant my place was roughly the same temperature as hell, but more humid.

The city of Chicago paid me a respectable wage for my services, but Mom's condo payment took a big bite. I had a private arrangement with her bank; she'd get a token monthly bill, easily covered by her pension and Social Security, and I took care of the lion's share.

In my quest to pinch pennies, I'd turned my apartment into a greenhouse. It was so hot I had wild orchids sprouting on the sofa. I set the air to *tundra* and took a cold shower, but the water never got any cooler than lukewarm. Wrapped in a terry cloth bathrobe, I attended to the Mr. Friskers situation.

My skiing days long behind me, I did own a pair of black leather gloves that would offer me some protection. I slipped them on, ready for battle.

Mr. Friskers sat patiently in the carrier, probably plotting the downfall of the United States. I opened the door latch, but he made no attempt to howl or attack.

Perhaps he'd worn himself out.

I took two bowls from the clean side of the sink and poured water into one. The other I filled with some of the dry cat food I'd purchased. I set the bowls on the floor in front of him.

Mr. Friskers walked out of the carrier, sniffed the food, and gave me a look of utter disappointment.

"Your cream-from-the-bottle days are over, buddy. And come to think of it—"

I reached down and grabbed him by the diaper. He morphed into the Tasmanian Devil, whirling and clawing and spitting and hissing, catching me a good one on the right forearm. But I proved to be the stronger mammal, and managed to pull off the tabs and remove the diaper before losing too much blood.

The aroma was heady. When the dizziness passed, I wrapped the diaper in a plastic garbage bag, then wrapped that garbage bag in another garbage bag, and walked it out into my hallway, depositing the package down the garbage chute.

When I returned, the cat was lapping at the water dish. Without the diaper, he looked less demonic, and more like a plain old cat. After slaking his thirst, he again sniffed at the food dish. He gave me a look that on a human would have counted as a sneer.

"This guy likes it," I told him, pointing to the cat on the bag of food.

He seemed to consider it, then began to eat.

Now for phase two.

I set the cat box on the floor and read the instructions on the back of the kitty litter bag. Simple enough. I tore the corner and filled the box, getting a noseful of sweet, perfumey dust.

Mr. Friskers looked up from the food dish, cocking his head at me.

"Okay. Time for your first lesson."

I picked him up gently, and he allowed it, going limp in my hands. But when I tried to set him down in the cat box, he dervished on me, twisting and screaming and kicking up a spray of litter. I had to let go of him, for fear of losing an eye, and he bounded out of the kitchen and down the hall.

I spit out some kitty litter. The bag hadn't lied; the granules clumped like magic.

"We'll get to lesson two later," I called after the cat.

I picked some litter out of my damp hair and attended to my makeup. For work, I made do with a light coat of powder, some eyeliner, and a slash of lipstick. Tonight I went all out—base and mascara and eye shadow and lipliner and a touch of color on my cheeks and a final brush of translucent powder with highlighting bits of glitter in it.

Satisfied I looked as good as I could with my bone structure, I went into the bedroom to pick out special occasion underwear. I put on black satin French-cut panties and my only good bra, a cleavage-enhancer that Latham had only seen me in twice before.

I hated my clothes closet for more than simple fashion reasons, so I didn't dally choosing an outfit. I went with a classic black dress, low cut and strapless. It was calf length, but had a dramatic slit on the right side up to mid-thigh. I liked it because it hung rather than clung, meaning I didn't have to suck in my tummy all night.

I was searching through my sock drawer in a fruitless effort to find a pair of nylons without a run, when I noticed Mr. Friskers on my bed, clawing at my sheets. He wasn't tearing them, just kind of gathering them in a ball as if burying something.

"Hey, cat. What are you . . . aw, dammit."

So much for the litter box.

I stripped the bed and went to the kitchen for some stain remover. Cat litter blanketed most of the kitchen floor, trailing into the living room. Not a bad effort for an animal without opposable thumbs.

It was coming up on six, and I hadn't even started on my hair yet. I hurried back to the bedroom, dumped some cleanser on the stain, then did a quick blow-dry.

My intercom went off. I hit the button to buzz Latham through the lobby door, squeezed into my least-runny pair of hose, and managed to tug on some two-inch heels just as the knock came.

Mirror-check. Not bad. I gave my hair a final finger-fluff and went to let Latham in.

Only it wasn't Latham after all.

CHAPTER 10

"Hiya, Jackie. Wow, you're all dressed up and looking girly. How'd you know I was coming?"

Harry McGlade had gained a few pounds since I'd last seen him a few months back, on my solitary visit to the set of *Fatal Autonomy: Harry McGlade Meets the Gingerbread Man.* He wore his usual three days' growth of beard and a wrinkled yellow suit jacket over a solid red T-shirt.

"I didn't know the *Miami Vice* look was back."

Harry grinned. "I don't have socks on, either. Aren't you going to invite me in?"

"No."

"Come on, Jackie. You can't still be mad."

"I'm not mad," I lied. "I'm getting ready for a date. Why don't you stop by sometime after Christmas? Of 2012?"

"Jackie, partner—"

"We're not partners anymore, McGlade."

Harry spread out his hands. "Look, I'm sorry. I thought the screen credit would make you happy."

I'd visited a location shoot because McGlade had insisted on me meeting the director and the actor playing me. "So they get the authenticity right," he'd told me.

It turned out my character was there for comic relief, and so stupid she had mismatched shoes for half the film. I cringed, recalling the scene where the idiot with my name read a suspect his *Fernando* rights.

I crossed my arms, anger rising. "You had me listed as a technical consultant on a movie that failed to accurately portray one single aspect of police procedure."

"Heh, heh. Remember the *Fernando* rights scene? Biggest laugh in the flick."

I tried to slam the door, but Harry shoved a foot inside.

"Jackie! Please! I really need to talk to you. It's hugely important."

I pushed harder, leaning into it.

"It's life or death! Please! These loafers are Italian!"

If I knew Harry, and unfortunately that was the case, he'd continue bothering me until I gave in. I considered arresting him, but as much as that would amuse me, Latham would be here any minute and I didn't want to spend our date at the district house booking McGlade.

"Thirty seconds, McGlade, then you go."

"Sixty."

"Thirty."

"Forty-five."

"Twenty."

"Fine. Thirty seconds, then I'm out of here."

I released the door. Harry grinned.

"Thanks, Jackie. You going to let me in?"

I stood to the side, allowing him entrance. He sauntered in, trailing a fog of Brut.

"So, this is your place, huh? Kind of dumpy."

"You have twenty-five seconds left."

Harry stopped fingering my couch and faced me.

"Okay, I'll get to the point. I need a favor. You know a sergeant out of the one-two, name of Pierce?"

"No."

"Well, he's—"

My buzzer sounded. Nice timing, Latham. I hit the intercom button.

"I'll be right down, Latham."

"Could I come up? These need to get in some water."

I pressed Talk, unsure of what to say. I really didn't want Latham to have to deal with McGlade.

"Jackie!" Harry yelled. "Come back to bed!"

I punched McGlade in the ribs, hard. Though I didn't weigh a lot, I was working on my second-degree black belt in tae kwon do, and knew how to hit. McGlade yelped.

"Jack, who was that?"

"Harry McGlade. He's just leaving."

McGlade pulled a face. "You promised me thirty seconds!"

"Jack," Latham sounded flustered. "We can go out tomorrow, if you've got something going on."

"No! Come on up."

I buzzed him in, then jabbed a finger at McGlade's spongy chest.

"You. Out."

"But you said . . ."

"If you don't leave right now, I promise that I'll dedicate my life to making sure you never get whatever favor it is you want from me."

McGlade considered it.

"So if I leave, you'll do the favor?"

"I don't even know what the favor is."

"When would be a good time to discuss it?" Harry dug into his jacket pocket, pulled out a PDA. "I think I'm free for lunch tomorrow."

"Fine. Lunch tomorrow. But you have to leave right now."

I shoved Harry out the door, hurried to the bathroom to check my hair and makeup, and swallowed two aspirin; McGlade never failed to induce a headache.

When the knock came, I did my damnedest to put on a nice smile.

"Hi, Latham."

Latham stood in my hallway, a dozen roses in his hand and a puzzled look on his face. Standing next to him, arm around his shoulders, was Harry.

"Good news, Jack. We can cancel lunch tomorrow. Your boyfriend invited me to dinner with you guys."

Latham shrugged.

"He said it was life or death."

I gave Harry a look I normally reserved for rapists and murderers.

"McGlade . . ."

"I won't stay long. And I'll pay. The best bar and grill in the city is right around the corner."

"Wait out here," I told him, tugging Latham into my apartment and closing the door.

Latham looked good. He wore a dark gray suit, a light gray shirt, and a rich blue silk tie. Businessman chic.

"So that's Harry, huh? He's older and fatter than the guy who played him on TV."

"He's stupider too. Are those for me?"

Latham handed me the roses. I took a compulsory sniff.

"They're gorgeous."

"You're gorgeous."

Latham moved in for the kiss, and when his lips touched mine I felt it all the way down to my toes. I had a sudden urge to forget about dinner, and

McGlade, and drag Latham into the bedroom. And I might have done just that, if my bed hadn't been covered with cat stains.

"We should put those in some water." Latham brought the roses into the kitchen, stopping when he saw the mess.

"What happened in here? It looks like Pompeii after Vesuvius."

"Long story. I'll tell you over a romantic dinner."

"Jackie!" McGlade pounded on the door. "What's taking so long? You guys bumping uglies in there?"

Latham laughed. "Romantic dinner, hmm?"

"My gun's in my purse. Want me to shoot him?"

"Let him pay for dinner first."

I found a vase in the cabinet while Latham cut an inch off the bottom of the stems. When the flowers were arranged, I kissed him again, then wiped a smudge of my lipstick off his lips.

"So what's this big thing you wanted to ask me, Latham?"

Latham smiled, eyes twinkling.

"I'll tell you soon enough."

CHAPTER 11

"So this was back in the '80s, and crack was still pretty new to the streets, and me and Jackie catch an *officer down* squeal at this known crack house."

Latham nudged me. "You two used to ride together?"

I took a large swig of Sam Adams and frowned.

"No one else would ride with Harry, so I got stuck with him."

"That's true. It's because I was reckless."

"It's because you're obnoxious. Every partner Harry ever had put in for a transfer."

Harry shook his head. "Wrong. Steinwank got shot."

"Steinwank shot himself in the foot to get away from you."

"Whatever. Anyway, we pull up to this crack house, and sure enough, there's a uniform down on the sidewalk right in front."

I drank more beer and looked around the room. We'd wound up at the Cubby Bear, a Chicago bar and grill across the street from Wrigley Field, just a few blocks from my apartment. Harry's face was a mess of BBQ sauce, and he gnawed at his two-dozenth buffalo wing while he spoke.

"So Jack gets out of the car, checks the guy. He's out."

"Was he shot?" Latham asked. He'd been humoring McGlade for the last half an hour, and I wished he'd quit it. Neither he nor Harry had gotten around to telling me the reasons they wanted to talk to me, and I was antsy, overdressed, and getting very bored with the cigarette smoke and loud noise and college kids bumping the back of my chair.

"That's the thing. He wasn't shot, but he's got this big goose egg on his head. Won't wake up—the guy's even snoring. Anyway, Jackie uses this as probable cause for entering the crack house. She marches right inside, which was suicidal. Crack houses are like fortresses. I even remember a raid where Vice nabbed a rocket launcher. Those guys don't play around."

Latham looked at me with such frank admiration I almost blushed.

"They didn't have a rocket launcher," I said.

"Let me finish the story. So anyway, because I'm Jackie's partner, I go in after her. Jackie's in there, screaming and waving her gun, and scares the absolute shit out of them. They practically trip over themselves trying to surrender. We made eighteen felony arrests, all by ourselves, not a single shot fired. Even made the nightly news."

"What about the cop?"

"That's the best part. Turned out the cop was there to score some coke for his personal use, and he tripped on a shoelace and knocked himself out."

Harry laughed, slapping his thigh and staining it with sauce.

"That's a great story," Latham said. He took a pull on his beer. "Jack really doesn't talk about herself."

"Do you know about the time she loaned out to Vice to go undercover as a hooker?"

"No. I'd like to hear that one."

I didn't mind hearing stories about my past so much as I minded Latham getting chummy with Harry McGlade, whom I couldn't stand for a handful of reasons. This was a good time to change topics.

"So what's the problem you're having with Sergeant Pierce?" I asked Harry.

"Oh. I tagged his wife."

"Tagged?"

"Slipped her the Harry Special, with extra sauce. She's a fine woman—too good for him." Harry licked his fingers and reached for the last wing.

"And you need me because . . . ?"

"Apparently—and Mrs. Pierce failed to mention this before we did the worm—her husband plays golf with the mayor."

"And?"

"And now the City of Big Shoulders refuses to let me renew my PI license."

I was about to express my amusement at this fortuitous news, when the *pop-pop* of handgun fire cut through the bar.

Harry and I, both instantly recognizing the sound, dropped to the floor. I yanked Latham down with me.

"You get a fix?" McGlade had his gun already out. A .44 Magnum, one of the biggest hand cannons on the market. Insert Freudian overcompensation joke here.

"Near the entrance," I told him, thumbing open my purse and yanking out my S&W .38.

Another gunshot. Half of the crowd still didn't know what was happening, and stood around looking confused or oblivious. I peered through the sea of legs and spied the perp by the front door. He was white, thin, his face nearly as disheveled as his clothing. He had a semiautomatic in his hand—looked like a 9mm—and was waving it around without direction.

At his feet, the bouncer lay in a widening pool of blood.

"Looks homeless and whacked out on something. Nine mil. One person down that I can see."

"I'll flank him. Cover me."

Harry scooted off to the right, heading for the far wall. I dug out my badge with my left hand.

"Stay down," I told Latham. Then I stood up and raised my badge over my head.

"Police! Everybody get down!"

The people around me screamed, yelled, ran, panicked, and some actually listened. The rock music playing through the house speakers stopped. I slipped off my heels and drew a bead on the perp, who stared up at the ceiling with his mouth open.

"Drop the weapon!"

No response. I couldn't tell if he even heard me. I glanced to the right but couldn't see Harry with all of the people running around.

Three steps closer, right arm at full extension, left arm supporting it from underneath, my gun fully cocked. I aimed for his heart.

"Drop the weapon, sir!"

He might as well have been deaf. I closed the distance between us to less than fifteen feet. An easy shot. I didn't have extra rounds, and I hoped six would be enough.

"This is your last warning, sir! Drop the weapon!"

He didn't move. I had no other options.

Breathe in, breathe out, *squeeze, squeeze, squeeze.*

Three rounds, a tight grouping in the chest.

He staggered back, stared at me, raised his 9mm.

Harry's cannon went off just as I fired my last three bullets.

I hit high, two in the shoulder and one in the neck.

Harry hit all over the place. His slugs were larger, faster, and ripped through the perp like stones through tissue paper.

The guy went down, hard. I moved in, kicked away his gun. There were cuffs in my purse, but I didn't think I'd need them; he looked like chicken Parmesan with a slice of Swiss cheese on top.

I turned my attention to the fallen bouncer. Stomach wound. Pulse strong, but irregular. I heard sirens coming closer, looked around for something to stop the bleeding.

"Well, shit on my head and call me a toilet."

Harry tapped me on the shoulder. He'd been removing the spent brass from his cylinder, and when I looked up at him he pointed forward with his chin.

The perp, our perp, was running out the front door.

I glanced at Harry. He shrugged.

We went after the guy.

I bolted out the door, barefoot, the heat pressing down on me. The blood trail went left, and I saw the shooter sprinting through traffic—a helluva lot faster than should have been possible.

Harry whistled. "Damn. You miss every shot?"

"I landed all six. How did you miss with a barrel that long?"

"All mine were sweet. That guy had more holes than a golf course."

We jogged after him.

The pavement was hot underfoot, and little bits of rock and debris dug into my soles. For the first time in my life I was grateful for my ugly calluses.

"Jesus!" McGlade huffed next to me. "I'm not used to exercise in the vertical position."

"Have another buffalo wing."

The perp rounded the north entrance to Wrigley Field, bystanders giving him a wide berth. He was bleeding, but not as much as I would have guessed. Maybe the layers of filthy clothes were absorbing it all.

McGlade dropped a few paces behind me, lost to a coughing jag. I lengthened my stride. My dress clung to my legs, but the slit was big enough to give me room. I still had the gun in my right hand, where it was beginning to get heavy. With my left hand I tried to adjust my underwire, which dug painfully into my ribs.

I took a short detour to avoid a broken beer bottle, turned a corner, and almost wet myself.

The perp had changed directions and was charging straight at me.

I skidded to a halt, losing some skin on my pinkie toes, and recovered quickly enough to fall into a front stance; right leg straight behind me, left leg forward, knee slightly bent, left fist clenched and parallel with the leg. A blocking position.

Tae kwon do originated in Korea. Students progress through ten belts before reaching black. Testing for each belt was broken down into four parts: forms, which were memorized steps similar to karate's *katas,* breaking boards, which partially accounted for my callused feet, Korean terminology, and sparring.

My forte was sparring.

The perp swung with his right arm, bringing it down overhead in a chopping motion.

I blocked easily, spun, and back-kicked him in the spine, adding to his momentum.

He ate pavement, hard, then rolled onto his side. The sidewalk under him was soaked with blood. I stared into his eyes—nothing but pupil, focused on someplace other than the here and now. His chest wounds oozed like a squeezed sponge.

I'd seen corpses in better shape.

But this guy didn't die. He sat up, trying to get to his feet.

I switched the grip on my gun and tapped him, butt-first, on the forehead.

He fell back, then sat up again, head wound gushing.

For years I'd heard the stories about PCP crazies breaking out of handcuffs, jumping off ten-story buildings and surviving, getting shot a dozen times and still putting up a fight. But I'd never believed them.

Until now.

Wheezing, coming from behind me. Harry trotted up, gasping for air like an asthmatic who'd just snorted pollen.

The perp looked at Harry, screamed something unintelligible, and launched himself at the PI.

Harry screamed as well, an octave higher, and whipped his Magnum across the perp's face.

Again the guy went down.

Again the guy sat up.

McGlade took a step back. "This isn't right, Jackie. Maybe we should just let him go."

"If he gets away, he'll bleed to death."

"And that would be bad?"

The man made it to his knees, and then his feet. I didn't want to hit him with the gun again, so I went with a roundhouse kick to the side of the head.

He went down. Came up.

Harry scratched his chin. "It's like one of those old toys. The little egg-shaped people that wobble but don't fall down."

"Weebles. But I don't remember them being this bloody."

Harry hummed the Weebles theme from the old commercial.

"I think I've got an idea." He turned and began walking away.

"You going to rent a tank?"

"No. Just need a running start."

McGlade took four quick steps toward the guy, then punted him square in the stones.

The perp's howl punched through the hot Chicago night and seemed to echo on forever.

"There." McGlade smoothed out his jacket. "That would knock the Terminator out."

He was right. The guy wheezed, then toppled over, hands clutched between his legs.

"He's all yours, Jackie. You can go ahead and read him his Fernando rights."

I fitted him for bracelets, then left McGlade with the perp while I went to find backup.

CHAPTER 12

The cab spit us out at my place just after four in the morning. Latham, gentleman that he was, stuck with me through two debriefings and a trip to the ER to get some glass removed from my foot. He walked me up to my apartment, and I gave him a hug.

"Some romantic evening, huh?"

He smiled, kissed my nose.

"Are you kidding? On our first date I get kidnapped by a serial killer, and tonight I get to see you save a bar full of yuppies from a drug-crazed maniac. Are you free tomorrow? Maybe we can find a bank robbery in progress."

He slipped his hand around the small of my back, pulled me gently against him.

"Would you like to come in?" I asked.

"That's the best idea I've heard all day."

I opened the door, knowing that I had no sheets and wondering if I was too old to do it on the sofa.

"Too late for a drink?" I asked. "Too early?"

"I'd drink muscatel from a dog bowl right now."

"Settle for a whiskey sour?"

Latham nodded.

I went into the kitchen, frowned at the gigantic mess, and built two serviceable highballs. Latham stood in the living room, his jacket off. A good sign.

"Do you like it here?" he asked, as I handed him his drink.

"Here with you?"

"Here in this apartment. I know you don't really like the neighborhood, and I know some—well—bad things happened here."

"I guess I never really thought about it. Why do you ask?"

He smiled; a little-boy smile tinged with mischief.

"I just bought a condo on the lake. Big place, plenty of room, killer view."

"That's great." I took a sip of my drink. "What about the house?"

"Sold. Move in with me, Jack."

Before I had a chance to answer, I noticed Mr. Friskers perched on top of my television, ready to pounce.

"Latham, don't move."

"But I have to move, I signed the papers—"

"Shh." I put my finger to my lips. "It's the cat. He looks like he's about to jump on you."

"Hey, I like cats. If you want to bring a cat along, that's fine with—Jesus Christ!"

Mr. Friskers launched through the air like a calico missile and attached himself to Latham's face, all four claws locking in.

Latham screamed something, but I couldn't hear it through the fur. I grabbed the cat and gently tried to tug him free. Latham's reaction was muffled, but came through.

"No! Stop pulling! Stop pulling!"

I let go, frantic. On the floor, next to the sofa, was the catnip mouse I'd bought at the pet store. I picked it up and held it under the cat's nose.

"Good kitty. Let go of his face. Let go of his face, kitty."

Mr. Friskers sniffed once, twice, then went totally limp. I carried him into the bathroom, keeping the catnip up to his nose, and then set both of them down in the bathtub and locked the door.

I found Latham in the kitchen, liberally applying paper towels.

"Oh, wow, are you okay, Latham?"

He forced a smile.

"I may need a transfusion."

"I'm sorry. I should have warned you."

"I thought it was illegal to keep mountain lions as pets."

I gave him the short version, helping him dab at his wounds. They weren't as bad as Herb's, so perhaps Mr. Friskers was mellowing down.

"So you're not keeping him?"

"Not if I can help it."

"Good. I mean, if he was part of the package, I'd accept him. But I wouldn't want to take off my pants with him in the room."

I opened my mouth to say something, but I wasn't sure what to say. Moving in with Latham would be great. He was right—I didn't like the neighborhood, and I didn't like my apartment, and having him to hold every night would go a long way toward helping my insomnia.

But instead of focusing on all of that, I focused on my mom, stranded on the floor of her bathroom.

"Latham, I'd love to move in with you—"

"That's great!"

"—but I can't. When my mom gets out of the hospital, she's coming to live with me."

I winced, watching the disappointment slowly seep into his face.

"The condo only has one bedroom."

My guard went up. "Latham, I didn't ask if my mother could move into your condo."

"I know. I mean, I'd want her to, if she's with you, but the place is only one bedroom. There wouldn't be any room for her."

"Hey, I didn't ask."

"That came out wrong." Latham touched my cheek. "Look, Jack, I really want to be with you. This whole *I-sleep-over-at-your-place, you-sleep-over-at-my-place* thing, we're too old for that, you know what I mean?"

"I know, Latham. I wish there was some way."

"Is there? Some way, I mean?"

I didn't like where this was going, but I baited him anyway.

"What do you mean?"

"How about she stays here, at your place? It's only a twenty-minute drive away."

"She needs someone around her at all times."

"Okay, fine. There are facilities. Good ones. Your mother could get the assistance she needs, the medical care, and we could visit her every—"

"I'm going to say good night now, Latham."

I took him by the crook of the arm and escorted him to the front door.

"Jack, all that I'm saying is that taking care of an elderly parent is a lot of work. I don't want you wasting your life—"

I opened the door.

"Caring for my mother is not wasting my life."

"I didn't mean it like that. Look, Jack, it's been an awful night and I'm not thinking clearly."

"Apparently not."

Latham's eyes got hard. I'd never really seen him angry before, and I didn't like the preview.

"I may be tooting my own horn here, Jack, but I think I'm a pretty decent guy."

"You're right," I told him. "You're tooting your own horn."

I felt terrible the moment it left my lips, but before I could apologize, Latham was halfway down the hall.

"Latham . . ."

He disappeared through the stairwell door, not giving me a backward glance.

Nice one, Jack. You just screwed up a relationship with the last decent guy in the Midwest.

From the bathroom, Mr. Friskers howled in agreement.

I walked back into my apartment, finished my drink, Latham's drink, and one more on top of that. Pleasantly tipsy, I let the screaming cat out of the john, took off my makeup, curled up on my sheetless bed, and slept for forty-five wonderful minutes before jerking awake.

For the next three hours, sleep was a stop-and-go affair, short stretches interspersed with bouts of anxiety, nagging questions, and doubt.

When I finally got up for work, the mirror was not kind.

I forced myself through some push-ups and sit-ups, took a cool shower, and dressed in a tan Perry Ellis blazer, matching skirt, and a striped blouse.

Venturing into my living room, I discovered I wasn't the only one who had a busy night. To my endless amusement, Mr. Friskers had clawed most of the paint off my grandmother's antique rocking chair. He perched on the sofa, staring, while I inspected the damage.

"Now I understand why so many people own dogs."

He didn't reply.

I cleaned up the kitty litter as best I could, poured him another bowl of food, forced down some Frosted Flakes, and went out to face the day.

Chicago was a furnace, hot enough to make my eyeliner run. Stopping for coffee seemed absurd, but I needed the caffeine. I bought an extra for Herb.

The district house still had an air-conditioning problem, which felt great for about two minutes, and then became painful.

Herb wasn't in his office, which was unusual. He always beat me to work. I set his coffee on his desk, then returned to my office and did some follow-up calls about the incident last night.

The gut-shot bouncer had stabilized, and the perp, defying all expectations, still clung to life. I left word with the doctor to call when toxicology finished the blood work, but she said it wasn't necessary.

"I'm ninety-nine percent sure he was high on Hydro."

"Water?"

"No. Hydro is the nickname for a new street drug. It's a mean mix of phencyclidene hydrochloride, phentermine hydrochloride, and oxycodone hydrochloride; basically angel dust, speed, and codeine. Why anyone would want to mix those is beyond me. Plus, someone is cutting the drug with mephyton phyonadione."

"Which is?"

"Vitamin K. It's commonly given to patients before surgery because of its ability to aid in blood coagulation."

"This drug turns people into psychotic supermen who don't feel pain or bleed?"

"Makes you long for the sixties and good old LSD, doesn't it?"

"Who would make something like this?"

"After working the ER for six years, I've lost count of the different ways people attempt to destroy themselves. I just patch them up so they can go do it again."

"You sound cynical."

"I'm the one who stitched up all the holes you put in this guy, and you're calling me a cynic?"

She had a point. Curiosity prompting me onward, I called the DEA.

"You've no doubt heard about the Big Bust."

The Big Bust the agent referred to was a capture of almost a billion dollars in heroin off the Florida coast. One of the largest drug seizures in history.

"That left a vacuum in the market," he went on. "The junkies still needed something to shoot, so a West Coast drug ring hired some chemists to cook up a replacement. We've already shut down three Hydro labs, but they're popping up all over the place. It's a bad high too. Causes some major freak-outs."

"I've seen it. We shot a man eleven times, and he took off like Carl Lewis."

"Eleven? Not even close to the record. Two cops in Compton cornered a Hydro-head with a Mac-10, took twenty-eight shots to bring him down. Bad drug."

"My guy's still alive."

"So's this guy. Has to be fed through a tube, though. We're thinking of using him as our new antidrug poster boy."

My faith in human nature restored, I checked Herb's office again. No Herb. I took his coffee, mine long gone, then went to check on Officer Fuller and the database.

"Just get in?" I asked.

He was hunched over his computer, squinting at a spreadsheet. I must have surprised him, because he flinched when he heard my voice.

"Oh, hi, Lieut. No, been here for a while. Why?"

"It's ten degrees in here, and you're sweating."

He smiled. "I've been blessed with a high metabolism."

"I wish I was that lucky. How's the database coming?"

"Slow. You've had a lot of arrests."

"I've been blessed with a long career. Any matches yet with County's sign-in book?"

He shook his head. "If I find one, you'll be the second to know."

"Thanks, Officer. Carmichael is retiring this October, which means a slot in the Detective Division is opening up."

Fuller mumbled something under his breath that I didn't make out.

"Pardon me?"

"Just saying a silent prayer, Lieut. I've been trying to get into DD for over a year, and you guys keep passing me over."

"You're a good cop, Fuller. But the cops that took those slots had seniority."

He mumbled something again, and I got the distinct impression I'd been insulted. I let it go. Fuller had a right to be disappointed—he went above and beyond the call of duty to help Herb and me whenever possible, even off the clock. Fuller had a nose for homicide, especially the violent ones, and more than once his input had proven valuable.

Still, he'd only been a cop for three years, and no one rose up the ranks that quickly. The system didn't allow it.

"Don't have anything yet, huh?" I asked.

"Not yet, but if there's something, I'll find it."

I thanked him, and noticed Benedict out of the corner of my eye. Actually, I'd heard him before seeing him. He was whistling.

"Good morning, Herb."

"Morning, Jack." He smiled, and then winked.

I eyed him suspiciously. "Everything okay, Herb?"

"Everything is wonderful. Couldn't be better."

"You're late this morning."

"I slept in." Herb winked again.

"Is something wrong with your eye?"

"No. Why?"

"You keep winking at me."

"Just in a good mood, that's all. Are we off to shake down the dealer?" He put his hands in his pockets and rocked back on his heels.

"Yeah. I'll stop by my office for a bag. You sure you're okay?"

"I'm absolutely perfect, Jack." And he winked at me again.

I went to my desk, followed by some weird alternate-universe version of my partner, and retrieved a plastic bag filled with powdered sugar. Davi's supposed dealer probably wouldn't be forthcoming with the police. The bag would help him loosen his tongue.

I handed it to Herb. In this day and age, it was risky for a woman to frisk a man, and vice versa. Sexual harassment laws protected criminals too.

After a quick stroll through the desert that was our parking lot, we got into Herb's Camaro and he cranked up the air. It was only a matter of time before the constant flux between hot and cold would give me pneumonia.

Herb pulled onto Lake Shore Drive, heading south. Chicago didn't seem to be bothered by the heat. People littered the walkways along the beach, and a few suicidal individuals were even jogging. Out on Lake Michigan, hundreds of boats competed for space. It looked as if someone sprinkled some kosher salt on a gigantic polished mirror.

Herb began whistling again, keeping tempo by drumming his fingers on the steering wheel.

"All right," I said after five minutes of biting my tongue. "Spill it."

"Spill what?"

"Why you're so damn happy."

"What do you mean?"

"It's like you've been possessed by one of the Care Bears."

He looked at me, and winked.

"There are some things best kept private, Jack."

"That's bull, Herb. We're partners. We have no secrets."

"You sure?"

"I'm sure."

Herb winked at me again. I made a fist, ready to slug him.

"Okay. Bernice and I were . . . intimate last night."

I stared at him.

"That's all? You're this happy because you got laid?"

He smiled. "Five times."

I did a double take.

"Five times?"

He nodded. "Three last night, and then two more this morning."

I looked at Benedict with newfound respect.

"You haven't been possessed by a Care Bear. You've been possessed by a porn star."

He winked at me again. "Viagra."

"Really?"

"Bernice and I have been doing the once-a-week thing for thirty years. So last night I decided to spice things up a bit."

"Apparently it worked."

"I was a dynamo, Jack. You should see the scratch marks on my back."

I had no idea how to respond to that. Pat him on the shoulder? Tell him to nail her once for me? I settled on, "That's great."

"She was begging me for mercy, Jack. But I kept a-goin'. I haven't heard her scream like that since—"

"Herb," I interrupted, "you were right. Maybe we should keep some things private."

Colin Andrews's neighborhood was primarily low-income. Gang-bangers flashing colors eyed us, trying to figure out what business a white couple in a new sports car had in their hood. At a stoplight, a kid with baggy pants pimp-walked up to the passenger side and tapped on my window.

"Y'all lost?"

I smiled at him. "Five-O. Y'all holding?"

He put his hands in the air and backed off, smiling at me with gold caps. The way he wore his bandanna told me he was a Gangsta Disciple. Couldn't have been more than twelve years old.

"I blame rap music," Herb said.

"That's much easier than blaming the parents."

"I'm serious. Think about how gang violence would be reduced if they all listened to Perry Como."

"Reduced? I think they'd riot. Hell, I'd riot."

Ninety-sixth Street had more potholes than asphalt, and Herb cringed every time his car took a dip. Andrews's apartment building was the nicest one on the block, but that didn't mean much. Graffiti still colored the sidewalk and walls, and three divots in the front door were obvious bullet holes.

Herb parked directly in front of the building, on the street. Our leather badge cases had cords attached, and we hung our stars around our necks. I got out of the car, feeling the same sense of uneasiness I always felt when on the South Side, being a white female cop. None of those traits were looked upon with respect here.

Herb turned to me. "What's your take on this?"

I knew what he meant. It was unlikely Davi McCormick got her drugs from Colin, unless he made frequent visits to the Gold Coast—dealers tend to stay local. And two severed arms planted in the county morgue wasn't your typical gang-related or drug-related crime.

"The calls from her apartment were to his cell phone. Maybe we'll get lucky."

The security door had a broken lock, allowing us an easy entry. The lobby reeked of heat and decay. More graffiti tags marked the walls, and someone had shattered two of the three hallway lights.

Colin Andrews rented an apartment on the first floor. The number had been removed from the door, but we figured it out by counting.

Herb rapped his knuckle on the door.

"Colin Andrews? Chicago PD."

No answer.

"Mr. Andrews, this is the police. We'd like to ask you some questions. It's in your best interest to open the door."

"How it my best interest letting cops in?"

"Because if you don't talk to us," Benedict said, "we'll start knocking on all of your neighbors' doors. It would be hard for you to live here if everyone thought you were a police snitch."

"I ain't no damn snitch."

We waited. I noticed Herb had his hand near his holster, and realized that mine had drifted there as well.

After a minute, the door opened a crack. A brown eye squinted out at us.

"What this about?"

I smiled pleasantly. "You want everyone to see you talking to us in the hall?"

He opened the door.

The apartment was air-conditioned, neat, nicely furnished. An entertainment center crammed full of state-of-the-art equipment sat next to a wide-screen TV.

Colin stood about Benedict's height, but rail thin. He wore an oversized Steelers jersey and a thick gold chain around his neck that seemed to weigh him down.

"Business must be good." I eyed his place, annoyed that the crooks always had better stuff than I did.

Colin shrugged.

"Colin?" A woman's voice came from one of the back rooms. "Who's there?"

"No one, Mama. Stay in your room."

"Mama know you deal?" I asked.

"I don't deal. That's all a big misunderstanding."

I fished through the pockets of my blazer and took out a folded head shot of Davi McCormick.

"Do you recognize this woman?"

I watched Colin's face. He glanced at the photo without changing his expression.

"Never saw her."

"She called your cell phone a few days ago."

"Don't got no cell phone."

I read the phone number to him.

"Don't got that phone no more. Lost it."

"When did you lose it?"

"Couple weeks ago."

Herb bent down, reaching for Colin's foot.

"I think you dropped something, Colin. Well—lookee here."

Herb held up the bag of powdered sugar.

"Dog, that ain't mine!"

Herb made an innocent face. "I saw it fall out of your pocket. Didn't you, Jack?"

"I don't even deal that shit, man. I just distribute the herb."

"Where's your phone, Colin?"

"I told you, I lost the phone."

Benedict dipped a finger into the bag, then touched his tongue.

"How much you think is here? Eight, ten grams? That's what—thirty years?"

I moved closer to Colin. "We found the arms. We know she called you."

"What arms? I don't carry, man. I'm low-key."

"Where's the phone?"

"I don't know."

Colin looked frightened. Though I couldn't arrest him for possession of a known confectionary, I decided to push my luck.

"You know the drill, Colin. On your knees, hands behind your head."

"I don't have the phone! I swear! You need to ask your people!"

"What people?"

"Cops. When I got arrested last month, they took my phone. I never got it back."

Out of the corner of my eye, I noticed Herb was dipping back into the bag for another taste. I stepped between him and Colin.

"You're saying we have your phone?"

"I had it with me when I got booked, and when I got sprung no one knew anything about my phone."

I had a pretty good internal BS detector, and Colin was either a much better liar than I was used to, or he was telling the truth.

"Have you canceled the service?"

"Haven't got round to it."

"Why not?"

I saw fear flash across Colin's eyes.

"Colin, do you know who has your phone?"

"No."

"Colin, the person who took your phone is very dangerous. If you tell us who it is, we can protect you."

"I told you I don't know."

"Maybe a trip to the station will help jog your memory."

Colin glanced at Herb and smirked. "I don't think you be charging me with nothing."

I looked. Benedict was licking a large mound of white powder out of his palm.

"I'm testing the purity," Benedict said. His beard was dusty with sugar.

Colin went to the door and held it open.

"Y'all can go now."

"Colin . . ."

"I know my rights. If I tell you to go, you got to go."

"We want to help you, Colin."

"Yeah, right."

I handed him my card. He took it, reluctantly.

"If a police officer stole your cell phone, you can file a formal complaint. You can help us get this guy."

"Whatever."

We left the apartment.

"Jesus, Herb. Real professional."

"I couldn't help it. I haven't had anything sweet in over a week. Once I had that little taste, I couldn't stop."

He drove his point home by upending the remainder of the bag into his mouth.

"Do you know how many carbs are in that?"

"I don't care. It's like an orgy on my tongue."

"During the orgy, did you manage to pick up on what Colin said?"

He nodded, his face turning somber.

The perp had access to my handcuffs, to the county morgue, and to Colin's cell phone.

All signs pointed to the killer being a cop.

Unfortunately, this did little to narrow it down. Chicago had a police force of over seventeen thousand. I had eight hundred working out of my district, plus cops from the other districts came and went on a daily basis. So did cops from out of town, Feds, lawyers, and government officials.

Benedict seemed to sense my thoughts. "Maybe we'll be able to narrow it down once we go through the complete phone log."

"Who's Colin's carrier?"

"FoneCo. They want a subpoena before they release his records."

"We can swing by the courthouse."

Benedict probed his goatee with his tongue, seeking out stray calories.

"Should we put a team on Colin?"

I considered it. If Colin saw cops hanging around, he might freak out and try to run. Plus, who could I trust to put on him? What if I accidentally sent the killer?

"No. We should talk to the assistant State's Attorney first. Colin's court case is coming up."

I didn't like driving away knowing that Colin was hiding something, but there wasn't much I could do about it. Coming to him with a deal might loosen his tongue.

"I hope it's not a bad cop, Jack."

Me too. If cops were viewed as the enemy, the tenuous balance of power could shift. Laws would be broken out of contempt. Authority wouldn't be acknowledged. Police officers might even be attacked, or worse.

I closed my eyes, and tried not to think about rioting.

"We're probably wrong, Herb. It's probably not a cop at all."

But deep down, I knew we were right.

CHAPTER 13

He watches them get into the sports car and pull away. That bitch Daniels, and her fat-ass partner, Herb Benedict.

He climbs out of his car and walks toward Colin Andrews's apartment.

He expected them to eventually find Andrews, but not this quickly.

No matter. He'll just jump ahead in the plan a little.

There's an empty plastic soda bottle next to the security door. He snatches it up and enters the building.

It's hot. Dark. He pulls a pair of latex gloves out of his front pocket, and they make a snapping sound. They're tight on his large, sweaty hands.

He has a slight headache, but the aspirin is keeping it under control. He's here for business, not pleasure.

But his arousal is apparent.

He knocks on Andrews's door.

"Chicago Police Department."

Silence. He knocks again.

"Open the door, this is the police."

"You ain't getting in without a warrant."

A male voice. Scared.

"We have a warrant," the killer lies.

"Slip it under the door."

He looks left, then right. All clear.

Taking one step back, he sets his shoulder, and then charges the door.

The frame snaps like balsa wood. Colin Andrews sprawls backward, hands clutched to a bleeding nose. The killer enters and shuts the door, shoving it hard so it fits back into the splintered jamb.

"Colin? Who's there?"

He grins. A woman. He hadn't expected that.

This is gonna be fun.

Colin is on the floor, scrambling backward, eyes wide as dinner plates.

He considers kicking him, decides he doesn't want to get blood on his pants, and pulls out his throwaway piece: a 9mm Firestar that he liberated from the evidence locker at the same time he'd taken Colin's cell phone.

The gun presses against Colin's forehead.

"Ask her to join the party."

Colin opens his mouth. No words come out.

He taps him on the skull, hard, with the butt of the gun.

"Get her in here, now."

The blubbering begins. Colin calls for his mama, voice cracking though the sobs.

Colin's mother is wearing a T-shirt and jeans. She's younger than the killer expected. Prettier too.

"Hi, Mama." He blows her a kiss. "Go sit on the sofa. The three of us are going to have a conversation."

Mama cops an attitude, hands rising to her hips. "What the—"

"Mama, sit down!" Colin screams at her, blood and tears rolling down his face.

His mother nods, then sits.

"Okay, here's the dealio." The cop smiles at his use of street slang. "I'm going to ask some questions. I get answers I like, I go away and never come back. I don't get answers I like . . ."

He slaps the gun across Colin's face, knocking him to the floor.

"Do we understand each other?"

He looks at the mother. Her eyes are cold, but she nods.

Colin is hugging the floor like a security blanket, trembling. The killer nudges him with his foot.

"Do you know who I am, Colin?"

Colin stares up. Nods.

"Tell me who I am."

"When I got brung in, you the one that locked me up."

"That's right, Colin. Do you remember what I said to you?"

Colin swallowed, his Adam's apple bobbing up and down like a basketball.

"You told me not to cancel my phone service."

"Or else?"

"Or else you'd hang my ass from the nearest lamppost."

"Good, Colin. You remembered. Did you believe me, when I said it?"

"I didn't cancel the service! I didn't!"

"I know, Colin. That's why you're not swinging from the streetlight out in front. But you did talk to the cops about me, didn't you?"

Colin shakes his head so fast it's comical.

"I din't say nothin'!"

"Are you sure?"

"Jesus, I din't say nothin'!"

"Get up, go sit next to Mama on the couch."

Colin pulls himself off the floor, plops down next to his mother. The cop knows he's broken him. Knows he's telling the truth.

He checks his watch. There's still a little time for some fun.

"Is your boy lying to me, Mama?"

She puts an arm around Colin's shoulders as he cries into his hands.

"Colin don't tell no lies."

The killer admires the defiance in her eyes. He becomes even more aroused. "He doesn't? But Colin deals drugs, doesn't he?"

She strokes Colin's head, as if petting a dog.

"I heard him, when those other cops came. He din't tell them nothin'."

The cop moves closer to the sofa. He feels ready to burst.

"You seem like a smart lady. If you and your boy want to live through this, you're gonna have to do something for me. You know what it is?"

Colin's mama stares at him, nods.

"There's a condom in my front pocket. Take it out."

Her hands are hot in his pants.

"Put it on me and get to work, Mama. Make me happy and I'll spare your life."

She's not the best he's ever had, and the condom limits some of the sensation, but she's much better than his bitch of a wife.

"Hey, Colin, I think your mama's done this before. She's got some good moves."

A few minutes pass. The only sounds are Colin's sobs and the killer's breathing, which gets faster and faster.

"That's right. Yeah. Good."

As he nears climax, he places the base of the plastic bottle he's been holding against the top of the woman's head. He puts the barrel of the 9mm into the bottle opening.

"That's it!"

His hips spasm, and at the same moment he fires into the bottle, the slug shooting straight through her forehead, embedding itself in the sofa.

The bottle traps most of the noise, and the sound is no louder than a hand clap.

Colin's head snaps up, staring as his mother falls away.

"Don't look so surprised, Colin. You know you can't trust cops."

He tosses aside the bottle, now filled with swirling white smoke. Then he picks up a sofa cushion and shoves it into Colin's face, jamming the gun into the fabric.

Four shots. Colin goes slack.

Condom still on, the killer zips up his pants, picks up the plastic bottle, and leaves the apartment. There's no one in the hallway, and no one outside.

His headache, happily, is gone.

The cop hops into his car and checks his watch. He's on his lunch break, and has already used up fifty-five minutes.

He speeds back to the station. After ten blocks, the condom goes out the window. A few blocks later, so does the soda bottle.

On his way back to the district house, the killer stops in front of the Wabash Bridge and pulls over to the curb. Palming the gun, he gets out and walks over to the Chicago River.

No one gives him a second glance as he drops the gun into the greenish water.

When he arrives back at the station, he doesn't see Benedict's Camaro in the parking lot. He's beaten them back.

The cop parks and walks into the building, wondering whom he hates more, Jack or that fat piece-of-shit Herb.

He climbs the stairs, heading for Benedict's office. His plan, such as it is, is deceptively simple.

He'll keep killing women and leaving various things belonging to Jack and Herb at the crime scenes.

Eventually, they might get close to figuring it out. When that time comes, he'll kill them both, making it look like they've killed each other.

Then he'll solve these current murders himself, framing his mortician friend Derrick Rushlo.

Sadly, Derrick won't make it to trial.

Simple. Effective. And so much fun.

The killer makes sure no one notices as he slips into Herb's office.

He's looking for something, anything, that Herb will recognize when he sees it on the next victim. A tie clip, a wrist watch, a picture of his ugly wife . . .

"Here we are."

In Herb's desk drawer, he finds a library card. Without hesitating, he picks it up.

"May I help you, Officer?"

His head snaps around. Benedict is walking into the office, holding a large coffee. One of his eyebrows is raised in silent inquiry.

"Hi, Detective Benedict. I was dropping these off for you."

In one smooth motion he slips the library card into his chest pocket and removes a small bottle of pills. He hands it to Benedict.

"Non-aspirin pain reliever?" Herb reads.

"Remember that bottle I borrowed last month?"

"Oh, yeah. Thanks." Benedict slaps him on the shoulder, like they're best buddies.

"Well, back to work," he says. "TOSAP."

"That's what we get paid for." Herb chuckles. "To Serve and Protect."

Too bad there's no one to protect you from me, old man.

Leaving Herb's office, he bumps into Jack, causing her to spill some coffee.

"Good afternoon, Officer."

"Good afternoon, Lieutenant."

Bitch.

Well, if things go as planned, Herb and Jack won't be around to irritate him for much longer.

He walks back to his desk, sits down, and takes a deep, full breath.

Close one.

He thinks about Herb Benedict, thinks about killing the man. He's never killed someone that big before. It might actually be a challenge.

A challenge could be fun.

He decides, when the time comes, he'll do it hands on. Mano a mano. No gun. No knife. He'll beat him to death.

As for Lieutenant Daniels . . .

The good lieutenant is tough, and strong. She'll be good for a whole evening's entertainment, in his little plastic room on the South Side.

And maybe, if he's careful, he could make her last the whole weekend.

CHAPTER 14

It took most of the afternoon to set up the surveillance.

After playing catch-the-subpoena at the courthouse, Herb and I managed to get access to the call log from Colin Andrews's cell phone. There were only three numbers on the list. One was to Davi McCormick's place, one was to a call girl named Eileen Hutton, and one was to a TracFone owned by someone named John Smith.

Eileen Hutton had a record—she worked for a high-roller escort service similar to Davi's. A search of her apartment found it empty and without any signs of foul play, and a call to her employer found them worried sick because Eileen had missed her last two dates.

A TracFone was one of those prepaid cell phones that could be bought at drugstores, electronics stores, or on the Internet. They're a cop's worst nightmare. It's simple to set up an anonymous account by using a fake name and then buying phone cards with cash.

We obtained another subpoena and secured the records from the TracFone that the killer had been calling. No calls listed going out, and the only calls coming in were from Colin's cell.

After talking at length with several people at the phone company, it proved impossible to set up any kind of tracking or tracing of the phone. But we were able to track the prepaid cards being used for minutes. The phone had been bought two months ago at an Osco Drug on Wabash and Columbus. Two weeks after that, a twenty-minute phone card had been purchased at the same place.

According to the recent bill, those minutes were due to expire tomorrow. Which meant a new phone card would have to be purchased, hopefully from the same drugstore.

Since we suspected the killer to be a cop, I was climbing the walls trying to figure out who to put on the surveillance teams. I played the sexism card, and put two teams of three female officers on eight-hour shifts. If the killer was a woman, I might have been blowing the entire stakeout, but I just couldn't reconcile a woman cutting off someone's arms.

Anyone who bought a phone card or a new phone at the Osco would be tailed. Anyone with access to the county morgue—cops, morticians, doctors—would be red-flagged and I'd get an immediate call.

According to the store, they sold between five and ten phone cards a day. I hoped three officers on the scene would be enough, but I did have the resources for more.

"We're getting close," Herb said.

"It's still a shot in the dark, Herb. The person who owns the TracFone might not even be an accomplice. It could be someone who doesn't even know the perp."

"If we look at the call logs, it works out. The perp called Davi's place at two forty-five P.M. She called him back at six fifteen. Then, at nine twenty, the perp calls the TracFone. In Eileen's case, the perp calls her yesterday at ten thirty A.M., then again at three twelve P.M. Three hours later, at six oh two, he calls the TracFone."

"You think he's abducting these women, then calling someone to join the party?"

"Or to help with the disposal."

I mulled it over. My eyes drifted to the phone. I'd called Latham three times, and he hadn't called back. I fought the urge to check my messages again.

I'd also called my mother, twice. She still wasn't accepting my calls.

I wonder if Alexander Graham Bell knew, back when he invented the telephone, how much control his device would have over the lives of so many people. Especially mine.

I switched gears. "We might be missing a connection between Davi and Eileen."

Benedict flipped through his notes. "There doesn't have to be a connection. Both have priors. The killer could have been searching for likely victims by going through arrest records. All cops have computer access."

Chicago had several psychiatrists specifically for its law enforcement officers. Cops had the same problems as everyone, but they tended to be amplified. I'd called the three doctors in the city's employ, and all gave me the same lecture about patient confidentiality. The off-the-record question of "Do you know of any cops who might be capable of this?" was met with three enthusiastic "yes" answers.

Herb popped something into his mouth, chasing it with old coffee. He looked at his watch.

"I've got to hit the road, Jack. These things kick in pretty fast."

"You took a Viagra? Herb, can't you give the poor woman a rest?"

"Do you want to try one? For Latham?"

I crossed my arms.

"Latham's fine in that area, thanks."

"You sound defensive."

"I'm not defensive."

"Jack, all couples have problems sometimes. I'm sure he finds you very attractive."

"We're not having any problems in bed, Herb. That is, when we find the time to go to bed."

"I thought, last night . . ."

"Did you hear about the shooting at the Cubby Bear?"

I watched Herb put two and two together in his head.

"You know, I was thinking that might be you, but when you didn't say anything this morning . . ."

I gave Herb a quick rundown of the events last night, ending with my argument with Latham.

"So I didn't get laid last night, because he was acting like a jerk."

"Wanting to move in with the woman he loves is him acting like a jerk?"

"I . . . uh . . ."

"He's told you he loves you, right?"

"Yeah, but . . ."

"Have you said it back?"

"I . . . uh . . ."

"You called him today?"

This I could answer.

"Three times. He hasn't called me back."

"When you called him, did you apologize for acting like a horse's ass?"

"Why should I apologize? He wants to stick my mother in a nursing home."

"He wants to figure out how to share his life with you, and you told him he was tooting his own horn."

Oops.

"Jack." Herb turned a shade of red usually reserved for apples. "I don't mean to cut out on you, but I have to run, and you might want to avert your eyes."

"Why? Oh—the Viagra's kicking in?"

"I just pitched a tent in my pants."

Herb picked up a manila folder and held it out well in front of his lap.

"That stuff really works," I said, for lack of anything better.

"Good night, Jack. Now if you'll excuse me."

"Good night, Herb. Give Bernice my best. Er, I mean, your best. Have a nice evening. Have fun. I'll shut up now."

Herb slunk out the door while I counted the ceiling tiles.

After he made his embarrassing exit, I picked up the phone, swallowed pride, and called Latham. His machine picked up.

"Hi, Latham. Look, I . . ."

Say you're sorry, I told myself. *Say it.*

But nothing came out.

". . . I'll call you tomorrow."

Why the hell had I choked? Why was apologizing such a big deal? I could admit to myself I'd made a mistake, why couldn't I admit it to Latham?

"Lieutenant?"

I looked up, saw Fuller standing in my doorway.

"Come in."

He set a computer printout on my desk.

"I finished the database. There weren't any connections between your previous cases and County's sign-in book."

"Thanks. I'll go over it later."

I'd intended that to be a dismissal, but he stayed put.

"Anything else?" I asked.

"Look, Lieut, I . . . I'd just like to help."

I considered it. The only person I really trusted was Herb. But Fuller had been extremely helpful to many of my investigations, going above and beyond his normal duties. I didn't know very much about him, personally, but as a cop he was smart, efficient, and always 100 percent professional.

I made a judgment call, and decided to let him in.

"Okay, there is something you can do. I want you to add some names to the database."

"Sure. What names?"

"Start with this district, then the surrounding districts, until you get all twenty-six."

Fuller furrowed his brow. "Cops? You think this might be a cop?"

I had to play this carefully, lest the rumor mill begin to turn.

"No. But if I find out which cops visited the morgue during the past week, I'll be able to start questioning them to see if they noticed anything strange."

"Got it."

"There's no rush. You can get started tomorrow."

He nodded, offered a grin, and left my office.

I finished typing the report of the interview with Colin Andrews (leaving out the powdered sugar fiasco), and then decided to head home. Perhaps Latham had left a message on my answering machine.

He hadn't. Neither had Mom. But Mr. Friskers, the lovable ball of fluff, had shredded both of the living room curtains.

"Tomorrow," I promised, "you get declawed."

I changed into an oversized T-shirt and wandered into the kitchen, cat litter sticking to the bottoms of my feet. I swept it all up, dumped it back into the litter box, and was surprised to find that Mr. Friskers had made several deposits of his own.

"Good kitty," I called to him, wherever he was hiding.

I went to the fridge to get him some milk, and stepped barefoot into another deposit he'd made, on the floor.

This required a shower. After the shower, I finished cleaning the kitchen, gave the cat some milk and food, and searched my cabinets for dinner. I found a can of soup. I wasn't in the mood for soup, especially mushroom, but it was expiring next month, so I ate it before I had to throw it out.

Halfway through, Mr. Friskers wandered in.

"I like the curtains," I told him. "Very feng shui. The whole room flows much better."

He ignored me, sticking his face in the milk.

I didn't finish the soup, so I set that on the floor for him as well, then I went into the bedroom and stared at my nemesis, the bed.

My sheets were in the dryer. I put them back on, climbed in, and closed my eyes.

It took all of five seconds for me to realize that I had a better chance of winning lotto than falling asleep. So instead, I flipped on the television.

Reruns. Sports. Crap. Movie that I've seen before. Crap. Crap. Reruns. Crap. Home Shopping Network.

I finally let it rest on an infomercial about the antiaging effects of juicing. A tiny ninety-year-old man did dozens of push-ups and exclaimed how celery shakes were life's elixir.

Did anyone buy that?

I did, and sprung for the rush delivery.

I also bought a Speedy Iron, guaranteed to do the job in half the time, a Bacon Magic, since the show proved beyond any scientific doubt that bacon was a health food, and a new home waxing system that promised it wouldn't hurt as much as the four other new home waxing systems gathering dust in my bathroom closet.

The only thing that saved me from plunking down serious cash for a countertop rotisserie oven was the fact that my counter space was barely large enough for a toaster. I toyed with the idea of buying one anyway, and keeping it in the bedroom. Even though I'm a single woman and rarely home, the novelty of roasting two entire chickens at the same time more than made up for that.

I drifted off sometime in the middle of a seminar on how to improve your memory, and slept on and off until seven A.M., when the phone rang.

I bolted up in bed, hoping it was Latham or Mom.

"Lieutenant? This is Officer Sue Petersen on the Osco stakeout. I just followed a man who bought a twenty-dollar phone card. ID'ed him as one Derrick Rushlo, thirty-six years of age. He's the owner of the Rushlo Funeral Home on Grand Avenue."

"Hold on a second."

I'd left Fuller's report in the kitchen. Rushlo's name was on the second page. He'd been to the county morgue last week.

"Are you still watching him?" I asked.

"Yes, ma'am."

"Stay on him. Call if he moves. I'll be there within the hour."

CHAPTER 15

The Rushlo Funeral Home faced the busy street of Grand Avenue, its storefront only ten yards wide. It was book-ended by a thrift shop on the left and a dental office on the right, all three of them done in the same cream-colored brick. On either side of the ornate front door were matching bushes in large concrete pots, carefully pruned to resemble corkscrews.

Herb and I entered. It looked like the inside of any funeral home; tasteful, somewhat opulent, with deep rugs and fancy lighting fixtures. The air-conditioning smelled faintly of lilacs.

"You okay, Herb?" Benedict had been walking funny.

"I strained a muscle in my back."

"Working out?"

"Making nookie. Viagra ought to come with a warning label."

We passed two parlors, and located the arrangement office at the end of the hall. Empty.

"May I help you?"

He'd come from a side door, next to the office. A squat man with a carefully trimmed beard that accentuated his double chin. He wore black slacks, a solid blue dress shirt, and a paisley tie, which hugged his expansive stomach.

"Derrick Rushlo?" Herb asked.

The man nodded, shaking Herb's hand.

"I'm Detective Benedict, Chicago Police Department."

Rushlo's eyes were bright blue, and spaced widely apart. The left one was lazy, and it appeared to be staring at me while the other stared at Herb. When Benedict mentioned the CPD, both eyes bugged out.

"I'm Lieutenant Daniels."

Rushlo hesitated, offered his hand, then let it fall when he realized I wasn't going to offer mine.

"Do you know why we're here, Derrick?"

"I haven't a clue, Lieutenant." His voice was high-pitched, breathy.

"We'd like to take a look around, if you wouldn't mind giving us a tour."

He blinked a few times in rapid succession.

"Normally, I wouldn't mind. But I'm in the middle of an embalming right now. If you could come back in . . ."

Benedict held up the search warrant.

"Now would be good."

Rushlo nodded, his chins bobbling.

"The embalming area is back there?" I indicated the door he had come through.

"Uh, yes. Come on."

We followed him behind the scenes. White tile replaced the beige carpet, and the area lacked adequate lighting. We walked through a hallway, which led to a large loft complete with two garage doors. A hearse and a van were parked off to the side. A gurney rested by the far wall.

"This is the, uh, back area. Feel free to look around."

"We'd like to see the embalming room."

His features sank, but he led us to another door.

When I stepped inside, I winced. It smelled like the morgue, but fresher. Brown spills marred the floor and the walls. Several buckets, crusted with dried bits of something, were stacked in the corner. An embalming machine, which looked like a giant-sized version of the juicer I bought last night, sat on a table. Behind it, bottles of red liquid in various shades lined the shelves.

In the center of the room stood a large, stainless steel table. It had gutters on all four sides, which drained into a slop sink at the foot. The table was currently occupied, a bloody sheet covering the body.

"Take that off."

Rushlo hesitated, then tugged the cover to the side and let it drop to the floor.

On the table were the remains of a woman. Caucasian, young, eviscerated from her pubis to her sternum. Her body cavity was empty, and I could see the ribs from the inside.

She had roughly the same build as Eileen Hutton, but I couldn't make a positive ID because her head was missing.

"Who is this?"

"Her name is Felicia Wymann. Just got her in yesterday."

"She's an autopsy?" I asked. That would explain why her organs had been removed.

"Yes. Not local, though. She's from Wisconsin. Hit and run. I know the family, and they asked me to take care of her. I've got the paperwork right here."

Herb looked over the death certificate, and I took a closer look at the corpse. The skin around the neck stump was smooth; it looked to me as if the head had come off cleanly. The likelihood of that happening from a car was slim.

Even more unlikely were the marks on her hands. Her fingertips were just fleshy stumps; they'd been cut off.

I looked higher, and discovered several bruises on her shoulders and arms. Angry, oval shapes. Some had flesh missing.

Bite marks.

Her legs were splayed open, knees bent as if she were giving birth. I noticed some soft tissue damage to the vagina, felt my stomach becoming unhappy, and looked away.

"Where's her head?" I asked.

"Her head? Um, it was crushed in the wreck."

"Shouldn't it still be here?"

"I cremated the head and vital organs earlier today. The family wanted her cremated."

"Why didn't you cremate her as well?"

Rushlo scratched the back of his neck.

"I was going to do that later today." One eye on me, one on Herb. "The crematory is sort of on the fritz, and it works better in sections."

"Where's the autopsy report?" Herb asked.

"The autopsy report? I have no idea. It should be around. You'd be surprised how often paperwork gets misplaced."

He giggled, manic.

"Do you have a cell phone, Derrick?"

"Um, sure. Doesn't everybody?"

"Is it the kind that you buy phone cards for, so there's no contract with the provider?"

He opened his mouth, lips forming a yes, but he stopped himself.

"I think I'd like a lawyer."

"You're not under arrest, Derrick. Why would you need a lawyer?"

He folded his arms.

"I'm not saying anything else without my attorney present."

I glanced at the corpse, 90 percent sure it was Eileen Hutton. I recalled seeing a hairbrush when we'd searched her apartment. All I needed was one strand of hair with the end bulb still attached, and I could get a DNA match.

But, contrary to cop shows on television, DNA testing took weeks, even the rush jobs.

In the meantime, we couldn't arrest Rushlo for anything. I needed something immediately incriminating. We needed to find the TracFone.

"I'm going to call my lawyer now."

He walked out of the room. I nodded at Herb, who followed. He'd watch who Rushlo called, making sure he didn't alert whoever his accomplice was.

I pulled on some latex gloves and began by searching the cabinets lining the rear wall. I found tubing, trocars, scalpels, a box of something called "eye caps," gallon jugs of various fluids, and a few extra scrubs.

The closet held a foul-smelling mop and bucket, some dirty rags, and several containers of bleach. Looking at the bleach, I thought of Davi's severed arms. Nausea be damned, I went back to the corpse and sniffed her cold hand.

Bleach. She'd been washed down, the same as Davi.

Several stained embalming books sat on the counter, along with a tray of sharp instruments. One drawer was stuffed with a large wad of cotton. Another had several unopened packs of large, curved needles.

In the final drawer, near the back, rested a small metal box with a wire handle. A cash box. It had a combination lock on the front.

I took it out, gave it a tiny shake. Something bumped around inside. Something that didn't sound like cash.

I picked up a clean-looking scalpel and spent about a minute trying to pry open the top. It held.

I left the prep room with the box, and found Herb and Rushlo in the arrangement office. Rushlo sat behind his desk, looking six kinds of nervous. Herb busied himself searching the bookshelves.

"What's in the box, Derrick?"

I tossed it onto his desk. The thud made him jump.

"That's private."

"We have a blanket warrant. That entitles us to search anything we're interested in. Open it up."

"I don't want to."

"Did he contact a lawyer?"

Benedict nodded.

"Not cooperating with us is just making it harder on yourself, Derrick. Open the box."

He folded his arms and tucked his chin into his chest, like a petulant child.

"I've got a crowbar in the Camaro. Want me to get it?"

"Thanks, Herb."

Benedict waddled off. I sat in the chair across from Rushlo, leaning toward him.

"Let me tell you what I think, Derrick. I think you faked that death certificate. I think that woman in the embalming room is actually Eileen Hutton. I think I'll be able to prove that. The head may be gone, and the fingerprints may be gone, but we've got more than enough DNA to make a positive ID."

Rushlo began to rock back and forth, humming to himself.

"You're going to be charged with first-degree murder, Derrick. The jury will take one look at the pictures of that poor girl, and you'll get the death penalty."

More humming.

"We know about the TracFone. We know you have a partner. Your only chance at getting through this is by giving us a name."

"I'm not saying anything until my attorney gets here."

"You think your attorney is going to help you get out of this? You've got a murder victim in there. Give me a name."

Silence.

Benedict returned, holding his pry bar.

"May I?"

I handed him the box. He worked the thin side of the tool into the crack, and then popped the cover open.

It took me a second to understand what I was seeing. At first I thought they were white prunes.

But they weren't prunes. They were ears.

And the silver hoop earrings in the lobes were mine.

CHAPTER 16

"You should talk to them, Derrick."

Derrick Rushlo sat in Interrogation Room E, arms crossed, one eye focused intently on the ceiling and the other staring off into space. He continued to hum tunelessly.

His lawyer, a cousin named Gary Pludenza, had been trying for the last hour to get Rushlo to take the deal.

I leaned closer to Rushlo, talking softly so he had to strain to hear me.

"Prison isn't a nice place, Derrick. I promise, you're not going to like it. We know you've got a partner. Tell us who your partner is, and I can promise you a reduced sentence. Or else you're looking at life."

Rushlo kept humming to himself.

"Here, Derrick." I took my driver's license out of my wallet and showed him the photo, keeping my thumb over my address. "See what I'm wearing in the picture? Those same silver hoop earrings we found in your office."

Derrick said nothing, but the humming stopped. I would have liked to say we had his prints on the jewelry, but they'd been wiped clean.

"We know you falsified that death certificate. That's not Felicia Wymann from Wisconsin. We checked. No one named Felicia Wymann died recently. There was no autopsy."

I'd mentioned that three times already, trying to hammer it into his head.

"Now look at these."

I showed him two pictures, one of Eileen Hutton in a bathing suit, and one of the corpse's right shoulder.

"See the birthmark, Derrick? The pear-shaped one right here and here? It's identical in both pictures. And soon, we'll have the DNA tests back, and they'll prove without a doubt that the woman on that table is not Felicia Wymann. It's Eileen Hutton."

Silence. I tried a different tactic, and slammed my palm down on the table. Both Derrick and his lawyer jumped.

"Don't you get it, Rushlo? You're going to spend the next fifty years sharing a twelve-by-twelve cell with some body-building rapist who's going to trade your ass for cigarettes. We found the TracFone. We've got you connected to two homicides. Is your partner worth that?"

Pludenza gave me a weak smile. "Can I speak to my client privately, for a moment?"

I stormed out of the room, my anger not entirely playacting. I needed some coffee, but had no idea where the vending machine was. Because Herb and I were convinced Rushlo's accomplice was a cop, possibly from our station, we'd brought him to the 12th District rather than the 26th. For all I knew, the bad cop might be from the 12th, so we tried to do this on the hush-hush.

I flipped a mental coin and chose to go right. After turning two corners, I found a coffee machine.

Unfortunately, all I had in my wallet were two nickels and a twenty-dollar bill.

"How's the interrogation going?"

Herb walked toward me, coming down the hall. He held a stack of papers.

"Do you have seventy-five cents?"

"That's what you need to break him? Seventy-five cents?"

"For coffee, Herb."

He fished around in his pants pockets and came up with a crusty penny and a stick of gum covered in lint. He ate the gum.

"Nailed the ID on the body," Herb said, chewing. "Eileen Hutton broke her leg in a skiing accident two years ago. We got her X-rays, and they match with the ones Blasky just took at County."

Herb offered me the papers. Even though the faxes weren't perfect, the match clearly was.

"How soon before he finishes the autopsy?"

"He's almost done—the organs are missing, so it's going quick. He estimates she's been dead for about eighteen hours. Neck wound is consistent with some kind of wire or garrote. He's got pictures and casts of the bite wounds, and is confident he can match them up with a suspect's teeth. Found semen. Should be able to type it if the guy's a secretor—Phil said it's only a few hours old."

"I thought she was killed eighteen hours ago."

Herb gave me a pained look, and I put two and two together.

"Rushlo?"

"Yeah. He's got the new high score on my personal Yuck Scale."

I got an involuntary image of Derrick, naked and grunting on top of Eileen's corpse, and immediately buried it. While the concept unnerved me, it didn't completely surprise me. Being a cop for so long, I had zero faith in humanity.

"Necrophilia isn't a crime, right?" I asked.

"If not, it should be. He hasn't cracked yet?"

"Hasn't said a word. You want to take a shot?"

Herb nodded. We walked back to the interrogation room and Herb popped his head inside.

"Ready to deal?"

The lawyer sighed, loud and long.

"I'm sorry, Detective. He refuses to say anything."

Herb sat in the chair across from Rushlo, and I stood behind him, wearing my no-BS face.

"We just got some X-rays, Derrick. They confirm the woman is Eileen Hutton. We're going to charge you with first-degree murder. I've spoken with the assistant state's attorney, and if you make a statement and name the partner, we'll go easy on you."

Rushlo began to hum again. I felt an urge to whack him upside the head.

"Are you not talking because you're worried about your partner? Or are you embarrassed to admit what you did to Eileen after you received the body?"

Rushlo's lawyer furrowed his brow.

"What do they mean, Derrick? What did you do to the body?"

I dropped the papers on the table. "We have evidence that your client had sexual relations with the corpse, roughly two hours ago."

I'd never seen a lawyer look so completely disgusted. In a way, it was refreshing.

"Derrick—I think you need to get other representation."

Rushlo turned to him, panicked.

"You're my cousin! You can't desert me!"

"I don't know if I can handle this, Derrick. My specialty is DUIs, not humping dead bodies."

"I don't have anyone else!"

The lawyer gathered up his things and stood.

"I'll make some calls, see if I can find someone. Don't say anything without counsel present."

He made a sick face, then left the room.

I wanted to keep going at Rushlo, but no lawyer meant no questions. We booked him, taking prints and mugs, and tossed him into a holding cell.

"Dammit, Herb. I really don't think he's going to give up his partner."

"We can check Rushlo's background. Try to narrow it down."

"That will take time. And meanwhile, we've got a crazy cop running around, slicing up call girls."

"How about a mole ploy?"

I considered it.

"What if one of the cops here is the killer? Maybe that's why Rushlo is so scared."

Herb rubbed his mustache.

"Bring in someone from the outside? Stick a wire on him, stick him in the cell, maybe he could get Rushlo to give up a name."

"Do you know anyone other than cops? Someone who would know how to get information out of him?"

"I know a few retired cops. I could make a few calls. How about you?"

I shook my head. "No one."

"How about your ex-partner? That McGlade guy?"

"No. He'd find some way to make everything worse."

"We've only got tonight, Jack. Tomorrow they'll ship Rushlo to the county lock-up. We wouldn't be able to get a mole in there."

"McGlade is an idiot."

"He used to be a cop. Plus he owes you one, from the way they depicted you in that awful TV movie. Remember how they made you into a binge eater, constantly shoving things into your mouth? That must have been humiliating."

I thought about McGlade's suspended PI license, and knew I could use that to get him to help. But, dammit, it was using a machine gun to kill a gnat.

"If the choice is working with Harry, or letting a maniac run free, I'm not sure which is the worse of the two."

"Call him."

"Maybe I can dress up as a man and do it myself. I can paint on a mustache with mascara."

"Call him."

"Ah, hell."

I needed to dial directory assistance to get McGlade's number. As his phone rang, I silently hoped he wouldn't pick up.

"This is Harry McGlade, World's Greatest Private Detective, featured in the television movie *Fatal Autonomy*. Talk to me."

I swallowed a gallon of pride. "Harry, it's Jack."

"Jackie! Calling to give me good news about my license?"

"Sort of. I need a favor."

"Consider it done, sugar. I had no idea you wanted to ride the Harry Rocket, but I'm more than happy to give you a taste. I usually like them younger, though."

"Even if you tied me down, McGlade, I'd chew off my own arms to get away. I need you to run the mole ploy for me."

"Gimme details."

I filled Harry in, lowering my voice when a pair of cops walked past.

"And if I help you out with the stiff-sticker, you'll get me my license back?"

"You have my word."

"I'll be there in half an hour, ready to be wired. See you soon."

Harry hung up. Herb gave me a pat on the shoulder.

"It's for the greater good, Jack."

I took a deep breath and rubbed my temples.

"That's what Oppenheimer said."

CHAPTER 17

"Want to help me tape on the wire?"

McGlade waggled his eyebrows at me. He'd unbuttoned his shirt, exposing a flabby chest completely carpeted with curly brown hair. It was like looking at a gorilla, if the gorilla used Rogaine.

"Is it a full moon?" Herb asked.

"Could be," McGlade answered. "Does the full moon turn you into a fat pig?"

Herb narrowed his eyes. Harry had a wonderful way of immediately getting on a person's bad side.

"Don't get angry, Porky." Harry grinned. "It's just a joke."

Herb folded his arms. "For your information, I just lost ten pounds."

"You didn't lose them—they're hiding in your ass."

I stepped between them and used some tape to attach the lavaliere microphone to Harry's chest. More tape than necessary.

"You're so gentle, Jackie. You're turning me on."

Harry put his hand on my hip, and I pinched his nipple hard enough to draw milk. He yelped and dropped his hand.

Herb shook his head in disbelief; Harry got that reaction a lot. "You were right, Jack. He's an idiot."

"Herb," I warned.

"A fourteen-karat, card-carrying idiot. How did you survive all those years with him as a partner?"

"Why are you in such a bad mood?" Harry asked. "Your local grocery store run out of Sara Lee?"

Benedict pointed a finger in McGlade's face. "You make one more fat joke . . ."

"And you'll do what? Eat me?"

Benedict got in McGlade's face, and I had to pull him away.

"Can you both please act like professionals?"

"Careful, Jackie, when he's done with me he may still be hungry."

Benedict grabbed a fistful of Harry's chest hair and yanked out a patch. McGlade screamed, then went for his shoulder holster.

"Sit!" I ordered Harry. "And back off, Herb."

Harry glowered at Herb, then sat back down. Benedict rolled his eyes and walked over to the other side of the room, giving Harry his back.

"Here's the deal, McGlade. We know Rushlo's got an accomplice, and we believe it's a cop. We need a name."

"No problem."

"You have to play it cool in there, try to get him to open up. You've read the file."

"Yeah. He's a mortician, and he likes his sex partners at room temperature. I'll get the info, Jackie. I'm good at this."

Benedict chortled.

"You may scoff, Detective Butterball, but I've worked undercover many times before. In fact, I'm a master of disguise. Guess who I am now."

Benedict took the bait and looked. Harry crossed his eyes and scrunched his neck down, giving himself a big double chin.

"I lost ten pounds on the donut diet," Harry grunted.

Herb made a fist, looked at me, and then excused himself from the room.

"The guy's got no sense of humor, Jackie. He probably eats to compensate for an inadequate sex life."

"I don't think that's Herb's problem. Let's get a level."

I turned on the receiver, a black box the size of a car radio, and adjusted the volume. The room filled with the squelch of feedback.

"Take a few steps back, McGlade, and say something."

McGlade walked near the door, singing about his lovely bunch of coconuts. He came in clear, lousy voice aside.

"The desk sergeant is going to put you in the holding tank. I want Rushlo to give up a name, but any other info you get out of him, I'll be recording. You know what he looks like?"

"I saw the mugs. He looks like a toad with a Lincoln beard."

"Probably not wise to use that as your opening line. What's your approach going to be?"

Harry grinned, his smile as wide as a zebra's hindquarters. "Trust me."

I had a sudden need for an antacid.

I put the bracelets on Harry and led him to the holding area. After signing him in, I took off the cuffs and let the desk sergeant escort him to his cell.

When I returned to the office we'd appropriated, Herb was already there, signing a piece of paper. It was the authorization to give a prisoner a full body-cavity search. McGlade's name was on the top. I took the paper and crumpled it up.

"Herb, you're being childish."

"Yeah. He'd probably just enjoy it anyway."

The radio made a clanging sound. Cell door closing. I hit the Record button.

Footsteps. White noise. Shuffling.

"Hey man, got any smokes?" Harry's voice.

"No. Sorry." Rushlo.

"I don't believe this shit. I shouldn't even be in here. She said she was sixteen, man. It was so worth the hassle, though. The younger the beaver, the softer the pelt, right? Right?"

"Yeah, I guess."

A grunt, perhaps McGlade sitting down.

"You guess? I can tell you like sex, just looking at you. You've got that vibe. I bet you're a real lady-killer."

Herb sighed and shook his head. "I know people who work at the zoo, Jack. We could have sent a trained monkey in there instead."

I shushed him.

"Actually, I'm not very good with women."

"You're kidding, right? With a face like that, I bet you get laid all the time. When was the last piece of ass you tagged? Come on, don't be shy. When was it? Last week? Yesterday?"

Seconds of silence went by.

"You're not a virgin, are you?"

"No."

"I didn't think so. So when was the last time you got some?"

"This morning."

"I knew it! I knew it the moment I saw you. I bet you like that kinky shit too. Little rope action, little spanky-spanky. Am I right?"

"Sort of."

"Look at you, smiling like that. What's your kink?"

"It's . . . private."

Hand-clapping sounds, and McGlade laughing.

"I bet it's real private. I can see it in your eyes. Well, your one eye. Your other eye is all screwed up. I bet you have a hard time watching 3-D movies."

Herb sighed again.

"So what's your kink, man? Kids? Animals? Getting pooped on?"

"Nothing like that."

"Tell me."

"I don't really talk about it."

"Got it. Secret stuff. I'm cool with that. What's you're name, man?"

"Derrick."

"Hi, Derrick. My name's Barnum. Call me P.T."

"Unbelievable," Herb said.

"What do you do, Derrick?"

"I own a funeral home."

"Funeral home, huh? How's business?"

"Business is dying."

They both chuckled. Herb and I managed to restrain ourselves.

"Hey, wait a second! A funeral home! Is that your kink, man? You boning the stiffs? That's freaking great, man! I bet you get a lot of tail working in a funeral home, and none of it ever says no. Am I right?"

"I don't want to talk about this."

"Why not? Nothing wrong with grabbing a little afternoon delight at work. I always wanted to nail a corpse."

"Really?"

"Sure. Don't have to buy her dinner, don't have to bother with foreplay, and she wouldn't want to talk afterward. Sounds like the perfect woman. Tell me the truth: How is it?"

Another long pause.

"It's beautiful."

"Not cold?"

"I use a heating pad to warm them up."

"That's genius, man! When we get out of here, maybe you'd let me stop by some time? I'd, you know, pay for the privilege. As soon as we both get out . . . hey, what's wrong, man?"

"I'm never going to get out of here." Rushlo's voice was cracking.

"Why not? What are you in for?"

"Murder."

"No shit! You killed somebody?"

"No. I didn't kill anybody. They think I did."

"Well, if you didn't do it, they'll let you out. Do you know who did it?"

Sniffling. *"Yes."*

"Did you tell them?"

"No. He'll kill me if I tell."

"Won't the cops protect you?"

"He is a cop."

"No shit? Man, that sucks. You wanna tell me his name?"

"No. Why?"

"I'll give you twenty bucks."

Herb slapped himself on the forehead.

"Why do you want to know his name? Are you a cop?"

"Sure, I'm a cop. I'm even wearing a wire. They sent me in here to see if I could make you talk."

Herb nudged me. "When this is over, let's leave McGlade in there. He's too stupid to be allowed in society."

"You're not a cop." Rushlo talking.

"Of course I'm not a cop. I hate cops. Hey . . . you wanna hear a secret?"

"Sure."

"I killed a cop once." Harry was whispering. I turned up the volume.

"Are you kidding?"

"No shit, man. I was on a street corner, talking to this cute little girl, and this cop starts hassling me. I didn't need that kind of hassle, know what I mean? He wants to pat me down, and I'm carrying."

"You had a gun?"

"Hell yeah, I had a gun. So before he gets a chance to take it away from me, I put

him down. Bam Bam! Two in the face. Maybe you read about it, happened a few weeks ago. You wanna hear the cool part?"

"Sure."

"I liked it."

"Wow."

"Yeah, I'm a stone-cold demon, man. I'm the real deal. Hey . . . you rich? I heard funeral homes make a lot of money."

"I have money."

"Maybe I can help you out."

"How?"

"Maybe I could take care of this cop for you. Sneak up on his pig ass and give him a little Bam Bam."

Nice, Harry. I was actually a little impressed.

"I don't think I want to kill him."

"He's a pig, man. All pigs should die."

"I don't know."

"Would he kill you, if he had the chance?"

"Yes."

"You've got to take this guy out."

"But he's my friend."

Harry's laughter made the speakers shake.

"Do all your friends want to kill you?"

"No. Most of my friends are dead."

Benedict snorted. "There's a shock."

"Well, maybe you and me can make this one dead too, Derrick."

"I don't know."

"Your call, man. I'll tell you something, though—if this guy's a cop, and you think you're safe in here, you're crazy."

"He's not from this station."

"Don't matter. He can still get to you. Sneak in when you're sleeping, stick you

a few times, and then blame it on one of the convicts. Or put something in your food. Or pay one of the other cons to do it. There's a million ways."

"Jesus."

"You could maybe ask to go into protective custody, but that's even worse. Then he'd have a shot at you when you're alone. You should let me take the porker out."

Another long pause.

"I can't."

"I could do it for twenty grand. You got twenty grand?"

"Yes."

"Groovy. Let me whack the guy. Tell the cops he forced you to help him, and they'll let you go. You could be back at work and getting it on with dear, departed Aunt Sally in a day or two."

"I can't."

"Whatever, man. You're the one who's gonna get iced."

There was no talking for over a minute. Only Rushlo's off-key humming.

"What if . . . what if I said yes?"

"Half the money up front, the other half when it's over."

"How?"

"Cash. You talk to your lawyer, have him deliver it to me."

"And what if you can't do it?"

"I can do it. Trust me."

"He's a big guy."

"Size don't matter if you aim for the head. What's the pig's name?"

I noticed I was holding my breath.

"Hey man, if you want me to kill the guy, I got to know his name."

"It's Barry."

Herb and I looked at each other. There was only one Barry we knew on the job. I tried to make it fit, to picture the cop on my team as the one responsible for these atrocities.

"Barry what? Barry Houdini? Barry Flintstone? Barry Manilow? You gotta give me more than that."

Fuller had access to my office, and to Colin Andrews's phone. Fuller was angry I passed him over for promotion. Fuller kept butting into this investigation, offering to help.

"I don't want to say any more. I can't say any more. I'm sorry."

"You already said too much, you little squealer." McGlade's tone had become harsh, menacing. *"Barry knew you'd try something. He sent me to take care of you."*

Rushlo made a sound somewhere between a gasp and a yelp.

"Leave me alone!"

"Barry can't afford to keep you around."

"I'm sorry! Tell him I'm sorry!"

"Tell who you're sorry?"

"Fuller! Tell him I'd never betray him."

"Get him out of there," I told Herb, the phone already in my hand. We needed to find Barry Fuller, fast.

Before anyone else died.

CHAPTER 18

Barry Fuller cruises Irving Park Road. He's off duty, dressed in civvies and driving his SUV.

His headache is explosive.

The morning began on a bad note. Holly, his bitch of a wife, had some stupid complaint about the living room curtains. He told her, several times, to buy new curtains if she hated these, but she couldn't shut her goddamn mouth and kept yapping and yapping and finally he had to leave because if he didn't he would have gutted her right there.

He needs a substitute, fast. Normally, he'd drop in the station and use the computer to locate a neighborhood hooker. But the pain is so bad he's practically blind with it, and he needs relief ASAP.

Luckily, the streets are littered with disposables.

He tails a jogger for a block. Blonde, nice ass. She blends into the crowd, and he loses her.

Another woman. Business suit. High heels. He idles alongside, visualizing how to grab her. She walks into a coffee shop.

Fuller fidgets in his seat, sweating even though the air is cranked to the max. He turns down an alley, searching, scanning . . .

Finding.

She's walking out the rear door to her apartment building. Twenty-something, wearing flip-flops and a large T-shirt over bikini bottoms, a towel on her shoulder. Planning on walking to Oak Street Beach, just a few blocks away.

He guns the engine and hits her from behind.

She bounces off the front bumper, skids along the pavement face-first. Fuller jams the truck into park, jumps out.

"My God! Are you okay?" In case anyone is watching. There doesn't seem to be.

The woman is crying. Bloody. Scrapes on her palms and her face.

"We have to get you to a hospital."

He half helps/half yanks her into his truck, and then they're pulling out into traffic.

"What happened?" she moans.

Fuller hits her. Again. And again.

She slumps over in the seat.

He makes a left onto Clark Street, turns into Graceland Cemetery. It's one of Chicago's oldest, and largest, taking up an entire city block. Because of the heat, there are few visitors inside the gates.

"We're in luck," Fuller says. "It's dead."

The cemetery is green, sprawling, carefully kept. Winding roads, obscured by clusters of bushes and hundred-year-old oak trees, make sections of it seem like a forest preserve.

Plenty of room for privacy.

He pulls into an enclave and parks next to the large stone monument marking the grave of millionaire Marshall Field. Drags the woman out of the car, behind the tomb, rage building and head pounding and teeth grinding teeth so hard the enamel flakes off.

Fuller unleashes himself upon her, without a weapon, without checking for witnesses, without putting on the gloves he has in the front pocket of his jeans for this purpose. Punching, kicking, squeezing, grunting, sweating.

Fireworks go off behind his eyes, erasing the pain, wiping his brain clean.

When the fugue ends, Fuller is surprised to see he somehow pulled off the woman's arm.

Impressive. That takes a lot of strength.

He blinks, looks around. All clear. The only witness is the green, delicately robed statue, sitting high atop Field's monument. A copper smell taints the hot, woodsy air.

The grass, and his clothes, are soaked with blood and connective tissue. Fuller wonders if the woman might be still alive, goes to check her pulse, and stops himself when he realizes her head is turned completely backward.

He returns to his truck, opens up the hatch. Takes out a large sheet of plastic, a roll of duct tape, a gallon of blue windshield wiper fluid, and his gym bag.

It takes the whole bottle of cleaning fluid to get the red stuff off his skin, and he uses his socks to wipe himself clean. These get rolled up in the tarp, along with the girl, her arm, and his shirt, shoes, and pants.

His workout clothes are in the bag. They stink of sweat, but he puts them on.

Fuller loads the bundle into the back of the truck, gets behind the wheel, and leaves the cemetery.

Pain-free.

On Halsted Street he calls Rushlo.

The mortician doesn't pick up.

Alarms go off in Fuller's head. Rushlo *always* picks up. That's part of their deal. He turns the truck around, heading for Grand Avenue, for Rushlo's Funeral Home.

Another call.

No answer.

Fuller worries his thumbnail, tasting the sour bite of windshield washer fluid. Could they have found Rushlo already? What if they did?

Rushlo won't talk. He's sure of that. The guy is too scared of him.

But that might not matter. If Rushlo got picked up before disposing of the body, there might be trace evidence. Hair. Saliva.

Jack's earrings.

He told Rushlo to wipe off the prints. Had he done it?

Worry creeps up Barry's shoulders and crouches there.

He calls Rushlo again.

No answer.

He hangs a right onto Grand. Cops are everywhere.

Fuller does a U-turn, hitting the gas and making the tires squeal. In the rear of the truck, the body rolls and bumps against the hatch.

It's over. Time to leave the country.

Fuller's bank is ten minutes away. He parks at the curb, jogs inside the lobby. The security guard stops him.

"You need shoes to enter, sir."

Fuller looks down at his bare feet, sees some blood caked on his toenails. He digs his wallet out of his pocket and flashes tin.

"Police business. Get your rent-a-dick face outta mine or I'll beat your ass right here."

The guard gives him steely eyes, but backs down. Fuller uses his star to get to the front of the line.

"I need to open my security box. Now."

The clerk gets him some assistance, and Fuller is ushered off into the vault. They turn their keys in unison.

"I'll need a bag."

The clerk returns a few moments later with a paper sack, then leaves him alone. Fuller empties out the contents of the box: a 9mm Beretta and three extra clips, six grand in cash—shakedowns from his patrolman days—a forged passport in the name of Barry Eisler. He stuffs everything into the bag and exits the bank.

A meter maid is writing him a ticket.

"Sorry, sister. I'm on the job."

She eyes his feet, skeptical. He shows her his star, climbs into the truck, and peels away.

Mexico has tougher extradition laws, so Mexico it is. He spends a few minutes on the phone with an airline, reserves a seat on the next flight to Cancún. It leaves in three hours.

Just enough time to pack and take care of some important business.

Fuller doesn't want to get caught. He knows what happens to cops in prison. If they're on to him, they'll be staking out his house.

But he can't leave the country without killing that bitch he married. That just wouldn't do.

He dials home, rehearsing the lines in his head.

"Hello?"

"Hi, Holly. It's me."

"What do you want?"

No fear in her tone. No nervousness or hesitation.

"Everything okay, babe? You sound strange."

"Everything is not okay. These damn curtains are driving me insane. How could we have lived with them for so long, Barry? They're hideous."

So far, she seems normal.

"Hon, I'm expecting some guys from the office to drop by later. Are they there yet?"

"Nope."

"Maybe parked out front?"

"Why would they be parked out front?"

"Can you check for me, babe? It's important."

"Just a second." Rustling, footsteps. "I'm looking at the street. No one out front."

Fuller considers this. Maybe they haven't found out about him yet. Maybe he can go home, do the bitch, and be able to pack his bags and some things.

He instantly rejects the idea as too dangerous.

"Baby, do you remember where we bought our bedroom set?"

"Sure. Why?"

"Meet me there in an hour."

"What for?"

Fuller smiles. "We're shopping for curtains."

"Really?"

"Really. Oh, and bring me a change of clothes and some shoes."

"Why? What are you talking about?"

"Long story. Some street lunatic threw up on me, and I'm wearing my workout sweats. Just bring me shorts, a T-shirt, and my Nikes. Meet me in Home Furnishings."

"Okay, Barry. See you in an hour."

Fuller puts the cell phone away and turns right, heading for State Street. He'll kill her inside Marshall Field's. She's a clotheshorse, and it won't take much to get her to try on an outfit. He'll break her neck in one of the dressing rooms. It's not the fillet knife that he always wanted to use, but it should be satisfying enough.

Hands-on treatment always is.

CHAPTER 19

"She's on the move."

Holly Fuller walked out of her apartment building and hailed a Yellow Cab.

Herb pulled into traffic behind her. I removed the earpiece, shoved it in my blazer pocket. After McGlade made Rushlo sing, we secured a quick subpoena to tap Fuller's home phone. A fake telemarketing call to the Fuller household proved Barry wasn't there. Since it was his day off, we decided to keep vigil until we heard from him.

The phone call disturbed me. Fuller seemed extra careful not to mention the name of the store where he wanted to meet his wife. And why would he need a change of clothes? Did he know we had Rushlo? I hoped not. Barry Fuller was not the kind of man who would be easy to subdue if forewarned.

I picked up the receiver on Herb's police band.

"This is Two-Delta-Seven, tailing Yellow Cab number six-four-seven-niner Thomas X-ray. Passenger is Holly Fuller, thirty-two, blonde, five-eight, hundred and ten pounds. She's wearing a red and orange summer dress, and carrying a red Nike gym bag. They're turning south onto Michigan Avenue. Do not engage. Repeat, do not engage. Over."

"Roger, Two-Delta-Seven. Twelve-Homer-Nineteen flanking South on Wabash, over."

"Roger, both. Sixteen-Angel-Niner turning east on Grand to intercept, over."

My team was unmarked, but a plain white sedan still screamed *COP* to all who saw it, so I ordered them to hang back. Even if we lost her, a call to the cab company would tell us where she was dropped off.

"Think she's headed for Water Tower Place?" Herb asked.

"Could be. Or State Street. Seems like a woman with expensive tastes. Her shoes are Ferragamos."

"You could tell through the binocs?"

"I've had my eye on that same pair for two months. Five hundred and fifty dollars."

"Do they come with a trip to Rio?"

"Don't pretend to understand fashion, Herb. And I won't make any comments about this big red penis you're driving around in."

Herb humphed.

"My Camaro? I bought this solely for comfort."

"So did Holly Fuller."

Traffic was tight, befitting a weekend on the Magnificent Mile. This was the best-known part of Chicago. The skyscrapers, John Hancock and the AON Center (formerly Amoco, and before that, Standard Oil). Nieman Marcus and Saks. Navy Pier. The Art Institute. Orchestra Hall. Further south, Buckingham Fountain, the Field Museum, Shedd Aquarium, Adler Planetarium.

The sidewalks were packed—not quite shoulder to shoulder, but personal space was at a premium. The sun beat down on everyone and everything, and I couldn't use the binoculars because I kept catching glints off of cars and hurting my eyes.

"She passed Water Tower. Continuing south on Michigan. Ease up, Herb—you're riding her bumper. There's a pedal next to the gas that I don't think you've tried yet."

Benedict slowed down, let the cab gain several car lengths.

"Jack . . . what if we have to take him down?"

I knew how he felt. Cops were fiercely protective of their own. Arresting one, or shooting one, was a hard idea to get your head around. The us-against-them mentality ran deep in the force. Us-against-us was anathema.

"Then we do our job. We take him down."

"I can't believe it's Barry. I can't believe he could do that. I consider him a friend, for chrissakes."

I couldn't believe it either. I tried to replay every meeting I'd ever had with Barry Fuller, tried to recall any signs or hints that he was a serial killer.

There were none. Fuller had fooled us all.

"You know as well as I do, Herb. The scariest monsters have the best masks."

Benedict made his mouth into a thin, tight line.

"He's supposed to be one of the good guys."

"Good guys don't slice up hookers."

The taxi hung a right onto Randolph, and then another right onto State. It stopped in front of Marshall Field's.

"The passenger has been dropped off at the northwest corner of State and Randolph. All units converge, but remain out of sight until target is spotted, over."

Holly Fuller paid the driver and walked into the department store, while Benedict double-parked. I shoved my earpiece in and pinned the lapel mike to my blouse. After informing our backup that Holly was in the building, Herb and I hurried into Field's.

The store was packed. An equal mix of men and women, their attire running the gamut from business formal to T-shirts and sandals. Heat waves were good for business, especially if you had decent air-conditioning.

We spotted Holly stepping onto the escalator, and lagged behind thirty seconds before following. A lighted sign informed us Home Furnishings occupied the fifth floor.

There was a line for the escalator, and we wedged ourselves on, surrounded by shoppers.

"Do you see her?"

"There. Eleven o'clock."

I followed his index finger and spotted Holly on the escalator two floors above us. She was easy to spot, which made me aware of how conspicuous Herb and I were. Benedict didn't exactly blend in.

"I'll need you to stay on the third floor, Herb. See if you can spot Fuller coming up. Lay low."

Benedict nodded. I spoke into the mike, requesting further backup to converge on all exits at my command.

Benedict got off the escalator. I pressed onward and upward. On the fifth floor, I searched for Holly and found her examining Oriental rugs. A quick survey of the area failed to reveal Fuller, but the several dozen shoppers milling about made me very uneasy. Too many people, only one me.

I didn't like this. Not a bit.

I could feel my heartbeat kick up a notch. My palms got damp and my mouth got dry. A crowded department store was not a place for a shoot-out.

I blended into the crowd, pretending to examine loveseats. A saleswoman came up, asked if I needed assistance. I told her no, keeping distance from Holly as she left rugs for window dressings.

Best-case scenario, I sneak up on Fuller, he surrenders without incident.

Worst-case—well, take your pick. He's a homicidal maniac and a trained marksman. He knows everything I'll do before I do it. Knows he's surrounded, exits blocked. Knows he has a much better chance to make a stand when there are this many bystanders hanging around.

"Any sign of the target?"

I received a round of *negatives* in my earpiece.

"The locale is too crowded. We'll tail him as he leaves, over."

That calmed me a bit. We could just hang back, take him down when he's back on the street, where there were fewer . . .

"I've got him." Benedict, from the third floor. *"Taking the escalator. Dressed in green gym shorts and a gray sweatshirt with the sleeves cut off. He's also barefoot, over."*

"Hold your positions. We will not engage until he's off site. Repeat, hold your positions. Over."

I changed directions, facing the escalator. A minute passed, and I realized I'd been holding my breath. I let it out, slow.

Fuller rose up out of the floor, seeming much bigger than he looked around the office. His manner was edgy, irritated, and his eyes darted this way and that. I squatted behind a display of bath towels, watched him through a gap in the terry-cloth layers.

He passed within twenty feet of me, beelining to window dressings.

"The target's on the fifth floor. I have him in my sights, over."

Holly had her back to him, absorbed in examining a valence. Fuller spotted her, quickened his pace. He reached his hands out before him, huge hands, at neck level.

I stood up, adrenaline surging. It was too far away to take a shot. I broke into a jog, hand going for my gun, and then skidded on my heels when Fuller put his hands over Holly's eyes and played *guess who.*

She giggled, turned around, and kissed him on tiptoes. Fuller held out his hand, and Holly handed him the Nike bag she'd been carrying. They exchanged a few sentences, another kiss, and then he led her away from window dressings, back to the escalator.

I spun around, absorbed in the price tag on a bronze floor lamp.

"Target and his wife are heading for the escalators. Going up. Everyone stand their ground, over."

I gave them half a minute's lead, then followed the pair up a floor. Women's Evening Wear.

"They're on the sixth floor, looking at cocktail dresses. He's picking one up off the rack, handing it to her. She's shaking her head. He's laughing. Now they're walking over to the dressing rooms. They just went in."

I examined my options. Keep my distance and wait for them to come out, or move in closer to make sure he isn't adding to his body count.

They seemed fine. No animosity. Smiling and kissing.

I decided to hang back. It was just a husband and wife, out shopping. Even as crazy as Fuller seemed, he probably wasn't going to kill his wife in the middle of a busy department store.

Right?

CHAPTER 20

He's ready to kill the bitch. The excitement of it makes him giddy, lightheaded. As soon as she opens that door, shows off that pretty little Dolce & Gabbana dress, he's going to wrap his hands around her throat and squeeze until his thumbs meet his index fingers.

He knocks on her dressing room door. "You okay in there, honey?"

"Just a second. This isn't the right kind of bra, I have to take it off. You really like this dress?"

"I have to see you in it."

"I didn't know you cared about fashion, Barry."

Fuller grins, thinking about the corpse in the back of his SUV.

"There's a lot of things you don't know about me, dear."

Fuller wipes some sweat from his forehead, hands shaking. The store's swamped with customers, and there's no one chaperoning the dressing room. He'll be able to kill his wife in less than thirty seconds, and then slip out before anyone knows what is happening. Remember to take her ring and tennis bracelet, he tells himself. Might not hurt to stop at the jewelry department on his way out and max his credit card on diamonds. He won't get even half their value at the pawn shop, but he doesn't plan on sticking around to pay the bill.

"You ready, honey?" Holly's voice is like a dinner bell.

"I'm ready."

"The shoes don't match."

"I don't care. Let me in so I can look at you."

The door opens. Fuller goes in.

Holly smiles at him, the same fake smile she gives photographers.

"What do you think?"

Fuller smiles back, full wattage, his eyes wide and the muscles in his neck stretched taut.

"I'll show you what I think."

He reaches for her neck.

CHAPTER 21

I learned to trust my instincts years ago, as a rookie. If a situation didn't feel right, it usually wasn't.

Something about the eager way Fuller followed his wife into the dressing room set me on edge. I'd never met a man eager to play fashion show, and the quick way he convinced Holly to try on the dress made me suspicious.

"Change of plan. All units converge on the sixth floor, at the northeast dressing room. We're taking the target down. Repeat, we're taking the target down. Over."

I hung my star around my neck and tugged out my .38, which was happy to be free of its claustrophobic holster.

Several patrons stared at me, mouths open. I warned them to stay back.

Two steps into the dressing room, I heard gurgling and grunting. A muffled scream. I followed the sounds, found the right door. Locked.

I kicked off my flats, planted my left foot, and snap-kicked the door at knob level, grunting with the force of my effort.

The jamb splintered. The door swung inward. My gun came up.

Fuller had Holly by the throat. He spun her around, in the path of my .38, and I jerked the shot high, firing at the ceiling.

I recovered quickly, leveling the gun, bringing my left hand up to steady it. Fuller's massive forearm was locked around Holly's throat. Her face was a mess of tears, mascara, and spit, and her eyes were squeezed shut in pain.

Fuller was smiling.

"Hello, Lieutenant."

I aimed at his head.

"Drop her, Barry!"

"I don't think so."

His arm tightened. Holly went from red to purple.

My hands had begun to shake. I tightened my finger on the trigger.

"Dammit, Barry! We can work this out! Don't make me shoot you!"

I heard Fuller's shots a millisecond after I felt them, ripping through Holly's belly and slamming into mine. It was like getting kicked in the stomach.

I fired on reflex, my slug winging Fuller in the forehead.

All three of us went down.

The dressing room was carpeted, and the floor felt plush under my back. Comfortable. I looked down at my belly and saw blood and bits of flesh. Somewhere in the back of my mind, I realized my outfit was ruined, and that amused me for some reason.

To my left, lying less than two feet away, Holly Fuller stared at me. She blinked. Opened her mouth to say something, but all that came out was blood.

"Don't talk," I told her.

She nodded, once. Then she closed one eye, and the other continued to stare at me as her life left her body.

Behind her, Fuller was laid out on his back. His head spurted blood with his heartbeat, and I saw bits of bone tangled in his hair. His right hand was clenched around a bloody semiautomatic.

"Die," I whispered.

He didn't.

I heard screams, and then Herb's plump face was staring down at me, filled with anguish. I wanted to tell him not to be so sad, but I couldn't get the words to form.

He pried the .38 from my hand, and touched my cheek.

"It's going to be okay, Jack. It's going to be okay."

Not for Holly Fuller, I thought. And then it was getting too hard to keep my eyes open, so I went to sleep.

CHAPTER 22

When I woke up, Latham was holding my hand. He smiled at me.

"Hiya, sport. You got out of surgery an hour ago. Had two bullets removed from your abdominal wall."

I looked around, took in all the standard hospital surroundings, and then went to sleep again.

The second time I awoke, Herb was there.

"Good morning, Jack. How you feeling?"

"Stomach hurts," I said. Or tried to say. What came out was something that sounded like, "S'hurt."

"I'll have the doctor up your morphine."

I shook my head and tried to say no.

"Thirsty?"

I nodded. Benedict poured me some water from a pitcher and held the glass. I took two sips, and two more sips dribbled down my face.

"Day?" I managed.

"Friday. You've been out about twenty-four hours."

"Olly?"

Herb shook his head.

"Uller?"

"He's in recovery. I'll tell you more when you're feeling better."

"Ell me."

"This is how we figured it—lemme know if it's right. Fuller was holding Holly around the neck. Did you know he had a gun?"

I shook my head.

"He had it pressed to her back, and tried to shoot you through his wife. The slugs ripped through her and got lodged in your stomach muscles. I guess it pays to do sit-ups."

I grunted. It wasn't sit-ups. Holly's body slowed them down, so they didn't penetrate deep.

"Your round took off part of his head, above his right eye. Mostly skull. The docs picked bone splinters out of his brain for the better part of ten hours. Also, they found something else."

"What?"

"Fuller had a brain tumor. About the size of a cherry. They removed that as well. He's in stable condition."

I mumbled for more water, and we did the slurping/spilling thing again. A small voice whispered to me that I should have shot Fuller immediately, before he had a chance to kill his wife.

"Latham should be back any minute. Went on a burrito run. All of these flowers are from him."

Herb made a grand, sweeping gesture, and for the first time I noticed all of the bouquets surrounding the bed, replete with stuffed animals and Mylar balloons.

"He hasn't left your side since you got here, Jack. He's like Lassie."

"Case?" I asked. I wasn't up to talking about Latham.

"Airtight. We found a body in the back of Fuller's truck. She's wrapped in plastic, and his prints are all over her, not that it makes a difference at this point. The State's Attorney is making a case for the two other women, Eileen Hutton and Davi McCormick, plus the Andrewses."

"Huh?"

"Oh, yeah. You didn't know. The dealer, and his mother. Both shot. Witnesses saw a large Caucasian man leaving the scene. Fuller was making so many mistakes, it's almost like he wanted to be caught."

I took a deep breath, smelling rubbing alcohol and iodine. My arm itched where the IV was jabbed in, and I scratched the skin above the hole. My stomach hurt; not from the inside, like an ulcer, but from the outside, as if someone had kicked me. I pulled down my sheet and pulled my hospital gown to the side. Herb carefully examined his shoes, while I poked and prodded at the large gauze bandage taped to my lower body.

The poking made me realize how badly I needed to go to the bathroom, and I managed to sit up and plant my feet on the floor. The tile was cold.

"Where are you going?"

"Bathroom."

"I don't know if you should."

"You want to cup your hands and hold them next to my knees?"

Herb helped me into the bathroom.

When finished, I was a little dizzy, and held on to the sink until the room stopped twirling. The woman in the mirror looked like hell. Hair, a disaster. Face, scrubbed clean of makeup, letting age and exhaustion shine through. Pallor, not much better than one of Derrick Rushlo's dates.

So when I stepped out of the bathroom, it was a given that my boyfriend would be standing there.

He was wearing a smile that could charitably be called dopey, and in his hands was yet another floral arrangement, this one blooming from a coffee mug with a rainbow on it.

"Hi, Jack. You look great."

And I could tell that he meant it.

Maybe it was the drugs, or the pain, or the guilt, but I burst into tears right there. He held me, softly, so as not to hurt me. But I hugged him tight, with everything I had, not ever wanting to let go.

"I'm so happy you're okay, Jack. I'm sorry I didn't call you back. I love you." I sniffled, making a mess of his sport coat.

"I love you too, Latham. God, I love you too."

CHAPTER 23

The hottest summer on record eventually fizzled out, easing into autumn's first frost. One hundred and three degrees to thirty in three short months. It confirmed my belief that the Midwest would be much more hospitable if we moved it six hundred miles south.

It was a chilly Tuesday morning, and Mr. Friskers was clawing the hide off a pumpkin Latham had bought earlier in the week. The cat hadn't exactly cozied up to me, but he didn't attack me constantly either. It was more an uneasy alliance than a friendship, but I was grateful for his presence.

The twelve weeks had been tough.

I hadn't been back to work yet, and even though I was in love with the most patient, decent, understanding man in the northern hemisphere, I felt like I was losing my mind.

"Want some milk, cat?"

Mr. Friskers halted his attack on the intruder gourd and squinted at me. I went to the fridge, found the 2 percent, and poured some into his bowl. He waited until I backed away before stuffing his face.

I yawned, and gave my head a quick shake, trying to dispel the drowsies. I'd fallen into the habit of taking a sleeping pill every night, and the grogginess took time to wear off.

I yawned again, wondered if I was hungry, and when I'd last eaten. Dinner, last night. Two bites of pizza, with Latham. The leftovers were in the fridge, but cold pizza didn't sound like a good breakfast. I thought about making myself eggs, dismissed it as too difficult, and plodded back into the bedroom and onto the bed.

Picked up the remote. Put it back down. Picked it up again.

Mistake. Channel 5 was on, covering the prelims for the Fuller trial. I switched it off and stared at the ceiling, trying to stop the thoughts from coming.

They came anyway.

"I know," I said aloud. "I should have pulled the trigger sooner."

I would have loved to say I was talking to Holly Fuller. A large part of me wished that I *would* see her every time I closed my eyes, or dream about her whenever I nabbed a few precious winks.

But the truth was, I had a hard time remembering what she looked like. Her face had been replaced with my own.

I didn't need a shrink degree to know what that meant. When Holly died, I not only disappointed her, but myself as well.

It's tough being your own worst critic.

Someone knocked on my door, shave-and-a-haircut.

"Can you get that?" I yelled at the cat.

The cat didn't respond, so I tied my bathrobe closed, forced myself out of bed, and padded to the door.

My mother smiled at me through the peephole.

"Mom!"

I couldn't open the door fast enough. When I hugged her, I felt like a little girl again, even though I was four inches taller than she was. I buried my nose in her shoulder, smelling the same detergent she's been using for forty years. She wore a fuzzy white turtleneck and some baggy jeans, and her right hand clenched the hook of an aluminum cane.

"Jacqueline, honey, it's great to see you."

"Why didn't you tell me you were coming?"

"We wanted it to be a surprise."

I blinked. "We?"

"Hello, Jack."

The voice made me catch my breath. I stepped away from my mother, looking at the man next to her, holding a single red rose.

"Hello, Alan."

My ex-husband smiled boyishly at me. The past ten years had been kind. He'd kept his hair, still thick and blond, and his waistline, still trim. There were more lines around his eyes and mouth than I remembered, but he looked almost exactly the same as he did the day he left me.

"Alan was kind enough to pick me up at the airport. We've been planning this for about two weeks."

I cinched my robe tighter, and spoke to my mother while my eyes were on him.

"Mom, maybe you should have told me first."

"Nonsense. You would have said no."

"Mom . . ."

"You're both adults, Jacqueline. I didn't think it would be a problem. Now, are you going to invite us in, or are we going to have a reunion in your hallway?"

Alan raised his eyebrows at me, still smiling. I gave him my back and walked into my apartment.

"Do you have any coffee, Jacqueline?"

"I'll make some."

I entered the kitchen, lips pursed. Coffee used to be an important part of my day, but now that I lived without a schedule caffeine wasn't necessary. I managed to remember how the machine worked, and got a pot going as Alan came in and leaned against the breakfast bar.

"Is this awkward?" he asked. He wore blue Dockers, a white button-down shirt, and a familiar faded brown bomber jacket.

"Don't you think so?"

"No."

I wanted to say something, to hurt him, but didn't have the energy. Maybe after some coffee.

"How are you doing?"

"Fine. Okay. Good."

"I heard you got shot again."

"I wasn't aware that you knew about the first time."

"Your mother keeps me informed."

I folded my arms. "Since when?"

"Since always."

"What does that mean?"

"Ever since our divorce, Mary and I have been in touch."

I snorted. "Bullshit."

"Why is it bullshit? I always loved your mother."

I had him there. "Since when did love stop you from leaving?"

Alan nodded, almost imperceptibly.

"Jacqueline!" my mother called from the living room. "You didn't tell me you had a cat!"

"Mom, don't!"

I rushed past Alan, hoping to prevent the maiming, and was shocked to see Mom cradling Mr. Friskers in her arms and stroking his head.

"He's adorable. What's his name?"

"Mr. Friskers."

"Oh. Well, he's adorable anyway."

"You should put him down, Mom. He doesn't like people very much."

"Nonsense. He seems to like me just fine."

"Then why is he growling at you?"

"That's not growling, Jacqueline. That's purring."

Son of a gun. Damn cat never purred for me. Not once.

My mother made a show of looking around the apartment. She tapped her knuckles on a large cardboard box. "What's with all the packing, dear? Putting some things into storage?"

"Yes." I hadn't yet told my mother about moving in with Latham.

"Good. I'll need the room."

She beamed at me, so full of strength and life, so unlike the woman I saw in the hospital bed months before.

I tried to sound upbeat. "You've decided to move in?"

"Yes, I have. I know I've threatened to disown you whenever you brought it up, but I came to a different conclusion. I don't believe I need you to look after me, but I don't have too many years left, and I'd like to spend them in the company of my daughter."

I smiled, wondering how real it looked. I'd given up trying to bully my mother into living with me, which is why I finally relented with Latham.

He would be crushed.

And, truth be told, I was crushed too.

"I have a buyer for the condo in Florida. I brought some papers for you to sign."

"Great."

"I should be ready to move in next week."

"Great."

Mom set down the cat and hobbled up to me, putting a wrinkled hand on my cheek.

"We'll talk more later, dear. We caught an early flight and I'm exhausted. Do you mind if I take a short nap here on the couch?"

"Use my bed, Mom."

At least someone would be using it. For something.

"Go grab something to eat with Alan. I know you have a lot of catching up to do."

She gave my face a tender pat and limped into the bedroom.

Alan stood by the window, hands in his pockets.

"Are you up for breakfast?" he asked.

"No."

"Would you like me to go?"

"Yes."

"Are you taking anything for depression?"

"Why would you think I was depressed?"

He shrugged, almost imperceptibly. Much of Alan's emotional range was imperceptible.

"Your mother seems to think you need someone now."

"So you came running to the rescue? Isn't that odd, considering the last time I needed someone, you fled like a thief in the night."

He smiled.

"I didn't leave like a thief in the night."

"Yes, you did."

"I left in the mid-afternoon, and I didn't take a single thing with me."

"You took my jacket."

"What jacket?"

"The one you're wearing right now."

"This is my jacket."

"I'm the one who wore it all the time."

"Why don't we fight about it over breakfast?"

"I don't want breakfast."

"You need to eat."

"How do you know what I need?"

Alan walked past me, and I wondered if I hit a nerve. I followed him into the kitchen.

"I said, how do you know what I need?"

"I heard you."

He found a mug, poured some coffee, and handed it to me.

"I don't want coffee."

"Yes you do. You're always pissy until you have your first cup of coffee."

I whined, "I am not pissy."

Alan started to laugh, and I had to bite my lower lip to keep from grinning.

"Fine. Gimmee the coffee."

He gimmeed, and I took a sip, surprised at how good it tasted.

"If you don't want to go out, I can cook." Alan opened the fridge and pulled out a single egg. "It's your last one. We can split it."

"I'd like my half sunny-side up."

I sat at my dinette set and watched Alan search for a frying pan. It brought back memories. Fond ones. Alan made breakfast almost every morning, during the years we'd been married.

Having found the pan, Alan searched the fridge again.

"No butter?"

"I haven't been to the store in a while."

"I can tell. What's this, a lime or a potato?" He held out a greenish brown thing.

"I think it's a tomato."

"There's something growing on it."

"Save it. I may need it if I ever get a staph infection."

He tossed the tomato in the garbage, and found two red potatoes, half a green onion, and half a bottle of chardonnay. From the freezer he took a bag of mixed vegetables and a pound of bacon. Then he went through my cabinets, liberating some olive oil, several spices, and a jar of salsa.

"This doesn't seem like an appetizing combination of food items."

He winked. "I've got to work with what I've got."

I sipped my coffee and watched him for the twenty minutes it took to microwave, peel, and dice the potatoes, fry the bacon, and sauté the veggies, chopped onion, salsa, and assorted spices in olive oil and white wine. He added the potatoes and bacon, stirred like mad, and then dumped the contents onto two plates.

"Hash à la Daniels." He set the plate in front of me.

"Smells good."

"If it's lousy, there's always pizza. Hold on."

The egg was still frying on the stove. He slid it out of the pan, sunny-side up, onto my pile of hash.

"Bon appétit."

I took a bite, and that led to two and three, and pretty soon I was shoveling it down my throat conveyor-belt fashion.

We didn't speak during breakfast, but the silence wasn't uncomfortable.

When I scooped the last bite into my mouth, Alan whisked away my plate and refilled my coffee.

"Still angry?" Alan asked.

"A little. I thought we had an unspoken understanding all these years."

"Which was?"

"You don't call me, I don't call you."

He nodded, putting his plate into the dishwasher.

"I never called you, Jack, because I knew it would hurt."

"You didn't seem to mind hurting me when you left."

"I wasn't referring to you in this case."

"You're saying it would have hurt you to call me?"

"Yes."

What could I say to that? I chose, "Oh."

Alan closed the dishwasher, then sat across from me, leaning in.

"So, how are you?" he asked.

"Fine."

"I know you're not fine, Jack."

"How would you know that?"

"Still have the insomnia?"

I looked away. "Yeah."

"You feel guilty about that cop's wife."

"Not really. IA cleared me on the shooting. It was completely by-the-book."

"By-the-book isn't enough for you. You have to be perfect, or you can't live with yourself."

I felt the armor I'd built up over the last decade begin to flake away. I needed to hate Alan. That's how I got through it.

"You don't know me like you think you do."

He shifted back in his chair, giving me room to breathe.

"How's the injury?"

"Almost healed, thank God. Latham has been more than patient."

"Latham?"

"My boyfriend."

I stared hard at Alan, but he didn't react. I don't know why that disappointed me.

"That's probably why you think I'm not fine. I just need to get laid."

"That did make you cranky. Remember that time I threw out my back?"

I grinned. "The three worst weeks of our marriage. Productive, though. I doubled my arrest record during that time."

"Remember when I was finally healed?"

"Yeah. We made up for lost time, didn't we?"

"Sure did. And I threw out my back again."

We both laughed, and I wondered how he turned the conversation away from Latham so quickly.

"I love him. Latham, I mean."

Alan stood up and walked over to me.

"That's nice. You deserve it."

"He's wonderful. You'd like him."

He put his hand on my shoulder.

"I hope I get a chance to meet him."

He leaned down, getting in my personal space.

"What are you doing?"

"Do you think there could ever be an *'us'* again?"

"I don't think so."

"Prove it to me."

"How?"

"Kiss me."

"No. You don't have that right."

"I made a mistake, leaving. I want to make it up to you. But I need to know if your feelings are still there."

"Alan . . ."

"I still love you, Jack. I always have. I didn't leave because I stopped loving you. I left because I couldn't compete with your job. It took everything you had, and there was nothing left for me. Plus, the constant worrying you wouldn't come home."

"Nothing has changed, Alan."

"I've changed. I can handle it now. And seeing you again . . ."

I said, "Don't," but his lips met mine, and I didn't stop it, I didn't pull away, and all of our history came rushing back, all of the good times, and I closed my eyes and let my tongue find his and spent a moment wondering what might have been.

Then I found my center and pushed him gently away.

"I'm in love with another man."

"I know."

I traced my fingers along his jaw.

"You hurt me, Alan."

"I know."

"I don't want to do this."

But when he kissed me again, I knew that I did.

CHAPTER 24

I didn't sleep with him, but felt so damn guilty I might as well have.

After the kissing became light petting, I excused myself to check on Mom.

Mom was snoring peacefully, with a silly smile on her face. I wasn't stupid. Bringing Alan here was part of some grand plan of hers, and for all she knew, it was working out fine.

For all I knew, she was right.

I dragged my tired bones into the shower, a cold one, and dressed in the most unattractive outfit I had: one of Latham's ratty football jerseys and an old pair of size ten jeans (after Alan left I briefly went from an eight to a ten, having traded the comfort of a husband for the comfort of pie).

I was searching through my closet for my ugliest pair of shoes, when I heard the screaming.

Alan.

My gun was in the bedside nightstand, and I grabbed it and ran into the living room. Alan was writhing on the sofa, Mr. Friskers trying to gnaw off his ear.

I realized I was pointing my gun, relaxed my death grip and set it on the table, and then tried to goad the cat off my ex-husband.

"Bad kitty. Let go of his ear."

I tugged. Alan screamed.

"Careful, Jack! He's clamped down on cartilage!"

"Hold on. I'll be right back."

"Hurry! He's chewing!"

I found the catnip mouse under the sofa, and shoved it under Mr. Friskers's nose.

"Easy, cat. Let him go. Let him go."

The cat went limp, and I pulled him away from Alan and set him on the floor.

"I was just sitting there, and he attacked me. How bad am I bleeding?"

"Bad."

"Stitches-bad?"

"You're missing about half your ear."

Alan spun around, alarmed.

"Really?"

"Maybe we can pump the cat's stomach." I kept my voice neutral. "We might be able to sew it back on."

He figured out I was joshing him and threw a sofa cushion at me.

I went to the kitchen and pulled a bunch of paper towels off the roll. Since acquiring Mr. Friskers, I always made sure I had an ample supply.

"It hurts." Alan had a hand clamped to his ear. He frowned, petulant.

"Oh, quit being a baby. It's nothing."

"Easy for you to say. For the rest of my life, my sunglasses will be crooked."

"You'll be fine. If you want, I'll let you borrow some of my earrings." I dabbed at the blood. "You have enough holes for six or seven."

"Funny. What's wrong with that cat, anyway?"

"I haven't been able to figure that out yet. Hold this, here, while I get the rubbing alcohol."

Alan moaned, and I went off in search of supplies.

A liberal splash of Bactine knocked the ardor out of Alan, and he didn't make another pass at me during the time it took to bandage his ear. I silently thanked Mr. Friskers for the reprieve.

I suggested watching a movie until my mom woke up, and offered Alan a choice of *Breakfast at Tiffany's* or *Royal Wedding*, the only two videos I owned. While we debated the various merits of each, the phone rang.

"Jack? Herb. How you feeling?"

"Better," I said. And I was. "Calling to check on me?"

"No. We, uh, need you at the office."

"I thought I was still on medical leave."

"The leave has been canceled. Direct order from Captain Bains, we need you here yesterday."

"What's this about, Herb?"

"It's Fuller."

"Gimme twenty minutes."

Alan stared at me. I realized this was a micro-encapsulation of our marriage—me getting a phone call and then running to work.

But we weren't married anymore, so I had nothing to feel guilty about.

"There's an extra set of keys in the little ceramic frog on top of the refrigerator," I told him. "Tell Mom she can reach me on my cell."

I tiptoed into the bedroom and changed into a pantsuit without waking my mother. Rather than fuss with my hair, I tied it back in a short ponytail. I spent all of two minutes on my face, not bothering with foundation or eyeliner.

Alan was sitting on the sofa, facing a TV that wasn't on. I picked up my gun from the table and put it in my holster.

"Be careful." He didn't turn his head to look at me.

"Will you be here when I get back?"

He met my eyes and cocked his head slightly to the left, as if appraising me. "I've got a room at the Raphael for a week. I figured I'd look up some friends, visit a few old haunts."

I felt something that I realized was relief.

"I'll see you soon, then."

"Dinner tonight?"

"It might be late."

"I'm used to waiting up for you."

I nodded, grabbed my London Fog trench coat, and left the apartment.

Chicago smelled like fall, which is to say the garbage and exhaust fume stench carried a hint of dying leaves. The Windy City was suitably windy, temperature in the mid-fifties, the sidewalks damp from a recent rain.

There was a powwow waiting for me in my office when I got to the station. Benedict, who was wearing the new Brooks Brothers suit he bought himself as a reward for losing twenty pounds, our boss Captain Bains, and Assistant State's Attorney Libby Fischer.

Stephen Bains had been captain of the 2-6 for as long as anyone could remember. He was short, portly, and balding. He combated the latter with a hair weave, which looked realistic except for the fact that it lacked gray, whereas his mustache was practically white.

Libby Fischer was around my age, and a clotheshorse. She wore a beige Gaultier top with a matching knee-length skirt that probably cost more than I made in a month. A white pearl choker, red Kenneth Cole pumps, and a small red Louis Vuitton bag rounded out her ensemble.

Libby smiled a lot. If I had her wardrobe, I would have too.

"How's the stomach?"

That was as close to a pleasantry as Bains would get.

"Better," I answered. "I think I'll be—"

"We're going to lose the Fuller case," Libby interrupted. She smiled sweetly.

I didn't try to hide my surprise.

"How the hell can that be? Is something inadmissible?"

"No. The case is solid. It's that brain tumor, floating in a glass jar, labeled exhibit A."

Bains frowned. "As you're aware, Fuller has been claiming amnesia since recovering from surgery. He says he has no memory of any murders."

Libby stood up and went to the window. "And so far, our shrinks haven't been able to crack him."

I crossed my arms over my chest. "Fuller's blaming the murders on his brain tumor?"

Libby continued to stare out the captain's window. "He's doing just that. It was on his frontal lobe, the brain's behavior center. It controls emotion, personality, and understanding of right and wrong. Expert shrinks are falling all over themselves eager to explain to a jury how a tumor can radically alter someone's personality. Fuller's lawyers are going for the first ever insanity defense based on physical evidence."

My anger level continued to build. "If he's declared insane, he still gets locked up, right?"

"Wrong. If they prove he was insane at the time of his crimes, and the insanity was caused by the tumor, he's a free man. No more tumor, no more insanity. The bastard walks."

"Jesus."

Bains stared at me, hard.

"Are you one hundred percent, Jack?"

I didn't feel one hundred percent, but I sensed something coming. I nodded.

"Good," Bains continued. "I want you to talk to him."

"To Fuller? Why?"

"A confession would be nice. But I'll settle for your impression of whether he's bullshitting or not."

"If he's faking, we can plan a better attack," Libby said.

"Do we suspect he's faking?"

"It would be nice if he was," Libby sat back down, "but we just don't know. He's been interviewed by over a dozen people: shrinks, lawyers, cops, doctors. So far he's unimpeachable."

"Has he taken a lie detector?"

"One. Theirs. And he passed with flying colors. He's got another scheduled tomorrow, with one of our examiners."

After a moment, I asked, "Why me?" My job was to arrest criminals. Other people were much more qualified to do follow-up interviews.

Bains scratched his weave. "You worked with him for several years. You know him. You're biased to our side, so you'll try to see through the lies. I don't have to tell you what a media circus this case has become."

"I'm not a professional interrogator, Captain. I don't want to see him back on the streets, but I don't think—"

"There's something else, Jack."

"What?"

Bains caught me in his iron gaze. "Fuller asked for you. Specifically."

"For me? Why?"

Libby leaned in close, like we were best friends sharing a secret.

"We don't know. He hasn't given anyone a reason. But since his capture, he's inquired about you many times. His counsel has advised him to not talk to us, and lately he's been a clam. But Fuller agreed to an interview, and he'll even do it without his attorneys present, but only with you. Of course, his statements won't be admissible as evidence, so if he says anything we'll have to introduce it through your testimony."

I replayed the scene in my head again. Kicking in the door. Telling Fuller to let his wife go. The bullets erupting from Holly's stomach, drilling into mine.

"I'd be happy to take a crack at him."

"He's at Cook County. You'll meet with him in a private visiting booth. Alone. Plexiglas wall between you. You know the setup."

"Will I be wired?"

Libby placed her palms on her thighs and smoothed out the Gaultier. "We all know that it's illegal to record someone without their consent. It would be inadmissible as evidence. As an officer of the court, I can't be privy to any knowledge of criminal activity, and if I heard of any I'd report it immediately. On a completely unrelated note, I was reviewing some old case histories and came across some interesting legal terms. One is called *recollection refresh*, and the other is *transcript for impeachment.*"

Libby then spent five minutes explaining how an illegal tape recording could be used in a trial.

When she finished, Bains said, "I'd like to go on record to say there will be no illegal taping of any suspects in my district. Especially with this voice-activated tape recorder."

Bains placed a slim electronic unit on his desk. I put it in my pocket.

"When can I meet with him?"

"You've got a meeting scheduled in an hour. Good luck, Jack. I'll expect a full report on my desk in the morning."

Libby stood, shook my hand.

"You know, you could have saved us all this trouble if you'd just aimed one inch lower."

I was beginning to think the same thing myself.

CHAPTER 25

We'd folded ourselves into the colorful plastic extrusion chairs of a nearby submarine sandwich chain, Herb eating and me staring out the storefront window. It was raining, and gray clouds smeared together with the muted brown and black tones of the city and its dying trees, the few that it had.

Maybe somewhere in the suburbs there were piles of colorful autumn leaves waiting to be jumped into, but here we only had torn brown dead things that turned into mud when wet.

"When I was a kid, every fall, my mom would take me up to Wisconsin to watch the leaves turn. I never appreciated it. Maybe beauty is wasted on the young."

"Could be," Herb said, mostly to the meatball sandwich opened up and splayed out before him. The low-carb diet he was following restricted bread, and he'd pushed it off to the side, giving the protein his full attention.

"What do you think of when you think of autumn?"

"Thanksgiving turkey."

"How about winter?"

"Christmas turkey."

"Spring?"

"Easter ham."

"I sense a theme here."

"You gonna finish that roast beef?"

I allowed Herb access to my half-eaten sub, and he used a fork to pull out the meat.

"I don't understand how eating all of that fat is healthy."

"Got me." Herb opened up a packet of mayo, slathered it on the beef, and crammed it all in. "Works, though."

"Yeah. You look great."

He grunted, as if not believing it.

"Herb? Something on your mind?"

He grunted again.

"Got some cholesterol caught in your throat?"

"It's Bernice."

"Is she okay?"

He shrugged.

Usually, I got daily Bernice updates, but since I'd been out of work, I'd only seen Herb three times. Each time, I'd been unloading my problems, without bothering to ask if he had any.

Some partner.

"What's wrong, Herb?"

"We're at odds. She doesn't like my new lifestyle."

"What? Low carb?"

"The weight loss is only part of it. She doesn't like my car. She told me she's sick of all the constant sex. Vacation is coming up, and we always go to California, to visit her friends in wine country. Been doing that for twenty years. This year, I want to go to Vegas."

"You can compromise. Spend a few days in Las Vegas, a few with her friends."

"Screw her friends."

Which was as spiteful a thing as I'd ever heard come out of Herb's mouth.

I wanted to pursue the issue, but Benedict checked his watch, shoveled in the last meatball, and stood up.

"We're going to be late." Which is what I think he said, cheeks full.

He walked out of the restaurant, and I followed. I tried to bring up the topic in the car, but Herb insisted he didn't want to talk about it.

Cook County Jail stretched from 26th and Cal to 31st and Sacramento, making it the largest single-site pre-detention center in the US. Eight thousand six hundred and fifty-eight men and women resided there, give or take, divvied up among eleven division buildings. Most of the inmates were awaiting their trials, after which they'd be freed or more likely sent someplace else. Others were just commuting their short sentences, ninety days and under.

I did a quick voice test of the tape recorder, and found it in working condition.

After being cleared through the perimeter fence, we located Division Eleven, where they held Fuller. From the outside, the clean, white building looked more like a government office than a maximum security prison.

Inside, however, was all business. We were met by the assistant division superintendent, Jake Carver, a beefy man with a moist handshake. We signed in, checked our weapons, and followed Carver into the bowels of the prison.

"Been a model prisoner." Carver had a voice like a buzz saw. Smoking, drink, or both. "No problems at all."

"What's the security on him?" Herb asked.

"He's in isolation. Can't put a cop in with the general population."

"Have you met him?" I asked.

"Sure. Chitchatted for a while."

"What's your impression?"

"Seems like a nice enough guy."

"Is he lying about the amnesia?"

"If he is, he's the best liar I've ever seen, and I've been with the DOC for almost thirty years. Here we are." We stopped at a white steel door with a six-inch-square window at eye level. "Visiting room H. Got it to yourself for half an hour. Just bang on the door when you want to go, or if he starts getting rowdy. I'll be right here."

Carver unbolted the door and allowed me entrance. I hit the Record button on the tape player in my pocket, then went in.

The room was small, twelve by twelve, lit by overhead strips of fluorescence, one of them flickering. It smelled like body odor and desperation. In the center of the room stood a folding chair, facing an inch-thick, pitted and scratched Plexiglas barrier, reinforced with steel bars, that divided the space in half.

Barry Fuller sat on the other side, a pleasant look on his face. He wore prison clothes; a Day-Glo orange jumpsuit with his number stenciled on the breast. His hands were cuffed, and a chain trailed down, connecting to his leg irons. A large, puffy scar ran from his eyebrow to the top of his head, his crew cut unable to conceal it.

"Thanks for coming, Lieut. Please, have a seat."

I nodded, sitting across from him. I kept my knees together, both feet flat on the ground, my back ramrod-straight.

"Hello, Barry. You look well."

He smiled, lowering his head so his finger could trace the scar.

"Healing pretty good. How about you? They told me you took two in the stomach?"

"I'm managing." I kept my tone even. "Much better than your wife."

Fuller's face seemed to deflate. His eyes got red and teared up.

"Holly. My love. I can't believe I did that."

"Well, you did. I was there. I watched her bleed to death, right in front of me."

Fuller sniffled. He rubbed his eyes, which made them even redder.

"I know how it sounds, Lieutenant. Imagine if you woke up one day, and everyone started telling you about all of these horrible things you did. Things you have no memory of."

"It was the brain tumor, huh?"

"I loved my wife!" Fuller's voice cracked. "I never would have killed her if I knew what I was doing. Jesus, Holly."

His shoulders sagged. A good actor? Or someone who really felt remorse?

"Why did you ask me here, Fuller? Without lawyers? What did you want to say to me?"

"I wanted to thank you."

That threw me.

"What?"

"To thank you. For stopping me, before I hurt anyone else. Also, to apologize for shooting you."

I gave him a once-over.

"Touching, Fuller. I'm deeply touched, really. Your tears make up for all of those women you butchered."

"I don't remember butchering any women. I'm thankful for that, actually. I don't know if I could live with myself if I remembered."

"You don't remember Davi McCormick? Cutting off her arms? Putting my handcuffs on her wrists, so your sicko buddy Rushlo could leave them in the morgue?"

Fuller shook his head.

"How about Eileen Hutton? You bit her so hard she was missing chunks of her flesh."

"Please stop."

"What did she taste like, Barry? Can you remember that?"

"I can't remember anything."

Time to get serious.

"I bet you do remember it. I bet you remember what a rush it was, to cut off her head. I bet it gave you such a sense of power and control. You fucked her too, didn't you? Do you remember if it was before or after you yanked out her heart?"

Barry was really putting on a show now, sobbing loudly. But I wasn't buying.

"Drop the act, Barry. I know you're lying. You remember every sick little detail. I bet you jerk off to those memories every night in your lonely little cell. You make me sick. I hope they fry your ass in the chair, tumor or no tumor, you piece of shit."

When Fuller pulled his hands away from his face, he was grinning. I'd expected anger or outrage, but he looked outright amused.

"You're wearing a wire, aren't you, Lieutenant?"

I didn't reply.

"You want me to be honest, but you won't be honest yourself? Let me see the wire."

I considered my options. Knowing Barry was faking this seemed more important than proving it. I took out the recorder, then switched it off.

"Fine, Barry. Just you and me. You ready to drop this stupid amnesia ploy and come clean?"

Fuller closed his eyes and clasped his hands together, as if in prayer. Then he lifted his arm and rubbed his face on his sleeve, back and forth.

"Onions." He blew his nose. "Under my fingernails. Instant tears, courtesy of the wonderful chicken soup served up nice and hot by the Department of Corrections. Pretty good performance, huh? Anything I need to improve before I give it in court?"

I felt myself get very cold.

"How much do you remember, Barry?"

"I remember everything, Jack."

"The murders?"

"Every detail. And you were right. At night, when I'm all alone in my cell,

I abuse myself thinking about them. Spit and a fist are a poor substitute for a bleeding, screaming whore. But I have to make do until they let me out."

He made a kissy face and winked at me. My stomach rolled over, and I felt something I hadn't felt in a long time.

"So there was no reason for this? Just bloodlust?"

"Just bloodlust? You say that like you're disappointed. What's a better reason for murder than that? Money? Revenge? Lust is so much purer."

"So you're a sociopath."

"Actually, no. I've had a lot of time in here to read, sort things out. According to the *DSM IV,* I suffer from disorganized episodic aggression. I feel empathy, I just choose to ignore it to get high."

"High on killing?"

"Headaches, Jack. Terrible headaches. Caused by the tumor, probably, but I've had them my whole life, and they tell me the tumor can't be more than a year old. Killing makes the pain go away. I figured out it has something to do with endorphin. Endogenous morphine. The body manufactures it to block pain, and it's a hundred times more powerful than an equivalent dose of heroin. Killing gives me an endorphin rush. At least, that's what I think. I'd like to ask all of these shrinks watching me 24-7, see what they think, but I've got to keep up appearances."

"So now that the tumor is gone?"

"Tumor doesn't matter, Jack. I'm addicted to killing."

He grinned, his eyes as black and lifeless as a shark's.

I stood up, not needing to hear any more. I got what I came for.

"Leaving so soon, Jack? But I haven't told you my plans yet."

"What plans?"

"For after they let me out. I'm going to be looking you up, Jack." He waggled his tongue at me, and began to rub his crotch. "We're going to have a real good time, Lieutenant. I got something special planned for you, and that fat partner of yours. I hated you before, because you wouldn't take me in Detective

Division. Since you put me in this hellhole, I've grown to hate you even more. I'll show you, soon."

I turned my back on him, and tried to walk to the door without shaking too badly.

"Don't worry, Jack. It won't be right away. First I'm going to kill everyone in your life. Everyone you know and care about."

I pounded on the steel, harder than I intended.

"Give my best to your mom and boyfriend, Jack. Be seeing you soon."

I pounded again, and Carver opened up.

"You okay, Lieutenant?"

I nodded. But I wasn't okay. My hands were quaking, and I had an overwhelming urge to vomit.

"Jack?" Herb had concern in his eyes.

"He's faking, Herb. Faking big time. We can't let him get out."

"What happened in there? Do you have the tape?"

I held Benedict's eyes and grabbed his arms, squeezing hard.

"We can't let him get out, Herb. We can't. No matter what."

CHAPTER 26

"Open cell eleven."

"Opening cell eleven."

The electronic lock disengages with a clang, and the cell door opens. Fuller eyes the prison guard escorting him; the man is eight inches shorter, with a neck so thin Fuller could strangle him with one hand.

The skinny guard unlocks Fuller's ankle irons, while the second guard, a fat guy with a face like a bulldog, stands at the ready palming a can of pepper spray.

Keep looking tough, punk. If I wanted to, I could take away that mace and stick it so far up your ass your breath would smell like jalapeños.

"Thanks," Fuller says instead. He smiles, playing his role. The thin guy takes off his handcuffs, and Fuller enters his cell. It's tiny, cramped. A lidless steel shitter dominates one corner, next to a steel sink. In the other corner is a steel cot, a two-inch-thick cotton mattress resting on top.

There isn't enough room in here to do a decent push-up, so Fuller compromises, putting his palms on the cool concrete floor and his feet on the sink.

"One, two, three, four . . ."

He touches his chin to the floor with each tip, feeling the burn build up in his shoulders and chest. His face begins to turn red, and he smiles.

Jack's expression was priceless. I practically made her wet her panties.

"Eighteen, nineteen, twenty . . ."

Fuller looks at the cot. There's a small slit in the mattress, along a seam, with more pieces of onion and some other things. Things that will produce dramatic court theatrics.

"Thirty-seven, thirty-eight—"

The lie detector tomorrow will be fun too. He still has the staple, secretly liberated from his attorney's paperwork. A staple is all he needs to pass with flying colors.

"Sixty-five, sixty-six . . ."

Everything is going his way. His bitch of a wife is dead, finally. He got his lawyer to pass on word to Rushlo to keep quiet—and the little toady will no doubt follow orders. If all goes as planned, Fuller will be back out on the street soon—probably in a few weeks. Then he'll pay Jack a visit, make good on his promise.

"Eighty-nine, ninety, ninety-one . . ."

Only one thing is bothering him. Though the doctors assure him his tumor is completely gone, he's still getting headaches. They aren't as sharp as before, but they've been increasing in intensity over the past few weeks.

"Hundred twenty, hundred twenty-one . . ."

So far, aspirin is helping. But he foresees a time when that won't be enough. He'll need to kill again. Soon.

"Hundred fifty."

Fuller's feet touch the floor and he stands and stretches, knuckles dragging across the ceiling. He's breathing hard. There's a metallic taste in his mouth—he's bitten his tongue.

The taste is arousing.

After a minute's rest, he puts his feet back on the sink and begins another set of push-ups. His teeth work on the cut in his tongue, making it larger.

"Twenty, twenty-one . . ."

He closes his eyes, pretending the blood he's swallowing is Jack's.

CHAPTER 27

I dialed Libby from Benedict's car and gave her the short version. The excitement in her voice was obvious.

"I knew he was playing us!"

"We don't have evidence."

"But now that we know for sure, we'll get some. The polygraph examiner we've got is the best. He pegged Ted Bundy. He'll get Fuller too. You did good, Jack."

"Thanks."

Except I didn't feel like I did good. I felt like I'd just gotten my ass kicked.

"You want to be there? Tomorrow?"

"For the lie detector?"

"Sure. It'll keep him off guard."

I wanted to say no. I didn't want to be there. Fuller unearthed feelings I thought I'd buried.

Feelings of fear.

In crisis situations, cops need to have a certain amount of fear. It precedes adrenaline, which makes reactions faster. When I shot Fuller, months ago, I'd been afraid. But the fear worked for me then, heightening senses, forcing me to act automatically, as I'd been trained to do.

Now—the sick feeling in my stomach, the sweaty palms, the dry mouth, the runaway imagination—did me no good at all, other than add to my pile of neuroses.

"Jack? You still there?"

"I just came back to work, Libby. I'm not sure what's going on tomorrow."

"The polygraph is at nine A.M., back at Division Eleven. I'll talk to Bains to clear some time for you."

"Thanks," I managed. "See you tomorrow, then."

Herb stopped at a light, squinted at me.

"Jack? You look sick."

"I'm fine."

"You let him get to you. Fuller."

I tried to smile. "Not a chance. I'm just tired, Herb. Nothing more."

The light turned green, but Benedict didn't go.

"I know you, Jack. You're not yourself."

Rather than answer, I played the role-reversal card.

"Me? You seem to be having the granddaddy of midlife crises, and refuse to speak a peep."

Someone behind us honked their horn.

"I'm not having a midlife crisis."

"Male menopause, then."

"That's not the case. Bernice and I are just heading in different directions."

"Different directions? Herb, you've been married for twenty years."

Herb turned away, facing the road.

"Maybe twenty years is too long."

Another honk. Herb hit the gas, squealing tires.

I closed my eyes and thought about yesterday, when my only concerns were what kind of pizza to order, when I'd be ready to make love again, and if I was becoming addicted to Ambien. My troubles seemed to have quadrupled overnight. And for the cherry on top, I got to deal with the very real possibility that a psycho would soon be out on the street, killing everyone I knew.

Herb and I didn't talk the rest of the drive back to the station. I went to my office, stared at the huge mound of paperwork that had grown on my desk during my absence, and then moved it aside to fill out my report.

After an hour of hunt and peck, I dropped off the report, and the recording, with Bains. Then I thought about getting started on my backlog, couldn't bring myself to do it, and called it a day.

Back at my apartment building, I was annoyed to hear piano music filling the hallway on my floor. Jazz, and someone playing it much too loudly. My mood was just foul enough to start banging on doors and flashing my badge, but when I discovered the source of the noise, I knew my badge wouldn't do much good.

"Mom?"

When I opened my door, the music hit me like a wind. I never liked jazz—I preferred my music to have structure and balance. I also never liked piano, having been forced into two years of lessons by a mother who thought it built character.

The living room offered more unpleasant surprises. My couch faced a different direction than it had this morning. It now also had three pink throw pillows on it, which matched the new pink curtains on my windows.

I liked pink about as much as jazz piano.

I hit the Off button on the stereo.

"Mom?"

"In the bedroom, dear."

I took a deep breath, blew it out, and walked into my bedroom. My mother was hanging a painting on my wall—one of those framed prints available at department stores for under twenty bucks. The subject was a tabby cat, with a pink bow on its collar, wrestling with a ball of yarn.

"Hello, Jacqueline. What happened to Midori?"

"Midori?"

"Midori Kawamura. The CD that was playing."

"It was too loud. The neighbors were complaining."

"Philistines. She's one of the greatest jazz pianists on the planet."

"I don't like jazz pianists."

"Perhaps you suffer from pianist envy."

I was too annoyed to smile at that.

"Mom, why is my sofa turned around?"

"You had it facing the wall. Now it's facing the windows. Do you like the pillows?"

"I don't like pink."

"You never liked anything girlish. When you were six, all of your friends played with dolls, and I had to buy you toy soldiers. What do you think of your new picture?"

She motioned, with both hands, at the cat with the yarn.

"Adorable," I deadpanned.

"Reminded me so much of your cat, I had to buy it. Frisky? Where are you?"

Mr. Friskers bounded into the room, onto the bed, and into my mother's arms.

"Frisky?" I asked.

"Look at him, isn't he a ringer for the cat in the picture?"

She held Mr. Friskers up, and he did, indeed, resemble his framed counterpart—right down to the pink bow my mother had tied around his neck.

"A dead ringer, Mom. Can you take off the bow? You're emasculating him."

"Nonsense. Frisky loves pink, unlike some people. Right, Frisky?"

She stroked his chin, and the damn cat purred at her. I sat on the bed, which my mom had made—much better than I ever had. Not so much as a wrinkle anywhere.

"How'd you do all of this?"

"Alan took me out, the dear man. He'll be back soon with the plant."

"Plant?"

"I asked him to pick up a floor plant. This place is so sterile and lifeless. You need a plant."

Resistance was futile, so I kicked off my shoes and shrugged out of my clothing.

"Jacqueline? You're not mad, are you?"

"No, Mom. I just had a tough day."

She set the cat down and put her hand on my head, stroking my hair.

"Would you like to talk about it?"

"Maybe later. I need a shower."

My mom smiled, nodded. Then she limped out of the bedroom.

A minute later, the jazz came back on.

I slammed the door to the bathroom and set the shower dial to poach. Ten minutes under the needle spray went a long way toward washing the Fuller meeting off of me. I shaved, deep-conditioned my hair, and used the shower mirror to do some serious eyebrow plucking.

I was wrapped in a towel, moisturizing, when the bathroom door opened.

"Jacqueline? There's a strange man at the door."

A jolt of panic gripped me, then let go when I realized it couldn't be Fuller.

"Does he have red hair?"

"Yes."

"That's Latham, Mom. My boyfriend. Didn't he use his key?"

"He tried to. I had the chain on."

"Can you let him in and tell him I'll be right there?"

Mom gave me a small frown, but nodded. I slipped on my bathrobe and wound the towel around my wet hair, turban-style.

Latham and Mom stood in the kitchen, Latham in his work clothes—gray pants, red tie, gray jacket. Mom stared at him like he was something she'd stepped in.

"Hi, Jack. I thought I'd stop by, take you out for a bite."

My mother smiled politely. "We have plans already."

I shot my mom with laser eyes, but she pretended not to notice.

"We weren't planning anything special, Latham." I smiled smoothly. "We'd love to have you join us. Right, Mom?"

Mom managed to fake an enthusiastic smile. "Absolutely. It would be just lovely, Nathan."

"Latham," he and I said in unison.

"I'm sure Alan won't mind either."

Shit. How'd I forget about Alan?

"Your boyfriend?" Latham ventured, looking at Mom.

"Jacqueline's husband," she answered, primly.

"Ex-husband. He was good enough to accompany Mom into town."

"He's helping me with the transition. Wonderful man."

"Transition?" Latham raised an eyebrow at me. I felt like going back to my bedroom and hiding under a pillow.

"Mom has decided to move in with me after all."

Latham, to his credit, barely flinched. I held his hand, gave it a hard squeeze that I hope conveyed everything I was feeling.

He didn't squeeze back.

"Well, that's wonderful. Jack has wanted that for a long time. She speaks the world of you."

"How sweet. It's a shame she never mentioned you."

I gave Latham another hard squeeze, and then released him to escort my mother before this got worse.

"Excuse us just a moment, Latham. Girl talk."

I steered Mom into the bedroom and shut the door.

"What is it, Jacqueline?"

"Cut the BS, Mom. You're acting horrible."

"Horrible? How?"

I raised an index finger, in scolding mode.

"I'm serious. I happen to love this guy. If you keep—"

"You love him? You never told me you loved him."

"I never had the chance, Mom. You only started taking my calls recently, and then the conversation has mostly been about you."

I regretted it as soon as I said it, and my mother's reaction held no surprises. She seemed to grow smaller before my very eyes.

"You don't want me here, do you?"

"Mom . . ."

"I would have never chosen to come up here if I'd known you were in love with this man. Has he asked you to move in with him?"

"Mom, we can talk about all of this later."

"If you love him, why did you kiss Alan this morning?"

It just kept getting better.

"I thought you were asleep."

"I was faking."

"That was a mistake. Mom, look, I've had a terrible day, I just want to get dressed and go out to eat. Can you please, *please,* go out there and make friends with Latham?"

"I'll do my best, dear. I'm suddenly not up for conversation."

I bit my lower lip, wondering how this could possibly get any worse.

Then I heard the front door open.

"Mary? I've got the plant."

Alan. I hurried over, preparing myself for damage control. Latham eyed me as I walked up.

"I should have called."

"I should have told you. We'll get through this. Be brave." I pecked him on the cheek, but he didn't offer me anything in the way of nonverbal encouragement.

Alan had a large floor plant in his hands, something with long green pointy fronds. He set it down, smiled at me, then noticed Latham and the smile vanished.

"I didn't mean to barge in."

"Alan, this is Latham Conger, my boyfriend. Latham, this is Alan Daniels, my ex-husband."

Neither moved to shake hands, and I watched them size each other up. If they'd been dogs, I would have expected each of them to lift a leg and start marking territory.

"Hello, Alan! What a lovely fern!" Mom made a show of limping up to him and kissing him.

I glanced at Latham. He was staring at his watch.

"So." I clapped my hands together and put on a big fake smile. "Who's up for pizza?"

CHAPTER 28

The two slices of pizza I managed to choke down sat like rocks in my stomach. Neither Latham nor Alan had said more than ten words during dinner, having expended most of their energy trying to ignore each other.

That left my mother to dominate the conversation, and she was on her third drink, inhibitions falling away by the sip. She hadn't mentioned the kiss yet, but it was only a matter of time.

"Spicy." Mom smacked her lips. "When you get older, your tastebuds—well—don't taste. But a good bloody Mary with a healthy dose of hot sauce makes this tired old tongue dance a jitterbug. Plus it's so much fun to order a drink with my name in it."

"Yeah," I said. "It's a hoot."

"Are you in town long, Alan?" Latham asked.

"I'm here until Mary settles in."

"So that's how long? A week? Two?"

"As long as it takes."

Latham played with his drink straw, spearing at the ice.

"Don't you have a job you need to get back to?"

Alan folded his arms—one of his defense postures.

"I'm a freelance writer. I'm not tied to an office job, stuck in that nine-to-five rut, making my employer rich from my efforts. But I'm sure it's not like that at all in the accounting world."

"I don't mind nine-to-five. It pays the bills."

"Boring, though, isn't it? Jack usually falls for creative types."

"Maybe she realized how badly that's worked for her in the past, and decided she needed a change."

I raised my hand. "Does anyone want to hear about my day? The crazy guy I put behind bars threatened to kill me."

I'd intended to provoke sympathy, but Latham took that as a cue to assert dominance. He put his arm around me, like we were drinking buddies.

"Stay at my place tonight, Jack."

"Jack doesn't look too thrilled there, Latham. Maybe you've begun to bore her already."

"Why don't you go run home and write about it?"

"Okay, guys. Enough." I pulled away from Latham and stood up. "You're all acting like jerks." I glanced at my mom, to let her know I included her in the statement.

"I'll drive you home." Latham stood up. So did Alan.

"I'll drive myself home." I dug into my pocket, threw some bills on the table. Both Alan and Latham fell all over themselves, trying to give me my money back. I left them there, heading for the front door, stepping out into the cold Chicago night air.

Home wasn't an option. I needed time to think. A Checker cab was at the stoplight, and I yelled to it and climbed in.

"Where you headed?"

Good question. After tonight, I was willing to swear off men forever.

Parents too. And police work. Where was I headed? Unemployed orphan spinsterhood.

I settled for Joe's Pool Hall.

The cab spit me out in front, and I beelined to the bar, ordered a whiskey sour, and scoped the action.

As usual, Joe's had enough secondhand smoke swirling around to cause cancer in laboratory animals. All twelve tables were in use, but I gave up being shy for my fortieth birthday, and got on the board for pickup games.

Four beers and two hours later, I'd done considerable damage to both my liver and the competition. Pool offered a refuge from my problems, and sinking ball after ball put me into an almost zenlike state. I'd forgotten all about Alan, Latham, Mom, Fuller, Herb, my job, my apartment, my insomnia, my life.

Then the balance shifted. The alcohol that had once calmed my nerves, now made me sloppy. I lost three games in a row, and decided to call it quits.

The night had gotten colder, and my jacket wasn't enough to keep the chill out.

Mom snored on the couch. My machine had eight messages on it, but I didn't feel up to dealing with them. I got undressed, curled up fetal on my bed, took my nightly sleeping pill, and cried softly to myself until it kicked in and ushered me into a blessedly dreamless sleep.

CHAPTER 29

They were torturing me with a horrible beeping sound, playing it over and over until it drove me to the brink of madness, and I couldn't get away and I couldn't make it stop, and finally something registered in my head and I opened my eyes and glanced groggily at my alarm clock.

Irritating little sound. But I suppose the pleasant melody of whales singing or frogs croaking wouldn't wake someone up.

I turned it off, and sat up, dizzily, in bed. My head hurt. I yawned, my jaw clicking from overnight calcium deposits, and then spent a minute trying to get my bearings.

Sleeping pill hangover. I forced my feet out of bed, thought about doing some sit-ups, touched the scars on my belly and decided I wasn't ready yet, and took a cool shower.

The soap, which promised to open my eyes, didn't. Neither did the cold water. When I got out, I was just as sleepy, and shivering as well.

"No more," I said to my face in the mirror. Along with making waking up one of the labors of Hercules, the pills also did wondrous things for my complexion. I hadn't had a pimple since junior prom, but now, staring at me like a third eye on my forehead, was a blemish.

I played fast and loose with my concealer, slapped on the rest of my face, and went to the kitchen to dump yesterday's coffee and make a fresh pot.

My mom, whom I knew to be an early bird, hadn't gotten up yet. I went to check on her.

She lay on her back, eyes closed, mouth slightly open. Absolutely still.

I moved closer, looking for the telltale rise and fall of her chest, but I couldn't see under the blanket. Closer still, holding my breath so I could hear her breathing.

I didn't hear a thing.

I considered panicking, realized I was being silly, and bent down over her, reaching for her neck.

Her skin was warm, and her carotid flittered with her heartbeat.

"Are you taking my pulse?"

I jumped back, almost screaming in fright.

"Mom! Jeez, you scared me."

My mother pinned me with her mother-eyes.

"You thought I was dead, and were taking my pulse."

I made a show of looking at my watch.

"I gotta run, Mom. I'll call you later."

"When did you get home last night?"

"Jesus, Mom. I'm forty-six years old. I don't have a curfew."

"No, but you have people who care about you, and it's selfish to make them worry."

Rather than argue, I went back into the kitchen for coffee. A quick caller ID check saw I had four calls from Latham, and four from the Raphael hotel—Alan. I didn't bother playing the messages.

I'd purposely added less water, so the coffee had a bigger kick. I added an ice cube to my mug so I could gulp it down quicker.

"Are you okay, Jacqueline?"

Mom had the blanket around her shoulders. She looked like Yoda.

"No, Mom, I'm not. And you really didn't help matters yesterday."

"I'm sorry for that. You know I love Alan like a son. Call me a foolish old woman, but I thought, you know, if I made him bring me here—"

"That we'd realize we still loved each other? He left me, Mom. Don't you remember how much he hurt me?"

"You hurt him too, honey."

"He's the one that left."

"You didn't give him much of a choice, working eighty-hour weeks, never taking a vacation."

I poured more coffee.

"You were a cop, Mom. You know how it is."

"And I regret it. All of those long hours. Working Christmas. I should have been spending more time with you. You practically raised yourself."

My veneer cracked.

"Mom, you were my hero. I never resented your job. You were out there doing good."

"I should have been at home doing good. Instead, I screwed you up, made you think nothing should stand in the way of your career."

"I'm not screwed up. I'm one of the highest ranking female cops in Chicago."

"And I'm the only woman in my bingo group that doesn't have grandchildren."

Mom saw my reaction, and immediately backpedaled.

"Jacqueline, I didn't mean that. It just came out."

"I'll be home late." I walked past her.

"Honey, I'm sorry."

I ignored her, grabbed my coat, and closed the door a bit louder than necessary.

If the anger didn't wake me up, the weather did. Cold, with stinging, freezing drizzle that attacked like biting flies.

I left the window cracked on the drive to Cook County Jail, letting the wind numb my face. The cell phone rang, but I ignored it.

Fuller's polygraph test was set for twenty minutes from now, and I needed to mentally prepare for seeing him again.

CHAPTER 30

Fuller works the staple under the nail of his big toe, digging it in deep.

There's very little blood, but the pain is electric.

With a quarter inch of metal left protruding, he puts on his sock and shoe.

It's lying time.

The guards come to get him, go through the ritual of putting on the restraints. Fuller's head hurts, but he doesn't ask for aspirin. A pain reliever wouldn't be in his best interests at this time.

They march him past other cells. Some cajole him, call out insults. He ignores them, staying focused on the task ahead.

The room is the same as before. Steel doors. Two chairs. A table, with the lie detector machine on it. Fuller is put in the chair, facing away from the machine.

Two of his doctors come into the room: shrinks, in suits. His lawyer, Eric Garcia, a Hollywood hotshot who seeks out high-profile cases so he can show off his five-thousand-dollar suits on television. The assistant DA, Libby something, who looks particularly tasty today in a pale pink jacket and matching skirt. The examiner, a different guy than before, round and soft and wearing a freaking white lab coat, for god's sake.

There's also a pleasant surprise: Jack Daniels and her fat partner, Herb Benedict, who doesn't seem as fat as he had a few months ago.

"Looking good, Detective Benedict. Diet seems to be working well."

"Please, Barry, no talking to them." Garcia pats Fuller on the shoulder.

The polygraph examiner rolls up Fuller's sleeve, attaches the blood pressure cuff. He puts sticky probes on Fuller's fingers to measure changes in electrical resistance resulting from sweat, and three elastic bands around his chest to record breathing.

"Ready to begin when you are, Barry," the examiner says, standing in front of him.

Barry smiles. "Let her rip."

"We're going to start by calibrating the machine. I'd like you to pick a card from this deck, and look at it, but don't tell me what it is. Then I'm going to ask you questions about the card, and I want you to answer no to all of my questions, even if it is a lie."

He holds out a deck. Barry picks a card, looks at it. A Queen of Diamonds. He smiles again, knowing that the deck is rigged; they're all Queens of Diamonds. This is to make him believe the machine is infallible, to make him even more nervous.

"Is the card black?"

"No."

"Is the card red?"

"No."

"Is the card a face card?"

"No."

"Is the card a ten?"

"No."

And on it goes. Fuller acts normally, and doesn't try to control his body's responses in the least. When the examiner finally says, "The card is a Queen of Diamonds," Fuller laughs, genuinely.

"That's terrific! Better than a magic show."

"As you can see, Barry, the machine can pick out lies rather easily. If you lie, we'll catch it."

"That's why I'm here. To show I'm telling the truth."

"We'll proceed, then. Please answer yes or no to the following questions. Is your name Barry Fuller?"

"Yes."

"Is the world flat?"

"No."

"Have you ever stolen something?"

Fuller knows this is a control question, one that sets the bar. The polygraph records the body's responses to the questions. The examiner understands that being accused about a crime will cause the breathing to increase, the palms to sweat, and the blood pressure to rise. The yes and no answers are irrelevant. The examiner is looking for the four markers on the scrolling piece of paper to jump when the subject is stressed.

So Fuller makes them jump. He curls his big toe, jabbing the staple deeper into the nail. His pain level spikes, his vital signs react, and the markers do their fast squiggle thing.

"No," he answers.

"Is the White House in Washington, D.C.?"

Fuller eases up on the toe pressure.

"Yes."

"Do you remember killing Eileen Hutton?"

"No."

Fuller realizes that his lie causes some spikes, but the spikes won't be as high as the spikes created by the stealing question, when he caused himself pain. The examiner will have to conclude he's telling the truth.

Easy as pie. The trick to beating a polygraph isn't staying calm. It's knowing when to act stressed.

"Have you ever lied on a job application?"

Control question. Toe pressure.

"No."

"Is a basketball square?"

Ease up.

"No."

"Did you remember cutting off Davi McCormick's arms?"

No toenail pressure.

"No."

"Have you ever cheated on your income tax?"

Force that staple in.

"No."

"Do you consider yourself an honest man?"

Another control. The staple feels like an electric wire, juicing him with pain.

"Yes."

"Did you kill Colin Andrews?"

Release the pressure.

"I don't remember. I've been told I did."

And so it goes on, for another half an hour. He takes his time. Makes it look good. Lets his body tell the tale.

"Are you faking this amnesia?"

Fuller smiles at Jack. He winks at her.

"No, I'm not."

"Thank you, Barry. We're finished here today."

Garcia walks over. "What were the results?"

"I'll need time to examine them thoroughly before I can give you my opinion."

"What's your preliminary opinion?"

"I wouldn't feel comfortable giving that. I'll wait until trial."

"Go ahead, Adam." Libby walks up as well. "Tell us your initial impression. No matter what side it falls on, you'll likely be subpoenaed anyway."

The plump man takes off his glasses, polishes them on the end of his sweater.

"In twenty years of administering polygraphs, I've never seen such a clear-cut case of honesty."

Fuller has to bite his lower lip to keep from giggling.

"This man is telling the truth. I'd stake my reputation on it."

Fuller's lawyer laughs, pats him on the shoulder.

Jack's look is worth a million dollars. Fuller mouths the words "see you soon" at her, and blows her a kiss.

The examiner removes all of the probes and sensors, and everyone begins to file out. Fuller's lawyer wants a moment with him, and makes the guards wait outside.

"This shouldn't even go to trial, Barry. The judge should have thrown it out."

"We're doing good, right?"

"Good? We're golden. After the experts testify, there won't be a doubt in anyone's mind. You'll be back on the street in no time."

"I want to testify."

Garcia loses the smile.

"You don't have to say a word, Barry. You can let the evidence speak for you."

"I want to."

"I don't think it's a wise . . ."

"I don't care. I have to speak my piece. It's important to me."

Another pat on the shoulder. "I understand, big guy. They'll be rough on you, but we can prepare you for that."

"I'll do fine."

"I'm sure you will, Barry. I'm sure you will."

CHAPTER 31

When I left the prison I was shaking, and couldn't decide if it was from cold, anger, or fear.

Since Benedict and I arrived in separate cars, we didn't have a chance to touch base after the polygraph. Herb seemed even more distant than yesterday, not carrying our exchange any further than "Good morning." I back-burnered my problems and confronted Herb when we got back to the station.

"I left Bernice."

"You left Bernice?"

"Last night. Not that big of an adjustment, really. I've been sleeping on the couch for the past month, anyway. At least the Motel 6 has a big bed I can stretch out in, and I've got a 'no nagging' sign on the door. It's refreshing, waking up without having to hear all of my problems pointed out to me."

"Herb, I'm sorry."

"No need. This was a long time coming, believe me."

"Are you okay?"

Stupid question. Of course he wasn't okay.

"Fine. I missed breakfast, though." He smiled, and it was an unpleasant thing. "First time in twenty-two years. Want to go grab a bite?"

I nodded. Herb drove, recklessly, to a diner on Clark, the kind of place that served pancakes twenty-four hours a day and boasted "fountain creations" on their storefront sign. Nothing on the menu was over six dollars, and our waitress moved so slowly I was tempted to take her pulse. I got two eggs, sunny-side up.

"Comes with toast," our server yawned.

I shrugged.

Herb ordered a ham and cheddar cheese omelette, with a side of bacon and two sides of sausage, hold the toast.

"This diet is killing me."

"I bet. I think I can actually hear your arteries harden."

He leaned in close, conspiratorially.

"It's the starch. I thought eating all the fatty foods I wanted would be great, but right now I would kill for a sandwich made out of french fries and macaroni."

"They've got that on the menu. It comes with a free angiogram."

Herb added a ninth packet of artificial sweetener to his coffee and stirred it with his fork.

"How are you doing, Jack?"

"You don't want to know."

"I do. Maybe it will help me take my mind off my problems."

I gave it to him. He paused, between noshing on fatty meat, to impart this bit of wisdom: "Damn, Jack, you're a mess."

I didn't feel like eating, but I forced the toast down because Herb's constant staring at it made me edgy.

"Thanks, partner. Misery loves company, I guess."

"Are you still in love with Alan?"

"I don't think I ever stopped loving him."

"Does he want you back?"

"I think so."

"Do you love Latham?"

"Yes."

"You're going to have to choose."

"I know."

"Who are you going to choose?"

"I don't know."

"Who do you love more?"

"I don't know."

"Are you going to eat your eggs?"

"I don't know."

"At least that's a decision I can help you with."

Herb did a quick plate-to-plate egg transfer, his fork a stainless steel blur. Apparently, separation hadn't hurt his appetite.

"What do we do about Fuller?" Yolk clung to his mustache.

I was happy to change the subject.

"I have a plan."

"Tell."

"Fuller mentioned to me that he kills to make the headaches go away."

"I read the medical. The doctors don't think the tumor is any older than a year or two."

"Right. But Fuller said he's always had headaches, his whole life."

Herb nodded. "So maybe he's killed before."

"We dig into his past, try to link him to an old crime."

"How do we do that?"

"Did you forget? We're police officers. Skilled professionals who solve crimes for a living."

"What if there's no crime to solve?"

"Then we have to find one."

I picked up the check, and when we got back to the station we went to work. We started with the department's file on Fuller. On paper, he seemed to be a good cop. Above-average arrest record. Showed up for work. Did well at the police academy, scoring high on all of his tests.

Prior to his law enforcement career, Fuller had been an NFL player. Herb pulled at that thread, while I traced his life back even further. Fuller went to Southern Illinois University, on a football scholarship. Majored in criminology. Minored in psych. Heavy subjects, for a jock.

A look at his four-year curriculum uncovered another interesting tidbit: Fuller was a member of the Drama Club, and had actually played Biff in a campus production of *Death of a Salesman*.

In the file Libby had put together on Fuller, there were no noteworthy incidents in his college career. He stayed out of trouble. Kept a B average. Apparently, he met Holly in college, and married her a year after graduation.

I wasted fifty cents of the taxpayers' money on a call to information, and was soon talking to the chief of police in Carbondale, a man named Shelby Duncan. He had a low voice and talked slowly, deliberately.

"During those years we had two unsolveds. One was a townie, sixty-two-year-old male, robbed and beaten to death outside of a 7-11. Another was a student, nineteen-year-old male, fell out a frat house window. BOC was triple the going rate, but the case has been kept open."

"How about missing persons?"

I heard fingers on a keyboard.

"One hundred and thirty-eight."

The high number surprised me.

"It that normal?"

"We're a college town, Lieutenant. Twenty thousand students attend classes every day. Some of them drop out, and don't tell anyone where they're going."

I asked if he could fax me the reports. He did me one better and offered the password to his database so I could peruse them on my own.

Herb leaned over. "What do you got?"

"He studied psychology and criminology in college, and also did some acting. Might come in handy, if you ever wanted to beat a lie detector. I've also got over a hundred MP files, which I'll try to sync up with Fuller's academic schedule. You?"

"Fuller's NFL career was mostly spent warming the bench. Constant knee injuries—in fact, his left knee is completely artificial. I'm surprised he could pass the department physical."

"No missing cheerleaders?"

"I talked to one of the assistant coaches. No problems at all. The guy was a team player, no obvious difficulties. Fuller was disappointed that he couldn't contribute more. Coach said he was a good guy."

"Fooled them just like he fooled us."

Benedict delved into his pocket and came up with a small bag of fried pork rinds. The bag art proudly stated "No Carbs." I wondered, yet again, what was wrong with the world when pigskin fried in lard was considered a health food.

"So, what now?" Herb asked, showing me what partially masticated hog strips looked like. It wasn't pretty.

"We get started on this list. You want to take *A* through *L*?"

"I guess."

I gave Benedict the password, and he nodded a good-bye and waddled off to his office.

I hit the computer.

Time passed slowly, as it always did with drudge work. Noon rolled around, and I declined Herb's offer of a cheezy beef, sans bun. By four o'clock I found a tenuous connection between Fuller and a missing girl named Lucy Weintraub—she'd been a cheerleader while he was on the football team. But a DMV search found Lucy alive and well and living in Chicago. I got in touch, and she admitted to dropping out of school and going to Florida, which her parents eventually found out about, but didn't bother informing the Carbondale PD.

Lucy didn't remember Fuller at all.

I dialed Benedict, and he'd had no luck either. If Fuller had been responsible for any of these missing persons, he didn't seem to have any clear connection to them.

It was creeping up on five in the evening, but home didn't seem tempting at the moment. I knew I had to make peace with my mom, but before that I needed to get in touch with my feelings.

I was doing that, unsuccessfully, when the phone rang. The desk sergeant informed me that a man was downstairs, asking to see me.

"Says he's your husband."

I felt my pulse jump. Anger, or excitement?

"Can someone escort him up?"

My mirror compact called to me, begging to check my hair and makeup.

I resisted, and read the same line on an arrest report fifteen times until the knock at the door came.

"Hi, Jack."

I didn't look up at him, reading the line two more times before answering. Then I gave him my slightly annoyed look.

"What is it, Alan? I'm busy."

"I wanted to apologize. For last night. I shouldn't have acted like that."

"I accept your apology. Now if you don't mind . . ."

"I'm leaving tomorrow."

The words hurt. I stayed silent.

"I shouldn't have come to Chicago. I didn't mean to intrude on your life. I guess . . . I don't know . . . I always questioned my decision. Leaving you. I wanted to see you again, to see if I was wrong."

"Were you wrong?"

His eyes softened. "Yes."

What do you say to a man whom you cursed ten thousand times, begged the universe to make him understand what a jerk he was, and then he finally agrees with you?

"Have a safe trip back, Alan."

His eyes got teary. Maybe mine did too.

"Can we be friends, Jack? Stay in touch?"

Don't play with fire, Jack. You got burned the last time.

"That's probably not a good idea."

He chewed his lower lip.

"You know, I never visited you at work, when we were married. Not once."

"I know."

"I can finally cross that off my list of should-haves." He tried to smile. "Have a nice life, Jack."

"You too, Alan."

He walked out.

The first time he left me, I didn't try to stop him. I always wondered what would have happened if I'd tried. Would we have lasted? Would we have worked out our problems? Would love have conquered all?

Was I destined to keep making the same mistakes, over and over again?

"Alan . . . wait."

He turned, eyes hopeful.

"Yeah?"

Looking at him, I knew.

"You're wearing my jacket."

Alan took off the bomber jacket, held it out.

I went to him.

Our hands met.

"Jack, I love this jacket too much to give it up."

"So do I."

"Maybe we can work out some kind of joint custody."

"Maybe."

"Can we discuss it over dinner?"

"That might be best."

I touched his face, wiped off a tear with my thumb.

"Can I call you? After work?"

"No. The work can wait."

"Excuse me?"

"The work can wait, Alan. Let's go."

We didn't go out to dinner. We went to his hotel room at the Raphael, where I played with fire.

Twice.

CHAPTER 32

I stared at the ceiling, naked and tangled in a sheet, sleep a faraway concept.

Alan slept curled up next to me. Looking at him, I felt an odd mixture of love and remorse. The sex had been good, like putting on an old pair of blue jeans you haven't worn in ages. Alan and I knew each other's buttons.

I'd called Mom earlier, explaining I wouldn't be home, without giving her details.

She figured them out anyway.

"I'll let Nathan know where you are if he calls."

"His name is Latham, Mom. And no, you won't. If he calls or drops by, have him call my cell."

Latham never did call, and I felt another odd mixture, of guilt and relief. I fleetingly wished I could feel just one emotion at a time, but that added confusion to my melting pot of conflicting feelings.

The ceiling had no answers for me.

I didn't have any sleeping pills, and my insomnia knew it; shifting, restless leg syndrome, unable to get comfortable in any position.

At two in the morning, heart palpitations and shallow breathing hopped on the symptom train, and I knew enough modern psychology to recognize I was having a panic attack.

It was horrible.

I'd had a physical, four months back, and been given a clean bill of health, so I knew this wasn't a heart attack. But still, I was enveloped by an overwhelming sense that I was going to die.

I got out of bed, paced, did some push-ups, tried yoga, drank two glasses of water, flipped through fifteen channels with the mute button on, and finally just sat in a corner, clutching my knees to my chest, rocking back and forth.

At five in the morning, in a near hysterical effort to simplify my life, I went into the bathroom and called Latham.

"Jack? That you?"

"I need to take a break, Latham. From us. Too much is happening too fast."

"You sound terrible. Are you okay?"

"No. I think I'm having a nervous breakdown. It's probably just a panic attack. I don't have my damn sleeping pills and I'm bouncing off the walls."

"Why don't you have your pills?"

Moment of truth time.

"I'm in Alan's hotel room."

I waited for Latham to scream at me, call me names. Hell, I wanted him to.

"You still love him."

"Yes."

"Do you love me?"

"Yes."

I heard him take a quick breath. A sob?

"You need some time apart, to figure things out?"

"Yes." I was crying now.

"A week? A month?"

"I don't know, Latham."

"I understand."

Dammit, why did he have to be so freaking nice?

"I might never come back, Latham."

"You have to choose what's right for you, Jack."

"Aren't you mad at me?"

"I love you. I want you to be happy."

I gripped the phone so hard my knuckles lost color.

"There's no goddamn way you can be that mature about this! Call me a cheating bitch! Tell me I ruined your life!"

"Call me when you've made a decision, Jack."

He hung up.

I raised the cell over my head, wanting to smash it against the tiled floor.

I settled for placing it on the sink and blubbering like a baby.

Alan knocked on the door.

"Jack? Are you okay?"

He let himself in, sat down next to me.

"Dammit," I cursed, rubbing my eyes. "Dammit, dammit, dammit. I'm not this weak."

Alan laughed.

"Why are you laughing?"

He put his arms around me.

"You're not weak, Jack. You're human."

"And that's funny to you?"

"I always suspected it. I just never thought I'd see it."

He held me until the tears stopped and embarrassment set in. I finally pushed him away and jumped in the shower.

If I hoped to get my life in order, I needed to start compartmentalizing. If I dealt with one thing at a time, I wouldn't get overwhelmed.

Number one on the hierarchy of importance was Fuller. He couldn't be allowed out.

After the shower, I got dressed, kissed my sleeping ex-husband on the top of his head, and went to the office.

One thing at a time.

CHAPTER 33

"Who's there?"

No answer.

I squinted, trying to see through the darkness of my bedroom. My digital clock displayed 3:35 in bright red; the only light in the room.

I sat up and reached for the lamp by my bedside. Clicked it on.

Nothing happened.

I reached higher and felt that the lightbulb was missing.

Carefully, slowly, I eased open my nightstand drawer, seeking out the .38 I put in there every night.

The gun was gone.

Something in the darkness moved.

"Mom? Alan?"

No answer.

I breathed in deep, held it, straining to hear any sound.

A faint chuckle came from nearby.

My digital clock went out.

The hair rose on the back of my neck. The darkness was complete, a thick inky cloth. Sweat trickled down my spine.

The closet.

"I've got a gun!" I yelled to the darkness.

Another chuckle. Low and soft.

Fuller.

Another movement. Closer this time.

My heart pumped ice through my veins. Where were Mom and Alan? What had he done to them?

How do I make it out of here alive?

My only chance was to get to the door, to get out of the apartment. Run hard and fast and don't look back.

I slowly drew back the covers, and eased one foot over the edge of the bed, resting it on the warm chest of the man with the knife who was lying on the floor beside me.

I screamed, and woke myself up.

Reflexively, I had the bedroom light on and the .38 in my hand in a nanosecond. My breath came in ragged gasps, and my heart felt like I'd just completed the last leg of a triathlon.

"Jack?"

Alan opened his eyes. They widened when he saw the gun.

"What's happening?"

"Just a bad dream."

"You're going to shoot a bad dream?"

I looked at my gun, quivering in my hand, and tried to put it back in the drawer. My fingers wouldn't let go. I had to pry them off with my free hand.

I sat awake, thinking about fear, until my alarm went off and I had to go to court.

I dressed in my best suit, a blue Armani blazer and light gray slacks, spent ten minutes dabbing concealer under my eyes, and met my mom in the kitchen, where she already had a pot of coffee going.

"Morning, Mom."

Mom wore a pink flannel nightgown with a cat stitched on the front. She sat at the breakfast bar, sipping out of a mug, you guessed it, with a cat on it.

"Good morning, Jacqueline. You look very pretty."

"Court." I poured coffee into one of the last drinking vessels without a feline picture gracing it. "You okay?"

"This cold weather is affecting my hip."

"It's got to be eighty degrees in here, Mom. You set the thermostat on 'broil.' "

"My hip is synced to the outside temperature, and it's freezing out there. I forgot how cold this city gets."

I wondered how cold Mom really was, and how much of this was her pining for Florida.

"Do you keep in touch with any of your friends back in Dade City?"

"Just Mr. Griffin. He keeps pestering me to visit. But I'd hate to travel in this weather. The cold, you know."

"Why not invite him here?"

"He's retired, dear. On a fixed income. I couldn't ask him to fly out here, and then pay those ridiculous hotel rates."

"He can stay with us."

Mom smiled so brightly she lost twenty years.

"Really?"

"Sure. If he doesn't mind sharing the sofa bed." I winked at her.

"Well, I think I'll give him a call, then. I could use the company. You work all day, and Alan spends all of his time locked in the bedroom, writing."

I searched the fridge for a bagel, finding nothing but Alan's health food. Soy and sprouts did not a good breakfast make. I chose some dark bread, and a non-dairy, low-fat, butter-flavored spread, which had such a long list of chemical ingredients on the package it should have been called "I Can't Believe It's Not Cancer."

"Thanksgiving is next week." I slathered the imitation stuff on the bread. "Invite him over for that."

"That's a wonderful idea. I'll call him now."

I took a bite, then spit the mouthful into my hand.

"What the hell is this?"

"Alan's soy bread. He has that gluten allergy."

I tossed it in the garbage. "It tastes like a sour sponge."

"Steer clear of his breakfast cereal. Tofutos, they're called. Beans and milk aren't a tasty combo. And whatever you do, don't let him make you anything in that juicer. He actually forced me to drink a celery sprout smoothie."

Mom got on the phone, and I finished my coffee and headed to the criminal courthouse at 26th and California.

Someone had forgotten to tell Chicago it was still fall, because a light snow dusted everything and I almost broke my neck on a patch of sidewalk ice.

My car started on the second try, and I played how-slow-can-we-drive-and-still-move-forward with my fellow Chicagoans. The first snowfall of the season and everyone seems to forget, en masse, how to drive.

I was late getting to the trial. The courthouse, a squat square building, had free underground parking for city employees. Heated. I took an escalator up to the main floor, bypassed the line at the metal detector with a flash of my star, and took the second group of elevators to the twenty-seventh floor.

Court had already begun, and the tiny room was crammed full to bursting. I shouldered my way through the crowd and sat next to Libby, who wore a lavender Vanderbilt jacket and skirt like it had been designed for her.

Her cocounsel, a brown-haired, twenty-something prosecutor named Noel Penaflor, had Phil Blasky on the stand. Phil had on an ill-fitting suit and tried his best to explain, in layman's terms, the results of Eileen Hutton's autopsy.

". . . thoracic cavity eviscerated and . . ."

I tuned him out, trying to organize my thoughts.

I didn't look at Fuller.

As the litany of atrocities ensued, Noel introduced pictures of Eileen as evidence. First came pictures of her with family and friends. Then came the autopsy photos.

As expected, this caused a general uproar in the courtroom. But no reaction was more impressive than Fuller's.

He vomited all over the defense team's table.

CHAPTER 34

A twenty-minute recess ensued, and the courtroom cleared.

Libby seethed.

"That son of a bitch. He did it on purpose, didn't he? How the hell did he do it?"

I shrugged. "Maybe he swallowed some ipecac, or something else to make him sick. Or maybe he can vomit on cue."

"Have you ever seen that done before?"

I knew what Libby was asking; could I somehow discredit the vomit episode through testimony?

"Sorry. I've never seen it."

She and Noel spent some time bantering back and forth. I went back into court and watched a janitor spritz the table with a disinfectant that smelled like oranges.

The trial progressed. Noel finished up with Blasky, which was followed by a brief cross-examination by Garcia. No redirect, and Blasky was excused and my name got called.

I took the stand and tried to keep the trembling under control.

Noel walked me through my testimony, and I gave a recount of the case, trying to remain professional and in control. The prosecution established me as not only a credit to my profession, but a hero as well.

I kept the dry spots to a minimum, elicited a few chuckles from the jury, and at the end of my statement repeated my encounter with Fuller at the jailhouse.

"So the defendant admitted that he was lying about the amnesia?"

"He did. And he said when he got out, he was going to kill again."

"Anyone in particular?"

"Me." My voice cracked when I said it. "He said he was going to kill me, and my partner, Herb."

Noel nodded at me, and I got a look of approval from Libby.

"Your witness." Noel took his seat.

Garcia, plump and confident, approached me smiling.

"Lt. Daniels, you mentioned you've been on the police force for twenty years, correct?"

"Yes."

"How many of those years have you been seeing a psychiatrist?"

"Objection. Relevance."

Garcia smiled at the judge. "I'm simply bringing into question the lieutenant's reliability as a witness."

Libby stood up. "Your honor, the very fact that Lt. Daniels has been a member of the CPD for twenty years is enough to establish reliability. It is also mandatory policy after a shooting for a police officer to receive counseling."

"Withdrawn." Eric smiled. "And I'd like to thank the assistant state's attorney for establishing that, as a member of the Chicago Police Department, an officer must surely have his mental faculties in order. Lt. Daniels, how long did you work with Barry Fuller?"

"Two years."

"And during those two years, what kind of impression had you formed of him?"

"I didn't know him personally."

"Professionally, then?"

"He did his job, as far as I knew. I never had any problems with him . . . until I had to shoot him."

That got a chuckle from the peanut gallery.

"Tell me, Lieutenant, how a twenty-year veteran, a hero who was responsible for bringing a heinous serial killer to justice last year, failed to realize the suspect she was chasing was working side by side with her all along?"

"Officer Fuller knows police procedure. Because he knows our methods, he knew how to avoid detection."

"And did that bother you, him avoiding capture?"

"Of course it bothered me. It's my job to catch murderers, and he was out on the streets, murdering people."

"Did it bother you beyond a professional capacity? Didn't it, in fact, get personal?"

"I keep my personal and professional opinions separate."

"Even though Barry is one of your own? You don't hold him in particular disdain, on a personal level?"

"No, I don't. My disdain is purely professional."

Another chuckle.

"Lieutenant, you testified earlier that, during your visit to Barry Fuller at Cook County jail, Mr. Fuller threatened you."

"Yes."

"During your conversation with him on that date, do you believe that you remained calm and professional?"

"Yes."

"Not personal?"

"No."

"Tell me, Lieutenant, is this your voice?"

He pulled a cassette recorder out of his pocket and hit the Play button. The female voice that emanated was both high-pitched and vicious.

"*Drop the act, Barry. I know you're lying. You remember every sick little detail. I bet you jerk off to those memories every night in your lonely little cell. You make me sick. I hope they fry your ass in the chair, tumor or no tumor, you piece of shit.*"

Both Noel and Libby screamed out objections, but my recorded voice could be heard above them, the murmur of the jury, and the sound of Judge Taylor banging her gavel.

"Objection, Your Honor! There's no foundation for this tape. This wasn't previously disclosed at the pre-trial hearing."

"Your Honor, the State had prior knowledge of this tape, and they failed to give this to us in discovery. Full disclosure goes both ways."

Libby made a face. "Foundation, Your Honor."

Garcia smiled. "Witness credibility, Judge. Lt. Daniels has previously stated she clearly separates personal and professional opinion. The tape is a gentle reminder of her true opinion."

"Privacy law, Your Honor. Lt. Daniels had no prior knowledge this tape would be used in evidence."

"But she did have prior knowledge of the tape's existence, Your Honor. In fact, she's the one who created it."

Judge Taylor turned to me. "Is that true, Lieutenant?"

"Yes."

"I'll allow it."

Garcia held up the recorder.

"Tape A for identification. Authentication by Lt. Jacqueline Daniels of the Chicago Police Department. Lt. Daniels, was that indeed your voice on that tape recording, made during your visit to the Cook County jail on October twentieth of this year, while interviewing the defendant, Barry Fuller?"

I felt ready to throw up myself.

"Yes. But that was taken out of context. There's more."

"I'd be happy to play the tape in its entirety. Let the record show that Tape A was identified and has been entered into evidence. Proceed."

After a brief moment of rewinding, the courtroom filled with my recorded voice.

In context, I came off even worse. Fuller's sobbing denial, and my escalating anger and accusations, destroyed my credibility.

The tape ended with Fuller asking me if I was wearing a wire.

"What happened after the tape was turned off, Lieutenant?"

"That's when Fuller said he really remembered everything, and would kill me when he was released."

"Why is it I expected you to say that? Even in view of your unmitigated, and very personal, hatred of my client, a wretched victim of a personality-altering brain tumor. I'm sure when he takes the stand he'll have a different account of what happened after the recorder was turned off. No further questions."

"Redirect?" Judge Taylor asked.

Libby stood.

"Lt. Daniels, why were you so hostile to the defendant in that tape?"

"It's standard police technique. I was trying to get him angry at me, so he would talk."

"And he did talk, after the tape was turned off?"

"Yes. Why else would he have asked me to turn off the tape?"

Libby turned to the jury. "Indeed. Why would he have wanted that tape shut off, if only to say something he didn't want recorded? No more questions."

"You may step down, Lieutenant."

Good recovery, Libby. But as I left the stand I noticed disgust on more than a few faces in the jury box. I was no longer the hero.

When I sat down, I glanced over at Fuller for the first time all day.

He was staring at me, and our eyes locked. His face was a study in sadness. He let out a big dramatic sigh, for the jury's benefit. Playing it to the hilt.

The judge broke for lunch, and I kept my composure long enough to get to the bathroom and splash some water on my face.

Libby walked in, and stood next to me by the sink. The bathroom was full, so I kept my voice down.

"How'd they get the tape? You've got the only copy."

"And it's in my office safe. They didn't get my copy."

She gave me an accusatory stare.

I sighed, too tired to get angry. "Give me a break. They crucified me up there. I want Fuller put away more than anyone."

"All I know is, no one has touched that tape since you gave it to me. That means it must have been copied prior to my receiving it."

I digested this.

"Unless we weren't the only ones taping the conversation. What if someone put a wire on Fuller?"

Libby's eyes got Betty Boop big.

"If there's another tape, that means there might be a record of Fuller admitting to the lies."

"Right. But who did the taping? His legal team? The prison? And even if we do find out who did it, how do we get a copy of the uncut version?"

"I know an audio guy. I'll get a copy of Garcia's tape, and compare it to yours. He should be able to tell if they're from different sources. That'll give me enough to be able to force Garcia into telling how he got the evidence."

A woman came over to use the sink, and Libby buttoned her lip. We left the washroom.

"How about Fuller's past?" Libby asked. "Any luck?"

"None. Maybe we could try Rushlo again."

"I've tried four times. The guy won't budge. His attorney keeps asking for extensions."

"Why?"

"Rushlo wants to stay in jail. He's afraid Fuller is going to get out and come after him. Jail is the only place he feels safe. He didn't even try to make bail."

"What's he being charged with?"

"Two counts of accessory. We've got him dead to rights. He's going away for a long time. But I'd trade that for Fuller in a heartbeat. The problem is, we can't find any connection. We don't even know how they met."

I rubbed my eyes, yawned.

"How long has he owned the funeral home?"

"Six years. Worked there eight years before buying it from the original owner."

"Before then?"

"His apprenticeship, Champaign-Urbana."

That was south, but still two hundred miles away from Carbondale, where Fuller went to school.

"Before then?"

"Worsham College of Mortuary Science in Wheeling."

Wheeling was even farther north.

"I'll keep digging. Maybe something will turn up."

"I hope so, Jack. You were my star witness, and the jury hates you. I've only got two more wits to call, and then it's the defense's ballgame. They're bringing in some big guns."

"How bad is it?"

Libby frowned. "If we don't get something fast, we're going to lose."

CHAPTER 35

Benedict was waiting for me in my office. "How'd it go?"

"The only reason I wasn't lynched is because no one in the courtroom had a rope."

He laughed, though it sounded forced.

"Why are you in such a chipper mood?"

"Freedom, Jack. Freedom at last."

"Freedom from what?"

"I saw a divorce lawyer this morning."

Herb smiled when he said it. I wasn't sure how to react.

"This is what you really want?"

"I've been living alone for almost a month, Jack. I love it. But I haven't really hit the scene yet."

"The scene?"

"The dating scene. Call me old-fashioned, but I don't want to start seeing other women while I'm still married. But that is gonna change real soon."

"How does Bernice feel about this?"

"She cried, but I know she realizes it's for the best. I'm getting close, Jack. I'm almost free."

Free from what, I thought? Free from a woman who loves you and devoted half of her life to you? Free from a home and a family? That's freedom?

"Congrats. I hope it works out for you."

"Up for a celebratory lunch? My treat. There's a new gyro place that lets you order without the pita."

"I'll pass. I've got some calls to make."

I was hungry, but didn't feel comfortable around Herb at that moment. Maybe because I thought he was making a colossal mistake.

Or maybe because I realized he and I were more alike than I cared to admit. Latham sprang to mind.

"Your loss," Benedict said. "I'll catch you later."

Herb left. The helpful drone at directory assistance gave me Worsham College of Mortuary Science, and connected me for an additional ten cents.

"I'm looking to speak with someone who might remember a student from fifteen years ago."

"Let me connect you with Professor Keevers. He's been here since the days before electricity. Hold a second."

I spent a minute listening to Muzak, then a smooth baritone picked up.

"This is Tom Keevers. Who am I speaking with?"

"I'm Lieutenant Daniels, from the Chicago Police Department. Do you remember a student from fifteen years ago named Derrick Rushlo?"

There was a pause.

"Derrick is in some kind of trouble, I take it?"

"Do you remember him?"

"Yes. Yes I do. We get people like Derrick every once in a while."

"What do you mean, people like Derrick?"

"I'm sure you know what I mean, hence your call."

"Necrophiles?"

"A distasteful minority in this profession. Has Derrick been caught with his pants down, so to speak? There are strict regulations against such activity, of course, but I wasn't aware of it being illegal."

"This is a homicide investigation, Professor. I take it you knew about Derrick's, uh, appetites?"

"I suspected. Never had proof. My best students remain aloof, detached, when embalming. Derrick was always a little too intimate with the bodies. Plus, there was that incident at SIU . . ."

"Excuse me? Do you mean Southern Illinois University?"

"Yes. They have an excellent mortuary school there. Derrick transferred from there to here."

And Bingo was his name-o.

"Was he expelled?"

"Not that I recall. Rather, he was encouraged to leave. If memory serves, one of their cadavers went missing, and suspicion fell on Derrick. There was never any evidence, though. It caused quite a stir in the academic community."

"Did he have any problems while at Worsham?"

"No. Excellent student. Did good work. I always had my suspicions about him, though. He murdered somebody, you say?"

"Accessory."

"That makes sense. I've always wanted to write a novel, with a mortician as the villain. It would be ridiculously easy, in our profession, to dispose of a murder victim."

"Cremation."

"There's that. But are you aware of how many closed casket funerals go on in this business? Some folks die beyond our ability to reconstruct them. Some families simply don't want to view the departed."

"So you're saying . . . ?"

"A mortician could easily place more than one body in a casket, and no one would ever know."

"Thank you for your time, Professor."

I hung up, excited. I not only had a connection between Fuller and Rushlo, but it gave me an idea on how we could get Rushlo to fess up.

I left Libby a message on her cell, and then occupied a few hours reviewing backlog cases. During my absence, Chicago lived up to its reputation of being the murder capital of the U.S. We averaged about 600 a year, but we were already at over 585 and the busy holiday season wasn't even upon us yet.

Immersing myself in paperwork turned out to be good therapy, and by the time five o'clock rolled around, I'd only thought about Fuller intermittently, rather than constantly.

I called home, got no answer, called Alan's cell, and got his voice mail. I told him I'd be home early, and left the office.

The snow had turned into freezing drizzle, and the ride took twenty minutes longer than normal, because every driver on the road collectively forgot how to drive in freezing drizzle.

After retrieving my mail, I went up to my apartment, walked into the living room, and caught sight of a very old and very naked man having sex with my mother on the Hide-A-Bed.

I immediately turned around and went into the kitchen. They hadn't seen me, having been too involved in the act. Perhaps their mutual moaning had masked the sound of my footfalls.

I considered my next move. Make a lot of noise, so they knew I was home? Sneak out? Ask them to quit it, because I was now scarred for the rest of my life?

I chose sneaking out. A twenty-four-hour coffee shop/diner was a few blocks away, but the freezing rain wasn't enough to erase the image branded on my brain, of Mr. Griffin's naked bottom rising and falling. I also found myself thinking, quite surprisingly, that it wasn't a bad butt for a guy his age. Firmer than I might have guessed.

I had coffee, and a Monte Cristo sandwich—hot turkey, ham, Swiss cheese, and bacon, on two pieces of French toast. The sandwich came dusted in powdered sugar, with a side ramekin of raspberry jelly. It didn't make sense that jelly went so well with turkey and ham, but for some reason it worked. I suppose some things that worked didn't need to make sense.

After killing an hour in the diner, which seemed to be more than enough time for my mom to finish, I called the apartment.

No answer. Perhaps they were napping in the post-glow.

Wanting badly to shower and change clothes, I again braved the inclement weather and made my way back home.

They were still going at it.

I didn't get an eyeful this time—the groaning was enough to keep me at bay. I turned and walked right back out.

My opinion of Mr. Griffin went up a notch. I'd always dated younger men. Perhaps I'd been missing out.

The local googleplex had a new Brad Pitt movie playing, and I plunked down ten bucks to spend ninety minutes with Brad.

Afterward, I called home. Thankfully, Mom picked up.

"Hi, Mom. Just calling to tell you I'll be home in about twenty minutes."

"Hello, dear. Um, can I ask a tiny favor of you?"

"Sure, Mom."

"My gentlemen friend from Florida, Mr. Griffin, is visiting. Would you mind giving us an hour or two to catch up?"

"An hour or two?"

"Yes. We haven't seen each other in a while and we've got some things to work out."

My mother made a frank, gasping sound. I rubbed my eyes.

"Sure, Mom. I'll catch a movie. I'll be home around ten?"

"Ten is fine," Mom said, an octave higher than normal.

I hung up.

Unbelievable.

I killed another two hours with Julia Roberts, and by then I was so tired I went straight home, my mother's sexual needs be damned. She just broke her hip, for heaven's sake. Shouldn't she be minding the injury?

Thankfully, Mom and Mr. Griffin were fully dressed when I returned. They were in the kitchen, sipping coffee. Mom's hair was a mess, and her cheeks were flushed.

"Nice to see you again, Jacqueline." Mr. Griffin was a student of the old school, meaning he stood up when I came into the room and offered his hand.

I shook it, and he winced.

"Are you okay?"

"Yes. My back is acting up a little."

I wonder why.

"We've got a pizza coming, if you're hungry."

"No, I ate. I'm going to turn in. Did Alan call?"

"He told me earlier he was going out with some old buddies, wouldn't be back until late."

I said my good nights, slipped in and out of a hot shower, and climbed into bed, determined not to take a sleeping pill.

After forty minutes of staring at the ceiling, I heard a deep moan come from the living room.

I took two pills, and fell asleep with the pillow over my head.

CHAPTER 36

Fuller lies awake in his cell. It's past midnight, and he needs to sleep. He has to look good for court. Appearance is everything.

He knows the jury watches him constantly. Looking for some trace of guilt or deceit. He'll only show them what he wants them to see.

The vomiting was a masterstroke. The piece of beef had been rotting in his mattress for days. Less than the size of a grape, the smell alone was enough to make him gag. Popping it in his mouth produced instant nausea. Disgusting, but effective.

The real show will begin when he takes the stand. He's hidden some red peppercorn flakes in his mattress—much more effective for bringing on tears than onions.

He knows the case will wrap up soon. Garcia wants to finish it before Thanksgiving, betting on the fact that the jurors will want to get the verdict in before the holiday. That leaves two days for testimony, and one for closing statements.

So far, everything is progressing smoothly.

There had been a bad moment, when Garcia told him about the tape. Some guard at Cook County jail had contacted Fuller's attorneys, willing to sell them a recording of his conversation with Jack at the prison. Blackmail, is what it boiled down to. Pay me, or I'll give this to the prosecution.

Fuller paid. He had to give power of attorney to Garcia, and authorized him to liquidate several things around the house—Holly's jewelry, a signed Dali litho she'd bought with her modeling money, the Lexus.

Fuller had been worried that Garcia might turn on him, once he found out about Fuller's deception. But the smarmy little bastard didn't bat an eyelash. In fact, he ingeniously used the tape to discredit Daniels.

Who says money can't buy a verdict?

The only problem at the moment is these damn headaches. They're getting worse. He hasn't explained to his doctors about how bad they've gotten, because he needs to give the impression that he's cured. If headaches made him kill, and he's still got headaches, they won't let him out.

So he makes do with Tylenol and sheer will.

But he can't hold out much longer.

There's only one thing that helps him when the pain gets this bad.

"Just a few more days," he whispers to himself. "Then I'll be free."

Fuller has Thanksgiving plans. He's going to drop by the Daniels household. Get a little pain relief. He's heard that Jack is living with her mom and ex-husband. What fun it will be to kill them both, in front of Jack, before ripping off her arms.

"Murder. The headache medicine."

When he finally falls asleep, it's with a smile on his face.

CHAPTER 37

"Dr. Jurczyk, in your eighteen years' experience as a brain surgeon, how many operations have you performed?"

Dr. Robert Jurczyk answered in a deep, resounding tone that radiated authority. "I've performed several hundred."

"Was one of them on the defendant, Barry Fuller?"

"Yes. I was in attendance at Northwestern when they brought him in."

"In technical terms, what was the defendant's condition?"

"He was brought in with a extradural hemorrhage caused by a bullet wound to the top right quadrant of the frontal bone, and after a CT scan it was determined the subject also had a neoplasm on the frontal lobe."

"Now in layman's terms."

"The bullet wound caused the outermost meninges to rupture. Meninges are the membranous layers that cover the brain. When this ruptured, it began to bleed, and the blood leaked into the space between the brain and the skull. Since the skull is a closed structure, this blood was pushing against the brain and would have resulted in death if a craniotomy wasn't performed."

"So you opened up the patient's skull to release the pressure?"

"Yes."

"Then you also removed the tumor on Barry Fuller's frontal lobe?"

"Yes."

"How big was that tumor, Doctor?"

"Approximately forty grams, about two centimeters in width."

"Your honor, and members of the jury, I'd like to present defense exhibit F, the tumor removed from Barry Fuller's head."

From the defense table came a glass jar containing a small gray thing floating in formaldehyde. The courtroom did its customary rumbling and the bailiff began to pass the jar around.

"Is that the tumor you removed from the defendant's brain, Doctor?"

"It appears to be. Yes."

"And how many of that type of operation have you done? Craniotomies, I believe you called them."

"Hundreds."

"Have there been any cases where a patient has had a craniotomy to relieve the pressure from an extradural hemorrhage, and later the patient experienced amnesia?"

"Yes. Almost eighty percent of patients with extradural hemorrhages experience some amnesia. In fact, after operations of this type, it's necessary to keep a constant watch on a patient in recovery because they usually wake up not knowing where they are or what happened to them."

"Have there been instances where the amnesia went back a few days, or even a week?"

"Yes. And further than that. I had one patient, brought in with a severe extradural hemorrhage caused by a car accident, and he completely forgot the last five years of his life. He didn't remember that he was married, and didn't know he had kids."

"Did those memories ever return to him?"

"Bits and pieces returned, but he never regained a significant amount of his memory back."

Things weren't looking good for the home team.

"How about personality changes? In your esteemed opinion, Dr. Jurczyk, could an intracranial neoplasm of the frontal lobe be sufficient enough to cause such a massive personality change that even murder could result?"

"Yes, it could."

Murmurs from the courtroom. Garcia faced the jury, smug. Libby gave me the briefest of sideways glances.

"Please elaborate, Doctor."

"The frontal lobe is the personality center of the brain. I've reviewed dozens of cases where damage to a patient's frontal lobe, either by an accident or by neoplasms, altered a person's personality to such a degree that even their own family members no longer recognized them."

"Are there any cases where a head trauma was associated with a personality change so dramatic that murder resulted?"

"There are many. Henry Lee Lucas, the notorious serial murderer who claimed responsibility for over one hundred victims, sustained several severe head injuries as a youth. John Wayne Gacy, Richard Speck, Charles Manson—all had records of serious head injuries."

"So it is possible that a normal, upstanding member of society like you or me, if afflicted with a meningioma of the frontal lobe, could undergo such a dramatic personality change that murder may be committed?"

"Assuming that the part of the brain dealing with morals and values was affected, which is also part of the frontal lobe, yes, it is possible."

"And if this person, before the tumor, was a nonviolent and caring individual, is it possible that the tumor could be the sole cause of such a dramatic personality change and the violent episodes that ensued?"

"Yes."

"And if that tumor—the sole cause of this violent behavior—were removed, would the person's personality then revert back to normal?"

"In my opinion, yes."

"Thank you, Doctor. Your witness."

Libby stood up but didn't even bother to move from behind the table.

"Have you ever, in your professional capacity, Doctor, treated an individual with an intracranial tumor who murdered anyone?"

"No, I haven't."

"And as one of the premier brain specialists in the world, have you ever encountered a case in your research where a person with an intracranial tumor murdered anybody?"

"No."

"How many cases have you reviewed, either in person or through research, throughout your career, Doctor?"

"Several thousand."

"Can you speak up, sir?"

"Several thousand cases."

"Several thousand cases, and not one case of murder. No more questions."

Garcia passed on the redirect.

I studied the jurors, and they seemed unconvinced by the cross-examination. Hell, if I didn't know Fuller was faking it, I would have been unconvinced too. When the world's leading brain specialist says it's possible that a tumor could cause someone to kill, you believe it.

"You may step down, Doctor. And we'll have an hour break for lunch." Taylor banged the gavel. "Adjourned."

Libby wasn't happy.

"Losing this case won't bode well for my career." She took my arm as we exited the courtroom. "I got a copy of the tape from Garcia yesterday. He claims it came in the mail, in a plain brown envelope, no return address, no note. Even gave me the envelope. I had it checked. Clean."

"I take it the tape didn't have Fuller's confession on it?"

"No. He says what he played in court was all that was on it, but Garcia is a sneaky little bastard, and he didn't get a name for himself by playing fair and nice with the other children."

"Did you get the tape checked?"

"It's being checked, but it's obvious the tapes come from different sources. I played it against the one you made, and the sound quality is completely different. It's better, and Fuller is louder than you. The mike must have been on his side of the room."

"Maybe it was someone from the prison. You know the warden better than I do. Ask him if he's had any no-shows lately. Guards calling in sick, quitting suddenly, that kind of thing."

"I'll do it today."

I switched gears. "I think I've got a way to get Rushlo to talk."

I gave her the short version. Libby frowned.

"Not my preferred course of action, but I'll swing it. Anything to save this sinking ship. I can have the paperwork ready by tomorrow. Cook County jail is right down the street, so we can do this on our lunch break."

I smiled, but it didn't quell the butterflies in my stomach.

CHAPTER 38

Herb and I were going through a list of every student who attended classes with Fuller at Southern Illinois University in Carbondale, and trying to make connections between them and any of the 137 missing persons from that time. We allocated my floor for the purpose, spreading out files in a big, uneven grid sorted semi-alphabetically. Benedict was on his knees, crossing off possibles, when Libby called.

"I've got a name. Marvin Rohmer. He's a guard at Division Eleven, been missing for the past week. A look into his personal finances revealed Rohmer has recently opened up eight checking accounts, each with cash amounts ranging from two to six grand. Probably got a large payment from that weasel Garcia."

"Spreading it out because banks have to report big cash deposits. Smart."

"Yeah, but he called attention to himself anyway by skipping work."

"We're on our way."

"Too late. Rohmer's a West Side boy, and I got a team to his place before the ink on the warrant dried. He skipped. Didn't find the tape, but we found a voice-activated recorder with some duct tape still on it. He probably taped it to the ceiling, or under a chair."

"Have you checked—"

"We're on it, Jack. We've frozen his assets, tracked his credit cards, and will soon release his name and description to every cop in the United States and Canada. If we find him, we don't even need the tape. I'll cut him a deal, force him to testify."

"Fax me Rohmer's file."

"It's already on its way."

I shared the info with Herb, and then we spent a few hours on the student records, ordering in a pizza with extra meat. Benedict ate most of it, but avoided the crust, leaving a cardboard box full of saucy white triangles.

I buried myself in the work. We were creating a big cross-reference grid; we listed all the students Fuller might have known from classes, sports, activities, and fraternities, and then tried to link them to any of the missing persons by doing the same thing. Tedium, and exactly what I needed.

"Got a possible." Benedict held up a paper. Not unusual, we'd had a few possibles so far.

"Name?"

"Missing person is Melody Stephanopoulos. Student. She had three classes with a kid named Michael Horton, who was on the football team with Fuller."

"Horton's girlfriend?"

"Could be. She was a science major, Horton was liberal arts, and she took two writing classes and a classics literature class with him, sophomore and junior year. Disappeared during the spring term, as a junior."

I looked up Horton in the Carbondale police files, got zilch. Then I called the SIU alumni organization, and spoke with a peppy lady named Missy who was hesitant to help until I gave her my badge number.

"I found him. Michael Horton is living in Seattle. Says he's married, a stockbroker, two kids."

I wrote down his number and dialed it.

"This is Michael."

"Mr. Horton, this is Lt. Daniels from the Chicago Police Department. We'd like to ask you a few questions—"

"About Barry, right? I've been following it on the news."

"Well, sort of. First we wanted to ask you about Melody Stephanopoulos."

"Have you found her?" The sentence came out so fast all the words ran together.

"I'm sorry, no. She was your girlfriend?"

"Fiancée. She disappeared."

"Did Barry know Melody?"

"Yeah. She didn't like him. Oh, Jesus, you don't think . . ."

"We don't know, Mr. Horton. We're trying to establish a connection. Were you and Barry friends?"

"Sure. We partied a lot together. Coach liked the team to hang out in our free time."

"Did Barry ever hang around with Melody, without you there?"

"Not that I remember. Melody was pretty much glued to my side all the time."

"When did she go missing?"

He paused.

"We had a fight, at a party. She didn't like me drinking so much. I told her to lighten up and quit being a nag. She left. That's the last time I saw her."

"Was Barry at the party?"

"Yeah. It was after the Florida game. Big celebration."

"Do you remember if Barry left after Melody?"

"I wish I could remember, Lieutenant. But I got pretty trashed that night. When I went to Melody's dorm the next day to apologize, her roommate told me she never came home."

Horton spent ten minutes filling me in on his relationship with Melody. He'd loved her deeply, and her loss devastated him. He spent another five giving me personal insights into Fuller, whom he called "a team player, a regular guy."

Which is how I would have described Fuller, before I found out about his extracurricular activities.

When the conversation wound down, he promised to call if he remembered anything else.

Herb, who'd been on the extension, hung up.

"Could be a lead. Maybe you can hit Rushlo with it."

I looked at my watch. Almost seven in the evening. I yawned. Herb gave me a look of disapproval.

"Jack, you need to get some rest."

"I'm fine."

"You look like a shit sandwich, with extra corn."

"That's sweet. You read that in a Hallmark card?"

"Go home."

"I'm afraid to go home. It's like walking into a geriatric version of *Last Tango in Paris*."

He frowned.

"What's wrong with you lately, Jack?"

Herb's voice took on a harsh tone, something that happened once in a leap year.

"What do you mean, Herb?"

"You're not yourself. You're edgy, short-tempered, and unhappy."

"If you're questioning my competency, Detective, then you're free to seek other employment opportunities."

Herb stood up.

"Maybe I should put in for reassignment."

"It wouldn't surprise me, considering you just did the same thing with your marriage."

Benedict shot me a very un-Benedict-like stare, and walked out.

I sat there for a few minutes, trying to get my breathing under control.

I couldn't.

CHAPTER 39

"Do you know why you are here, Barry?"

Fuller nodded, doing a damn good impression of a scolded puppy. He wore a dark blue suit with a light blue shirt, which was wrinkled by his slouching.

"Because I killed some people." His voice was soft, meek.

"Do you know why you killed these people, Barry?"

"I don't remember. I don't remember killing anyone."

"But you've watched the proceedings. You know that without a doubt you are the one who murdered these people."

"Yes. I know."

"But you can't tell us why you did?"

"I don't remember why. I don't remember anything for almost a month before the first murder. It's like all that time never happened. My God, I'd never . . . I'd never kill anybody. I can't believe . . ."

Fuller's voice cracked. Fountains of tears streamed down his face. His crying became sobbing and he wailed and moaned and Garcia held out a box of tissues and Fuller went through one after another, for almost two minutes.

"It wasn't me. I know it wasn't me. I couldn't have done that."

"Why not, Barry?"

"Because I'm not a killer. I'm not even violent."

"But weren't you a pro football player? And a police officer? Most people consider those violent professions."

"I mostly sat on the bench. Coach didn't think I had that 'killer instinct,' he called it. And I became a cop so I could uphold the law and help people. I had a terrific record, until, oh God . . ."

More sobbing and more Kleenex. It made my stomach turn.

"Take your time, Barry. You say you can't remember any of the murders. What is your last memory, prior to your brain operation?"

"The last thing I can really remember clearly was getting drunk on my couch after work, trying to make it go away."

"Trying to make what go away, Barry?"

"The pain. In my head."

"Your last memory is of a headache?"

"A terrible headache. I thought my head would explode. Aspirin didn't help, so I drank a bottle of rum to make the pain stop."

"When was this?"

"Sometime in late spring. May, maybe."

"Why didn't you go to a doctor?"

"I don't remember. I don't remember anything after that. Maybe I did go to a doctor."

"When you woke up in the hospital, after your operation, what was your first thought?"

"I thought I was in the hospital because I drank too much and fell down some stairs or something."

"And how did you react when you were told you'd been shot after murdering your wife?"

More sobbing. Garcia made a show of getting a second box of tissues from the defense table.

"I thought it was some sick joke. I still can't believe it. Everyone is telling me I've done horrible things, things I would never do. And all the evidence says I did them. But I can't remember them. How would you feel if someone said you murdered your wife? Oh my God . . ."

More crying.

"Settle down, Barry. It's okay."

"No, it's not okay. It will never be okay. Do you know I haven't slept for more than two hours a night since this began? I should have gone to a doctor, or a shrink, or . . ."

"Or what, Barry?"

"Or killed myself. If I had killed myself, all of those people would still be alive."

Amen to that, I thought. But a glance at the jury told me they didn't share my sentiments.

"Is there anything you'd like to say to the families of those people?" Garcia asked.

"Yes. Yes there is."

Fuller stood up and removed a crumpled piece of paper from his jacket pocket. He held it tenderly in his hands, as if it were a kitten, but as he spoke he didn't have to look at it once.

"I can't say anything that would justify my taking six lives. I can't say anything that would make you forgive me. I can only say that I'm, I'm . . ." He began to cry again. "I'm so, so, so sorry. I wish I could remember their deaths, because that would give me something I could use to hate myself even more. I don't know how any of this happened. My doctors and my attorneys say it was a brain tumor. Maybe that's the case, because I really don't know how I could have done all of this, hurt so many people. If I could return any of those lives I took with my own death, I would. Oh God, I would in a second."

Fuller stood there, blubbering like a baby, for several minutes. Every time he began to speak the sobbing would take over again. And in a moment that would forever be embedded in my brain, I turned to look at the courtroom, and saw at least eight people dabbing their eyes.

Two were on the jury.

"What's your plan of action?" I whispered to Libby. She had on a double-breasted gray pantsuit with champagne stripes. Emanuel Ungaro, she'd told me earlier. I also wore a gray pantsuit, which I picked up at JCPenney's for $89.99. I felt like a hobo about to spit-roast a hot dog over some Sterno.

"No plan."

"You're going to wing it?"

"I'm not going to cross-examine."

"Why not?"

"So Fuller can spout more lies and gain more audience sympathy? Noel and I can't look like bullies—you already did more than enough of that. I don't want to give Fuller's testimony credence by acknowledging it."

The Garcia and Fuller Show went on for another hour, Garcia gently asking questions, Fuller striving for a Tony Award. He managed to produce more tears than an entire season of *All My Children.*

When the judge broke for lunch, Libby and I hauled tail across the street to Cook County jail.

Rushlo was being held in Division 2, a medium security facility. Dorm living, fifty cots to a room, no barred cells. For a man as private as Derrick, I could guess the effect this had on him.

Rushlo's lawyer, Gary Pludenza, met us at the first security checkpoint. He apparently hadn't been able to slough off Rushlo on other counsel.

Libby shook his hand. "Good afternoon, Mr. Pludenza. We've got a new deal for your cousin."

"What's the deal?"

"We have suspicions he's been covering up for Fuller longer than we thought. We want names."

"He won't turn on Fuller. He's made that clear to me several times. He's terrified of him."

"We realize that. We think he will."

"I don't see how. I've begged him, and I can't get through to the guy. He won't even acknowledge me."

"Maybe if you closed your eyes and played dead?" Libby suggested.

Pludenza frowned. "Can we get this over with, please? I have to be at the Daley Center in two hours for a bankruptcy hearing."

"Sounds exciting."

"Yeah, well, we all can't be characters in a Grisham novel."

Through the metal detector, through the security doors, and into the heart of Division 2. Two guards accompanied us, regulation rather than protection. This section of the prison was for nonviolent offenders. Still, Libby and I got a few obscene catcalls from the male population.

Well, Libby did. I convinced myself it was her suit. Even criminals appreciated fashion sense.

We located Rushlo in the rec room, sitting at a steel table, reading a dog-eared *People* magazine. When he saw us, he freaked out.

"I'm not saying anything." He jumped to his feet, head jerking this way and that, searching for an escape route. His cousin put a hand on his shoulder, squeezed.

"It's okay, Derrick. They're coming here with an offer. Hear them out."

"I don't want their offer. They tricked me before."

I sat down, smiled easily. "You don't have a choice, Derrick."

Rushlo stared at me. Well, one eye did.

"I'm not talking."

"You don't have to." Libby handed him some papers.

"What are these?"

Pludenza looked them over, then broke into a big grin.

"They're dropping the charges, Derrick. You're free."

Rushlo turned a pasty shade of white.

"No . . ."

"I'll have you out of here by this evening."

"No . . . you can't let me out."

Libby winked at him. "We can, and we just did. Good timing too. Your buddy's trial is almost over. You guys can have a nice little reunion."

Rushlo began to whimper. I put my hand on his forearm, hiding my revulsion.

"I'd watch your step, Derrick. Fuller is kind of annoyed you didn't cremate the body of Eileen Hutton. I think he'll want to speak to you about that."

Rushlo went from pale white to bright pink. I thought he was going to pop.

"You have to protect me!"

"We'd like to help you, Derrick, but you haven't helped us at all."

I nodded to Libby, and we stood up.

"Please, help me!"

"We can put you into the witness protection program, Derrick. Change your name, hide you someplace. Or, if Fuller stays in jail, you'll never have him to worry about again. Either way, you have to help us before we help you."

His whole body began to shake.

"I . . . I can't!"

"Have a nice life, Derrick. For as long as it lasts."

We walked away.

"Please! PLEASE!"

Libby and I made it back to the courthouse with enough time to indulge in a vending machine lunch.

"Think he'll crack?" she asked, her mouth around a triangularly cut cheese sandwich.

"I was going to ask you the same thing. I think so. The question is: Will he crack in time?"

"Closing arguments should only take a day. But even if the jury is deliberating, I can motion Judge Taylor to allow a surprise witness, and she can call them back into court. Rushlo's got to come clean before they reach a verdict. If Fuller gets off, we can't retry him. Double jeopardy."

I had a bite of tuna on wheat. Soggy.

"Can you filibuster?"

"This isn't Congress, Jack. If I try stalling, Taylor will jump all over me."

"How about trying for some kind of extension or continuance?"

"I've tried, several times. Taylor kept reminding me we had three months to prepare. She'll allow last-minute evidence, but won't postpone the trial so we can get it."

Libby ate more of her sandwich, and then glanced at her watch. A Movado, with diamonds around the bezel.

"Gotta get back to court. You didn't like your sandwich?"

"It tastes like wet paper towels."

Libby raised an eyebrow.

"You okay? Seem kind of off today."

"Got a lot on my mind."

"No kidding. Hey, all's not lost yet. Rushlo might still spill."

Everyone filed back into the courtroom, but didn't stay long. Libby's cross-examination of Fuller was a study in brevity.

"Mr. Fuller, I understand you were in the drama club at Southern Illinois University. What plays did you perform there?"

"I did *Death of a Salesman, Merchant of Venice,* and *Waiting for Godot.*"

"I bet you were excellent." Libby sat down. "No further questions."

Judge Taylor adjourned for the day, with closings to begin tomorrow.

When I got back to my office, Benedict was nowhere to be found. We hadn't spoken since yesterday, and I didn't like any bad blood between us. I called his cell.

"Where are you?"

"I'm meeting with my lawyer."

"Can it wait? The trial is going to end any day now, and we have to finish cross-reffing these missing persons."

"No, it can't wait. Some of us haven't gotten a day off in the past three months."

I bit back my response, and hung up. I'd told him to file for reassignment out of anger, but now I was thinking it might be a good idea. I didn't like the person Herb had become.

I tackled the project solo. Ruled out some names. Followed a few leads to nowhere. Cleared a small section of paperwork off of my floor.

By dinnertime I had a headache. I called home and spoke to Alan, who was getting together with some old friends over at Mirabell's, a German place on Addison. Did I want to come?

I didn't feel very social, but I agreed because I'd blown off Alan for the past few nights. Maybe being around company would help get me out of my funk.

I couldn't have been more wrong.

CHAPTER 40

"Hi, Jack." Alan had been waiting in the bar, and gave me a hug when I entered the German place. He looked good, in black slacks and a gray cardigan. When I pecked him on the cheek I could tell he'd just shaved.

"I'm not in the best of moods," I said.

"It'll be fun." He took my coat and led me through the restaurant. "This is an old friend of yours."

"What old friend?" Then I saw.

Harry McGlade winked at me from his seat. He wore the standard Harry outfit: a wrinkled brown suit and a stained tie.

"Hiya, Jackie. This is my new squeeze, Nora."

"It's Dora." Dora was half McGlade's age, blonde with a streak of pink in her bangs, and the blouse she wore would have been tight on a Barbie doll.

"Yeah, Dora. Sorry, honey."

"Harry called earlier." Alan beamed like a schoolboy after his first kiss. "He wanted to thank you for something. Since you've been in a funk lately, I thought it would be nice if he thanked you in person. He's the guy who was in that made-for-TV movie with you, right? I mean, his character and your character?"

"Yeah." I tried to sound upbeat and enthusiastic. I failed.

Harry didn't have to fake it. "I just got my PI license in the mail this morning. The Illinois Department of Regulations takes their time, but you made good on your word, Jackie. Dinner is on me."

"Great." That sounded even worse.

The waitress came by, a woman in her sixties dressed in a dirndl. Her English was heavily accented with German. She made the mistake of starting with Harry.

"Something to drink, sir?"

"Got any German beer?"

"We've got the largest selection of imported beer in Chicagoland."

"How about Schlitzkreig?" asked Harry.

"We don't have that."

"Krautweiser?"

She shook her head.

"He'll have a Beck's," I told the waitress. "And so will I."

"Make it three." Alan held up three fingers.

"Diet cola with an orange slice, a lemon slice, a lime slice, and a cherry," Dora said.

"Why not just order a fruit salad?" asked Harry.

Dora giggled. I shot Alan a pained look, but his nose was buried in the menu and he didn't see it. I suppose I couldn't blame the guy. Alan didn't know Harry, and I'd never had any reason to mention him.

"Would you like an appetizer?"

"Swastikabobs." This from McGlade, naturally.

"We do not have shish kebab."

Harry shook his head. "No, I said—"

"We'll think it over," I interrupted. The poor waitress loped off.

Alan set the menu down. "I'm going with the wiener schnitzel."

"What's that?" Dora asked in a forced-cutesy way.

"It's veal."

"What's that? Like pork?"

"It's a baby cow." Harry pinched her cheek. "You're so adorable."

Dora's face bunched up. "You're ordering a baby cow wiener?"

"Wiener is German for veal," Alan explained.

"Wanna see my veal?" Harry winked.

Where was that beer?

It came, eventually, and I ordered a second one before taking a sip. If you're stuck in hell, you might as well roast some marshmallows.

Conversation, if it could be called that, centered around McGlade and the various cases he'd been involved in. Dora remained glued to every word. Alan laughed politely when it was called for. I drank.

The food was wonderful, and I had to give Alan credit; he did manage to make me forget about Fuller for a few hours.

"What's the deal with the Fuller trial, Jackie?"

So much for that.

"The deal is, he's going to get off, unless his partner confesses or we locate a runaway prison guard."

"You gotta find someone? Why didn't you tell me?"

"We've got every cop in Illinois, plus Feds, looking for him. What could you do, McGlade?"

"I happen to be a world-famous private investigator, Jackie. And what do I do, Dora?"

She giggled. "You investigate privates."

"Indeed. And I also find people. Gimme the rundown."

The beer had loosened my tongue a tad, so I gave Harry the scoop.

"You got the file?"

"In the car."

"I'd be happy to assist you in this instance. And in return, I only ask a small favor."

"I don't think I can handle any more favors, McGlade."

"This one is easy."

"What is it?"

"I'll tell you when I catch the guard." McGlade winked at me.

Dessert was black forest cake and incredibly strong coffee. Harry made good on his word and picked up the check. Alan tried to reach for it, but I gave him a vicious pinch underneath the table to squelch that idea.

Afterward, McGlade invited us back to his place for a nightcap. Alan got another pinch as a warning, and he made up a nice excuse about having to get home early.

McGlade got the file, Dora gave me a hug good night, and we went our separate ways.

"I'm getting the impression that Harry isn't your favorite person." Alan grinned at me when we got into the car.

"You picked up on the subtle nonverbal clues?"

"That, and all night you kept muttering *'idiot'* under your breath."

"Was I right?"

Alan laughed. "You were right. He's a character, though. Think he'll find that guard guy?"

"He couldn't find snow in Alaska."

Alan put his hand on the back of my neck. Rubbed.

"You haven't been yourself lately. You okay?"

"Everyone keeps asking me that. I'm a little tense, that's all."

"Want to talk about it?"

"I'm fighting with Herb. We're losing this case. I walked in on Mom and Mr. Griffin."

Alan laughed. "You did too? He's spunky, for an old guy."

"Spunky? The man's a jackrabbit. He's going to break Mom's other hip."

"Anything else bugging you?"

There was an implied, *anything with us?*

I told him no, but that wasn't true. There *was* a problem with us. Every time I got home from work, I half-wondered if Alan would still be there. He left me once. He could do it again. So to protect myself, I was holding back.

I had to. Until I was sure.

"I'm glad." Alan moved his hand from my neck to my leg.

"Don't start something you can't finish."

"Oh, I may not be Jackrabbit Griffin, but I think I can finish okay."

And when we got back to my place, he proved that he could.

CHAPTER 41

The call came at four in the morning.

"I got him."

I tried to open my eyes, but the Ambien wouldn't let me.

"Who is this?"

"It's Harry. Duh."

"What do you want, McGlade?"

"The bull. The guard. I got him."

That got my eyes open.

"You're kidding."

"Why would I kid?"

"Where are you?"

"I'm in the lobby of the Four Seasons. He's in room 3604, under the name John Smith. Real creative, huh?"

I shook my head, tried to get my thoughts clear.

"How'd you find him?"

"I'll tell you when you get here. Bring a warrant."

Judge Taylor wasn't happy about being woken up in the middle of the night, but because she knew the immediacy of the situation, she understood. I stopped by her place on Cumberland, and then went to the hotel.

McGlade greeted me at the entrance with a canary-eating grin.

"How the hell did you manage this?"

"I told you. I'm a world-famous private investigator."

"Spill."

"Well, I knew you guys would have checked the airports, bus terminals, and train stations, and since the guy didn't have a car, I figured he'd still be in the city. You froze his accounts, so he couldn't use his credit cards. That meant he had to pay with cash. So I touched base with some of my friends at a few dozen local hotels, asking if anyone checked in lately paying in cash. Got a hit here, and confirmed it when the doorman saw the picture."

"Harry, I gotta admit it, I'm amazed."

"Yeah. Sometimes I amaze myself. You ready to crack some skulls, partner?"

I nodded. We entered the building, all crystal chandeliers and polished marble, and I hit the button for the lobby.

"So, you owe me a favor, right?"

"Anything you want, Harry, as long as it doesn't involve either of us getting naked."

"You wish. You remember my movie? *Fatal Autonomy*?"

"Unfortunately."

"Well, I'm talking with the producer, and he's considering turning it into a series."

"That blows my mind."

"Mine too. One of the Baldwin brothers is going to play me this time. They want to get that fat actress who played you to reprise her role. There's a little matter of permission, though."

My good mood lost a smidgen of goodness.

"Please, Jack? I found this guy for you, right? You owe me one. They love your character, and don't want to do a series without her."

I sighed. "Fine."

McGlade opened his arms to hug me, but I advised him against it.

The elevator spit us out on the seventh floor. We passed a table stacked high with cut flowers, and made our way to the second set of elevators. McGlade pressed the number 36.

"Nice hotel." He tapped the marble-inlaid floor with his shoe. "Reminds me of a HoJo I stayed at in Jersey."

When the elevator stopped, we found the room without difficulty.

"Mr. Rohmer! Chicago Police Department. Open up. We have a warrant."

No answer.

"Mr. Rohmer! Open the door, sir!"

Nothing.

"I'll get a manager." Harry trotted off. I continued knocking for another five minutes, before a desk clerk came over, smiling nervously.

"We'd like to keep this as quiet as possible, so as not to disturb the other guests."

"Sure. Just open up."

He opened it. I went in first, gun in hand. The room was dark, but I noticed two things immediately.

First, the television was on, playing the kind of movie that men watch when they're alone.

Second, Mr. Rohmer was on top of the bed, naked and grasping his veal. He was also quite dead.

"You could try mouth-to-mouth," Harry suggested. "He'd probably like that."

I might have tried, too, but I'd been around enough corpses to know he'd been dead for at least an hour.

Harry shook his head. "And they say pornography is harmless."

I turned off the TV, cursing bad luck, fate, and timing in the same breath.

"Oh, dear." The manager made worried mother-hen noises. "We can't let this get out."

"It'll make a good headline." Harry put his arm around the clerk's shoulders. "Crooked Department of Corrections Employee Wanks Himself to Death at Four Seasons."

"Oh, dear."

"At least he died happy."

I called it in, then flipped on the lights and spent ten minutes tearing the room apart. I found a few grand in cash, and nothing else.

"Get anything?" I asked McGlade.

"Just an almost new bottle of baby oil."

"No tape?"

"No tape. It's not here, unless he's hiding it in a body cavity. I'll roll him over if you wanna check."

I rubbed my eyes. Cops came, and paramedics.

"Probably a heart attack or a stroke," said a uniform.

"More like a lot of strokes," Harry said.

My cell rang. I went into the hallway to answer.

"Daniels."

"Lieutenant? This is Gary Pludenza, Derrick Rushlo's lawyer. Derrick would like to talk."

"I won't testify!" Rushlo screamed in the background.

"We need him to testify, Mr. Pludenza."

"He won't do it, but I think he might be able to help you anyway. Can you come here?"

"Where are you?"

He gave me his address, a house in the suburb of Naperville.

"How soon can you get here?"

"Gimme an hour."

I hung up, heading for the elevator. McGlade nipped at my heels.

"You're still going to sign the permission form, right? Jackie? I'll be by in a couple of days, okay? Sorry this didn't work out for you—"

The elevator doors closed, saving me from further pestering.

I took Delaware to Congress, and hopped on 290 heading west. Rush hour was in full effect, and the stop-and-go traffic was a perfect setting for inducing a panic attack. My heart rate doubled, my palms became slick, and I chewed on the inside of my cheek while my brain kept sending me still pictures, like a slide show, of every mistake I'd ever made over my whole life.

By the time I made it to Naperville, I was a wreck.

Pludenza's house reeked of money. It sat in a cul-de-sac in a ritzy development, two stories high with four alabaster Doric columns supporting the roof overhang. The doorbell was hooked up to real bells.

"Thanks for coming, Lieutenant." Pludenza looked about as agitated as I felt. He led me through a grand foyer, my short heels clicking on the terrazzo floor.

"Bankruptcies seem to be on the rise."

"Hmm? Oh. My wife comes from money. It's like living in the Taj Mahal. Derrick is in the den."

The den was an expansive room with vaulted ceilings, black leather furniture, and a beautiful Prairie Wind pool table in colonial maple.

Derrick sat in an armchair, hugging his knees to his chest.

"Is he out yet?" he asked.

"Soon. Closing arguments are today. If you want to keep him locked up, you have to testify."

His head shook violently.

"No. No testifying."

"Then he's going to get out, Derrick. And then he'll come for you. He was a cop. He knows how to find people."

Derrick began to hum, off-tune.

"Did you want something to drink, Lieutenant?"

I asked Pludenza for some coffee, and sat across from Rushlo.

"Derrick, we need to keep him in jail. Do you understand that?"

He nodded.

"I know that you're scared. We can keep you safe. I promise. But you need to help us make sure he doesn't get out."

He nodded again.

"Tell me about Southern Illinois."

His good eye locked on me.

"You know about Southern?"

"I know about you getting kicked out. I know that's where you met Fuller. I know about the body you stole."

"I took her out into the woods, where no one would see. He followed me and watched."

I ventured a guess. "Fuller turned you in."

Rushlo looked at me like I'd just grown donkey ears.

"Barry didn't turn me in. He was the one that told me to do it. He understood."

"How did you meet him?"

"He came up to me, after class. Wanted me to get him and some of his fraternity buddies into the morgue. For hazing week."

"Did you let them?"

"No. I would have gotten kicked out of school. But for fun, I let them see my embalming book. The guys were making jokes, acting tough, because they didn't want to admit being grossed out. But Barry was different. He seemed . . ."

"Interested?"

"More like aroused. Not by the embalming pages. By the reconstruction pages. He liked the trauma pictures. Extreme disfigurement. Stuff like that. So a week later, he came by again, alone. We got to talking. We have a lot in common, you know."

Yeah, I thought. You're both psychotic perverts.

"Were you helping Barry with disposals while in college?"

"No. That didn't happen until I had to leave. During my internship, at the funeral home in Champaign-Urbana. We stayed in touch, and one day he calls me up and says, 'Do you want a fresh one?' "

"A fresh corpse?"

"Yeah. He was still down at Southern. He told me she was untraceable, and he needed my help to get rid of her."

"This was someone he'd killed?"

"Yeah. So I drove down to Southern to pick her up. He'd bloodied her up pretty good, but she was still warm."

Derrick got a faraway look in his one eye; the other one always had a faraway look.

"You buried her in a closed casket with another body."

He fixed both eyes on me, a first for him. "How did you know that?"

"Do you remember the names, Derrick?"

"The girl's name was Melody. Such a pretty girl."

"Melody Stephanopoulos?"

He nodded.

"How about the name of the person you buried her with?"

"Last name was Hernandez, I remember that. Skinny guy. Tongue cancer. Most of his jaw was gone. I put them both in the same coffin, planted them in Greenview Cemetery. It was a beautiful ceremony. Lots of flowers."

I took out a pad and scribbled all of this down.

"How many others were there?"

"Kantner's Funeral Home in Urbana didn't have a crematorium. When I got a job in Chicago, it was much safer. I would still do an occasional two-for-one special, though, if I could get away with it. Cremation is such a waste. You might not believe this, but I think death is sacred. A funeral is a sacred ritual. I think everyone should have a wake, even if it isn't your family kneeling at the casket."

"How many, Derrick?"

"There were about eighteen women, total, over the last fifteen years. I buried nine of them."

"You have names?"

He smiled shyly.

"Of course. I remember them all. Each and every one of them."

"What if you didn't have to testify? What if you just made a statement?"

That flipped the switch in Rushlo. "I won't testify! You can't make me testify!"

"Easy, Derrick. Calm down."

"I won't do it!"

"But you wouldn't have to go to court. You could just . . ."

"I love him."

Pludenza chose that moment to return with the coffee. He handed me a cup and saucer, a wince etched into his face.

"Derrick"—I tried to sound soothing—"Barry wants to kill you."

"I can't betray him like that. He understands me. He's the only one that understands me. But I don't need to make a statement. You can prove Barry killed those women."

"How?"

"He likes to bite. All of the girls I buried had bite marks on them."

"You're sure?"

"I'm positive."

That would be enough. If we exhumed Hernandez and found Stephanopoulos in the casket, with Fuller's teeth marks on the corpse, he'd have to stand trial in Carbondale. And since this was years ago, he wouldn't be able to use the tumor insanity defense.

I set down the coffee without taking a sip, and dug out my cell. Derrick grabbed my pants leg.

"You have to help me."

"I'll send some guards over to watch the house."

"How about the witness program? Where they give people new names?"

I punched in Libby's number. "If Fuller gets out, that's a possibility."

"Can they set me up at another funeral home?"

"We dropped charges against you, Derrick, but I really don't think the FTC, IDPR, or OSHA is going to let you practice again."

He began to cry. I thanked Pludenza and left Libby a voice mail on the way to my car. Then I called Herb.

"What?"

"Look, Herb, we can deal with our squabble later. I'm driving down to Carbondale and I need you to run interference for me."

"Tell me."

I filled him in, and he agreed to set the wheels in motion.

Southern Illinois University was a five-hour drive.

I hopped back on the expressway, my car pointed south.

CHAPTER 42

I was sixty miles away from Carbondale when Libby called.

"The jury's out."

"How was your closing?"

"Not as good as Garcia's." I could picture Libby frowning. "If I were on that jury, I'd vote not guilty."

"If that happens, we need to keep tabs on Fuller until we can get an arrest warrant from Carbondale."

"What're the chances of that?"

"If Rushlo wasn't lying, chances are good."

"Keep me posted."

"You too."

I met the Carbondale chief of police, Shelby Duncan, at Greenville Cemetery forty minutes later. With him were a woman from the Health Department, the county coroner, the assistant director of the cemetery, and several workers.

Herb had made good on his word; the permits were in order, and everyone who needed to be there was there.

The day was cold and miserable, befitting a disinterment. We huddled together, hands in pockets and shoulders scrunched, while the guy operating the backhoe repeatedly dipped the big yellow shovel into the Hernandez plot.

After an hour, he struck concrete. The vault. Illinois cemeteries required all coffins to be placed in a burial vault or grave box. That prevented the earth from collapsing the casket, which would leave the cemetery pockmarked with hundreds of obvious indentations.

Two men in overalls went down the hole to widen the edges, and large spikes with eyeholes were driven into the vault cover. They secured ropes, and the backhoe lifted the section of concrete out of the grave. Straps were then attached to the coffin, and it was brought to the surface and gently placed next to the vault top.

The coroner, a thin reed of a man named Russell Thompkins, brushed off some dirt at the foot of the casket, then fit a special hex key into a small opening. He cranked it, counterclockwise, and the rubber seal broke, releasing a powerful hiss of putrid air that I could smell from ten feet away.

The casket unlocked, Thompkins lifted open the head and squinted inside.

"Two bodies." He pinched the nostrils of his pointy nose with long, slender fingers. "A man and a woman."

"Is that enough?" I asked Chief Duncan. Duncan looked like a stouter version of John Wayne, and must have known it, hence the plaid flannel shirt and cowboy boots.

"It's a damn good start. We need to establish that it's Melody Stephanopoulos, and that your Barry Fuller was involved in her death."

"Did you bring her dental records?"

"Yeah."

"How about the faxes of the bite marks?"

"I've got it all in the car."

I accompanied him to his vehicle, and took what I needed up to the casket.

"We need to find bite marks, ones that match these." I showed Thompkins the papers. He nodded, slipped on some latex gloves, and got to work.

I took out a pair of my own, from the deep pockets of my blazer, and looked into the casket for the first time.

Julio Hernandez occupied the left-hand side. He was skeletal-thin, swimming in the oversized brown suit he wore. His facial features were sunken, recessed, and he had no lower jaw—cancer, Rushlo had mentioned. His mouth and throat were packed with rotten cotton batting.

The smell was so bad I had to take breaths from over my shoulder. Even the best embalming job couldn't prevent decay, and the bacteria had eaten well for years before they too ran out of nourishment and rotted away.

Melody proved to be in much worse shape than Hernandez. She wore no clothing, and her flesh had a light gray cast. The atrocities committed upon her stood out in bas-relief black: a jagged tear across her throat, slits forming X-marks over each breast, a deep gash running from her pubis to her belly button. And dozens of dark, round sores, covering her head to toe like polka dots.

Bites.

The major wounds had been sewn up, the stitches expertly done, though hardly cosmetic. Rushlo's postmortem work.

The coroner snapped pictures, and I borrowed his scalpel and forced it between Melody's cold, dry lips, cutting the mortician's glue that sealed them shut. The blade clicked against teeth. I pried her lips apart and found the suture, looping under her lower gums and up through her septum. I severed the ligature, and attempted to open the mouth.

The mouth didn't comply.

Using the scalpel's handle as a lever, I pried open her mouth until I could get two fingers inside. It took considerable force, and felt like I was being bitten, but I managed to stretch her jaws wide enough to get a penlight inside.

There was a gold crown on her back molar, on the upper left side.

The crown matched the one on Melody's dental records.

The records also showed a filling on the upper right canine, and I easily found that with the light.

"It's Melody."

"Russell?" the chief asked the coroner.

"Too hard to tell. There's a lot of decay."

"I'll settle for your best guess."

"It's possible they're from the same man. I'd need more time, proper equipment, to know for sure."

My cell rang. Libby. I picked up.

"Verdict came in. They didn't take long to free the bastard."

"Hold on a second, Libby." I turned to the coroner. "Is there anything you notice that can prove our guy did this?"

Russell took out a handkerchief and blew his nose.

"Actually, there is something pretty incriminating. See these two bites here, on her inner thighs? There are bite marks in the pictures you gave me, in the exact same places."

Chief Shelby unhooked the radio from his belt. "That's enough for me. I'm calling Judge Dorchester."

"You're getting an arrest warrant?"

"Yes, ma'am, we are."

"Libby," I said into the phone, "don't let Fuller leave the building. Find a cop and arrest him."

"You've got a warrant?"

"Yes. He's being charged with the murder of Melody Stephanopoulos."

"Gladly. Nice work, Jack."

Chief Shelby walked away, barking into his radio, and I stripped off my gloves and headed back to my car.

I wanted to be relieved, but I only felt empty. Empty and tired. The cop part of me would have liked to be there, to see Fuller's face when he got arrested. But mostly I just wanted to put all of this death, this ugliness, behind me.

"Nice work, Lieutenant." Shelby came over, offered his hand. "We'll get started on these other names right away. Looks like you've closed a lot of cases for us today."

"I don't envy you the media circus you'll soon have."

"We'll manage. We're a tough little town. Anyway, thanks for your help. You interested in some supper? Wife's a helluva cook."

"Thanks, Chief, but I have to head home."

The ride back to Chicago was the loneliest five hours of my life.

CHAPTER 43

Melody Stephanopoulos. Barry hasn't heard that name in a long time, but he remembers her.

You never forget your first.

He wonders how they found her. Rushlo, probably. It doesn't matter. What's done is done.

Barry tries to scratch his chin, but the chain isn't long enough; his handcuffs are attached to his ankle restraints.

"I've got an itch on my chin. Can you help out?"

The uniform seated to his right, a cop named Stephen Robertson whom he'd worked with out of the 2–6, scratches his chin for him. Fuller sighs.

"Thanks, man."

The squad car is making good time down Route 57. No lights or sirens, but speeding nonetheless. Fuller can guess how anxious they are to get rid of him. Cops don't like it when one of their own goes bad. It hits a little too close to home.

"I have to go to the bathroom," Fuller says to the driver, a Statie named

Corlis. He has on a snap brim hat and reflector shades, even though dusk has come and gone.

"Hold it in."

"C'mon, gimme a break. I was in court all morning, got declared not guilty, and I'm free for two minutes and the cuffs get slapped on me again. It's been a real bad day, and I really need to take a shit."

"I'm sure Carbondale has johns. You can go there."

"I won't make it. There's a rest area coming up in a few miles. Please."

Corlis doesn't answer. Fuller clenches his sphincter, audibly passes gas.

"Jesus, Barry." Robertson fans the air in front of his nose. "That's disgusting."

Fuller shrugs, trying to look innocent. "Prison food. Not my fault."

"Stop at the rest area," Robertson says to Corlis.

"No stops."

"You can either stop, or trade places with me back here."

"I really have to go." Fuller puts on a million-dollar grin. "I'll be quick."

Corlis glances at his partner in the passenger seat, another state trooper named Hearns. Hearns shrugs.

Corlis flips on his signal, and turns into the rest area.

Route 57 is a divided highway, the lanes separated by thirty yards in stretches. This oasis sits between the north and south lanes, serving travelers going in either direction.

Perfect, Fuller thinks.

"Does anyone have change for the vending machine? I haven't had any junk food in three months."

No one answers. Fuller nudges Robertson.

"You got a buck? I'm good for it."

Robertson rolls his eyes, fishes a dollar out of his pants.

"Thanks, man."

The car stops, and Fuller's door is opened. He steps out, tries to stretch, but the shackles prevent it.

Hearns takes off his ankle irons. Fuller thrusts his wrists forward, but Hearns shakes his head.

"How am I supposed to wipe my ass with cuffs on?"

"You know procedure. I should cuff you from behind. That would make it even harder."

"Maybe Robertson will help you," Hearns says.

Snickering from Hearns and Corlis. Fuller chuckles too, and takes a quick look around. They've parked away from the other vehicles: four cars, plus two semis. On the other side of the rest area, the side servicing cars going north, there are three more cars and another truck.

Fuller guesses there are between ten and twenty people here, all taking potty breaks.

Corlis stays with the car, and Robertson and Hearns escort Fuller up the sidewalk to the building. It's typical of rest areas in Illinois—a Prairie-style ranch, brown with oversized glare-reducing windows, surrounded by a copse of firs. This one has a large roof, giving it the appearance of a toadstool.

In the lobby sits a large, illuminated map of Illinois, a brochure rack filled with tourist attractions, and the requisite vending equipment. Fuller pauses in front of a soda machine, feeds in his dollar, and selects an Orange Crush.

Robertson and Hearns herd him into the men's room. Fuller notes two little boys at the urinals, a black guy washing his hands, and a bald man adjusting his comb-over in the stained mirror. It smells of urine and pine disinfectant. The tile floor is wet from people tracking in rainwater.

Fuller goes into the nearest stall and closes the door, latching it behind him. He sits on the toilet seat with his pants still on, and removes his leather loafer and his white athletic sock. His shoe goes back on, sockless. He places the can of Crush into the sock and pushes it down to the toe. Holding the sock firmly by the open end, he stands and takes a deep breath.

Time slows. Fuller can feel his vision sharpen. Whole encyclopedias of sensory input bombard him; the sound of a toilet flushing, Hearns talking to Robertson about football, the two boys giggling, his bare toes rubbing against the inside of his shoe, the weight of the sock in his hand, the throbbing in his temples . . .

Throbbing that is about to stop.

He opens the door and sights Hearns, swinging the can at the trooper's right temple, putting his weight into it.

The Crush can explodes on impact, and there's a burst of orange soda and red blood that hangs in the air a millisecond after Hearns hits the floor.

Robertson reaches for his gun, but Fuller brings his large fists together and clubs him across the jaw, bouncing him off of the sink counter.

He kneels next to Hearns, and pushes the button on his safety holster to release the Colt Series 70, a .45 with seven in the clip and one in the chamber.

The first one goes into the back of Hearns's head.

A scream; the two little boys. Fuller winks at them. The comb-over guy scrambles for the door, and gets one in the back. The black guy is backing up into the corner, his hands over his head.

"I'm cool, man. I'm cool."

"Not anymore." Fuller shoots him twice in the face.

Robertson is on the ground, moaning, slapping at his holster in a most comical way.

"Thanks for the dollar," Fuller tells him, arm extending. "I guess I won't have to pay you back after all."

He ends Robertson with a cap to the dome, and it's the messiest one yet. He takes Robertson's gun, a Sig Sauer 9mm, and his wallet and badge. Then he goes back to Hearns and locates the handcuff keys in the trooper's breast pocket. He removes the cuffs, and also takes the trooper's badge and wallet; it will take longer to ID the body and sort out what happened.

Crying, to the left. Fuller swings the gun around.

The two little boys are hugging each other, hysterical.

Fuller smiles at them. "You kids stay out of trouble, you hear?"

They both nod so eagerly Fuller laughs. The pain in his head is a memory, the adrenaline pounding through his veins makes him feel like he's woken up after a very long slumber.

He steps out into the lobby. Two people stare at him, a man and a woman. As expected, people don't tend to believe violence when it happens around them. They had probably been asking each other, "Were those gunshots?" "No, they couldn't be."

Wrong.

He squeezes off three rounds. One catches the man in the chest, one hits the woman in the neck, and the last flies between them and finds the tinted glass window, punching through with a spiderweb of cracks.

Fuller drops the Colt, checks the Sig. It's a P229, chambered for 9mm. Thirteen-round clip, plus one in the throat. He thumbs off the safety and walks into the women's bathroom.

Empty, except for a stall. An elderly woman opens the door.

"You're in the wrong bathroom."

"Nope." Fuller grins. "You are."

The Sig has a lighter recoil than the Colt, and the results aren't as messy.

Fuller turns back to the door and eases it open a crack. Corlis bursts into the lobby, his .45 clutched in a two-handed grip.

Unfortunately for him, he's looking in the direction of the men's room, rather than behind him.

Fuller gives him four in the back. Corlis sprawls onto his face, arms and legs splayed out like a dog on ice. He's still clutching the gun in his right hand, but Fuller is on him in four steps and he stomps hard on Corlis's wrist. The hand opens, and Fuller shoves the Colt into the front of his pants.

He kneels next to Corlis and speaks above the man's whimpering.

"Thanks for stopping, buddy. I appreciate it."

At this close range, the Sig does quite a job on the trooper's crew cut.

Minding the blood, Fuller takes the wallet and badge, and exits through the opposite doors, the side where the cars are going north. The semi is still there, parked off to the side. Fuller walks over, then uses the side bar to hoist himself onto the running board. He peers into the cab.

The driver is at the wheel, eyes closed and snoring pleasantly. The guy is white, mid-forties, and his brown hair is cut into a mullet.

Haven't seen one of those in a while, Fuller thinks.

He holds up Robertson's badge and taps on the window. The guy wakes up, startled.

"What's going on, Officer?"

"Please step out of the vehicle, sir."

"What's going on?"

"I need you to step out of the vehicle, please."

The man complies. He's awake now, and copping an attitude. "What's the problem?"

"No problem. I didn't want to get your blood in my new truck."

Two in the chest, and Fuller takes the man's keys and wallet, hops into the driver's seat, and starts the engine.

He figures he has a twenty-minute lead. That will be enough to get him to Interstate 80, and from there, he can take back roads and side streets.

Fuller flips on the CB, and switches it to the police frequency. Standard chatter, no mention yet of his little dalliance.

He yanks the Colt out of his pants and sets it on the passenger seat. The Sig he keeps on the dashboard. Fuller pulls out onto the highway.

He's two miles away from I-80 when the news breaks. Fuller picks up the mike.

"This is car 6620. Suspect is an African American male, five feet ten inches tall, in his mid-thirties, driving a brown sedan. He was last seen heading south on Route 57. Over."

"Car 6620, what's your position?"

Fuller smiles, doesn't answer. That will keep them confused for a few more minutes. He merges onto I-80, squad cars screaming past him. A large green sign reads: CHICAGO 40 MILES.

"Ready or not, Jack. Here I come."

CHAPTER 44

"You've always been like this, since you were a little girl."

Mom sat on the sofa with Mr. Griffin, who had fallen asleep sitting up, his head tilted back and his mouth open wide enough to drive a car into. She removed the half-finished drink from his hand—I guessed it to be a bloody Mary from the red color and the celery stick—and raised it to her own lips.

"Been like what?" I asked.

"Been moody, when you should be happy. Remember when you won your first medal in tae kwon do?"

"No."

"You won it for sparring. You must have been eleven or twelve. I think you were eleven, because you were wearing pigtails and on your twelfth birthday you declared yourself a grown-up and that you'd never wear pigtails again."

"Do all old people ramble on like you?"

Mom smiled at me. "We do. When you turn sixty, you get a license to ramble from the federal government."

"Mine may come in the mail, in the time it takes you to finish this story."

Mom sipped the drink and shuddered. "No wonder he's asleep—he managed to fit a whole bottle of vodka into a ten-ounce glass. Now, what was I saying?"

"You were rambling about my tae kwon do competition."

"You'll miss my rambling someday. So anyway, there you were, with all the winners, and the grand master put the gold medal around your neck, just like he did with the others in the row. Every one of them was smiling. Every one of them, except for you."

"I remember now."

"You always tried too hard to win, but when you did, you never seemed happy."

"That's because I was thinking of the next match, and wondering if I'd win that."

Mr. Friskers hopped onto the sofa and bumped his head into my mother's thigh, demanding to be petted. She complied, eliciting a deep, throaty purr from the cat.

"You can't let the uncertainty of tomorrow interfere with the joy of today, Jacqueline. May I offer a little bit of wisdom?"

"I thought that's what you were doing."

"You should be taking notes. This is the meaning of life I'm talking about."

"I'm all ears, Mom."

My mother took a deep breath, sat up straighter. "Life," she said, "isn't a race that can be won. The end of the race is the same for all of us—we die."

She smiled at me.

"It's not about winning the race, Jacqueline. It's about how well you run."

That sounded vaguely familiar.

"In other words, it's not if you win or lose, but how you play the game?" I said.

"I prefer my analogy."

"How about something simpler? Like, 'Try to have fun'?"

"That works too."

I pulled myself out of the rocking chair, destination: kitchen. Alan had his head in the fridge.

"My mom says I need to have fun."

Alan looked at me. "I'll agree with that."

"So maybe we can go do something fun."

"A movie?"

"I just saw two of them."

"A few drinks?"

"That's a possibility. What else?"

"Dancing?"

"Dancing? I haven't been out dancing since kids were spinning on their heads on sheets of cardboard."

Alan held my arms, drew me close.

"I was thinking something more adult. Something that involved moving slowly to old Motown classics."

"I'll get my shoes."

I kissed Alan on the cheek and went back to the living room. Mom was trying, unsuccessfully, to get Mr. Griffin's mouth to stay shut. Every time she eased it closed, it yawned back open.

"Alan and I are going out dancing." I plopped on the sofa and slid on my flats.

"Good. Take your time. I may wake Sal up and do a little dancing of our own."

I leaned over, reaching for my cell phone on the table.

"Leave it, Jacqueline."

"My phone?"

"It's a phone? I'm sorry—I thought it was a leash."

I left the phone where it sat.

"Fine. See you in about two hours."

"No sooner. You're putting a cramp in my love life."

I pecked her on the forehead. "Love you, Mom."

"Love you, Jacqueline. And I'm proud of you. I raised a pretty good daughter."

"The apple never falls far from the tree. See you later."

From the sofa, Mom waved me and Alan good-bye.

CHAPTER 45

Fuller ditches the truck on the West Side and takes a cab to Jack's apartment. He pays with Robertson's cash, and quickly cases the building.

No doorman. The security door is a joke for a guy his size—one solid kick from a size thirteen and the door opens with a bang.

He knows Jack's apartment number. While in prison, he would recite her address over and over and over again. A mantra.

His patience is about to be rewarded.

Another kick. The apartment door buckles in.

Fuller, gun in hand, strolls into the living room and finds two old people on the couch, holding each other. He laughs.

"Were you just necking?"

The old man, eighty if he was a day, stands up with his fists bunched. Fuller ignores him, walking through the kitchen, finding the bedroom and bathroom empty.

"Get out of here, right now."

The old man points a finger at him.

Fuller asks, once, "Where's Jack?"

The man reaches for the phone.

Fuller hits him with the butt of the Sig, busting open the old guy's head like a piñata. The fossil falls to the ground, twitching and bleeding out.

The old woman is still on the sofa, gnarled hands trying to work a cell phone. Fuller slaps it out of her hands.

"You must be Mom. Jack's told me so much about you."

The woman stares at him. Fuller sees fear. But he sees anger too. And a hardness that he's never seen in prey before.

"You must be Barry. Jack has mentioned you as well. Still humping dead hookers?"

Fuller laughs, despite himself. Gutsy old bitch. He sits next to her. The sofa creaks with his weight.

"Where's Jack?"

"You're not only a disgrace to police officers everywhere, you're a disgrace to the human race."

"Yeah, yeah, yeah. I'm a big disappointment to everybody. Now, where's Jack?"

The mother sits up straighter.

"I spent half my life putting scum like you behind bars. I'm not telling you anything."

"Tough talk. But you'll tell me, sooner or later. I can be very convincing."

"I doubt that, Barry. I've seen you play football. You're a real candy-ass."

He doesn't use the gun—doesn't need to. Her bones are old and brittle.

Snap! There goes an arm.

Snap! There goes a leg.

Fuller laughs. "Didn't anyone tell you to take calcium supplements?"

He cuffs her across the face, feeling the cheek shatter.

The old woman's face is wet with tears and blood, but she doesn't make a sound. Not even when he grabs her broken arm and twists.

"Where's Jack?"

The attack catches him off-guard. Something hits him in the face. Something soft, yet sharp.

Fuller cries out in surprise. There's a yowling sound, and the thing attached to his face is digging at his left eye, scratching with needle-sharp claws.

A cat. Stuck tight.

Fuller grabs. Pulls.

Mistake. The cat holds on, and Fuller almost tears out his own eye.

He punches the cat. Once. Twice.

It drops off and limps away.

Fuller is in agony. The eyelid is rapidly swelling shut, his eye a hot coal burning in the socket.

Both hands pressed to his face, he stumbles through the apartment, finds the bathroom.

The Elephant Man stares back at him in the mirror. His left eye has puffed out to the size of a baseball.

Fuller lashes out, smashing his reflection with a meaty fist. He finds some gauze pads in the medicine cabinet, presses one to his face, and howls.

He needs a doctor. Without medical attention, he'll lose the eye. And the pain—Jesus—the pain! He searches the bathroom and finds a bottle of ibuprofen. He takes ten.

What next? What to do next? A hospital? No. Can't risk it. He needs a safe place. To heal. To plan.

Fuller hurries back through the kitchen, stepping over the mess left by the dead guy, and pauses briefly in the living room. Jack's mother is lying facedown on the carpet. Dead? Possibly. No time to check. He speeds out the door, down the stairs, and onto the cold, wet streets of Chicago. After a frantic moment of wondering what to do, Fuller hails a taxi and knocks on the driver-side window. The driver rolls it down.

"You need a cab?"

The guy has an accent. Indian, maybe, or somewhere in the Middle East.

Fuller says nothing.

"You okay? You are bleeding."

"You are too."

He places the Sig against the man's head and fires, causing quite a mess on the passenger side. Then Fuller opens the door, shoves the guy over, and hits the gas.

He stops the taxi under a bridge, searches the driver's pockets. A cell phone. A wallet, with a few hundred bucks. A set of house keys.

Fuller checks the driver's license. Chaten Patel, of 2160 N. Clybourn.

"Thanks for inviting me over, Mr. Patel. Do you live alone?"

Fuller pulls back into traffic.

"I suppose we'll find out."

CHAPTER 46

When I pulled onto my street and saw the flashing lights in front of my apartment, I knew. I threw the car into park, got out, and ran.

"Jack!" I faintly heard Alan call after me.

Herb was standing in the lobby. He saw me, and rushed over to hug.

"Jack, we thought he got you."

"Fuller?" I managed.

"Killed three cops and a bunch of others, escaping."

My eyes welled up.

"M-Mom?"

"They're about to bring her down."

"Dead?"

"No, but she's in bad shape."

I pulled out of Herb's grasp, raced up the stairs.

Cops, paramedics, a crime scene unit. Pained looks from people I knew. A black body bag, on the floor of my kitchen.

My breath caught. I unzipped the bag.

Mr. Griffin, half of his head missing.

I pushed into the living room, saw the stretcher, watched some horribly beaten body being intubated.

". . . oh no . . ."

I rushed to her side, unable to reconcile it in my head, unable to believe that this broken, bleeding thing was my mother.

Her hand was cool and limp. The paramedics pushed me away. I wanted to follow, wanted to go with her, but my legs gave out and I collapsed onto the floor.

Something brushed against my leg.

Mr. Friskers.

I grabbed the cat and held him tight and cried and cried and cried until nothing more came out.

CHAPTER 47

Doctors came and went, talking about Glasgow Scales and Rancho Los Amigos levels of cognitive functioning. I was too numb to pay attention. I only knew that Mom wouldn't wake up.

Two days passed, or maybe it was three. People visited and stayed for a while and left. Alan. Herb. Libby. Captain Bains. Harry. Specialists and nurses and cops.

Guards were posted outside my door. I found this amusing. As if Fuller could possibly hurt me more than he already had.

Benedict kept me updated on the manhunt, but the news was always the same: no sign of Fuller.

"She's probably going to die," I said to Herb.

"We'll get him."

"Getting him won't make her better."

"I know. But what else can we do?"

"I should have been there."

"Don't play that game, Jack."

"I should have killed Fuller when I had the chance."

"This isn't helping the situation."

I got in Benedict's face. "Nothing will help this situation! This is my mom, lying here. And she's lying here because of me. Because of my job."

"Jack . . ."

"To hell with it, Herb. To hell with all of it."

My star was in my pocket. I held it out, made Benedict take it.

"Give this to Bains. I don't want it anymore."

"He won't accept it, Jack."

"He'll have to."

Benedict clutched my badge and got all teary-eyed on me.

"Dammit, Jack. You're a good cop."

"I wasn't good enough."

"Jack . . ."

"I'd like you to leave, Herb." I watched my words register on his face. "And please don't come back."

CHAPTER 48

He watches Detective First Class Herb Benedict leave the hospital. Unlike Jack, Herb doesn't have an armed escort.

Big mistake.

Herb climbs into his late model Camaro Z28, starts it up. Fuller starts the cab and follows Herb out of the parking lot, turning left onto Damen.

It's nighttime, cold enough to need the defrosters. The cab smells like blood; Fuller never bothered to clean up after dispatching the hack. Normally it's a smell he enjoys, but pain is playing tug of war in Fuller's head, his injured eye and his unrelenting headache each vying for top honors.

The eye has gotten worse. It's infected, there's no doubt. Fuller can't open the lid, and it's leaking a milky, foul-smelling fluid.

Goddamn cat.

The throbbing in his head has returned with a vengeance too. It's even worse than before the operation. Fuller wonders if the doctors really got all of the tumor out. Perhaps they'd left a teeny-tiny piece in his brain, and it keeps getting bigger and bigger every day, growing like a seed.

Benedict parks alongside the street, in front of a health food store. Fuller waits until he leaves the vehicle and enters the shop. Then he pulls into an alley.

Fuller doesn't think Herb will be tough to handle, but he's no geriatric, either. He has a plan to keep the cop under control.

Two days ago, Fuller shot a street corner dealer and relieved him of his stash. He scored a lot of reefer (which Fuller thought might help his eye but didn't do a damn thing), a few grams of coke, and three balloons of black tar heroin, complete with works.

The heroin went down smooth. Fuller boiled the needle first and had no problem tapping a vein—it reminded him of his steroid days.

Blessed pain relief.

The last hit he took, a few hours ago, is wearing off. He has one syringe left, resting safely in the inside breast pocket of his jacket, a piece of cork on the tip.

He prefers to use it on himself, but if Benedict gets rowdy . . .

Speaking of, the portly detective comes out of the health food store with a protein bar. His attention occupied with unwrapping the snack, Fuller sidles up behind him.

Benedict spins around, reaching for his gun, but Fuller anticipates the move and grabs Herb's wrist. His grip tight, he gets behind Benedict and applies a hammerlock, one arm around his neck, another pinning Herb's wrist behind his back.

"Hello, Detective. Glad to see you're watching your health."

Benedict reaches for his shoulder holster with his free hand and Fuller tightens the submission hold. Benedict is strong, but not strong enough. With a quick jerk, Fuller yanks upward on the older man's arm. Benedict's elbow hyperextends, and then blows out.

Herb is yelling now, fighting like crazy, but Fuller has a firm grip on his bad arm and levers him into the alley. He forces Benedict to his knees, pulls the cork from the needle with his lips, and jabs the fat man in the neck.

Benedict continues to resist, but slowly, sweetly, the energy goes out of him.

Fuller replaces the cork, tucks away the syringe, takes Herb's gun, and muscles him into the back of the cab.

Then he goes prowling for more smack.

The taxi makes him invisible—urban camouflage—so he's free to cruise parts of the city where a Caucasian might ordinarily stand out. He drives to 26th and Kedzie, an area known as Little Mexico. It doesn't take long to find a young Hispanic male hanging out on a corner. Cold night to be just hanging out, alone.

He circles the block twice, and then stops. The youth walks over in the wide, unhurried gait of a young man whose pants are too baggy.

"Tienes cocofan?"

The Latino has a little peach-fuzz goatee, and a gold crucifix hanging from his ear. *"Que?"*

"Cocofan, puto. Zoquete. Calbo. Perlas?"

"Calbo?"

"Yes, jackass. Heroin."

"No tengo calbo. Tengo Hydro, vato."

Fuller sighs, and shoots the kid in his sideways-tilted baseball cap.

Rico Suave takes the big dirt nap, and Fuller steps out and gives him a quick pat-down. He finds three loose joints, and six vials of brown granules.

"No calbo my ass."

Fuller squeals tires, heading back to his hidey-hole on Clybourn.

Twice, people try to hail him. Fuller slows down, lets them get close, and then pulls away before they can get in the cab.

Good, clean, American fun.

Benedict moans in the backseat.

"We'll be home soon, Detective."

Chaten Patel shared a residence with his girlfriend. Fuller never got her name. They lived on the ground floor of a two-flat. A modest place, old but clean, with a large basement they used for storage.

The basement currently stores Chaten, and what's left of his woman.

Fuller parks the taxi in the alley behind the house, and half-carries/half-walks Benedict through the backyard and down the steps to the basement entrance. Herb obligingly has a pair of handcuffs in his pocket, and Fuller locks the detective's bad arm to a pipe under the concrete shop sink, and takes his keys.

The corpses have begun to smell, but Fuller won't be here for long. Once Daniels is dead, he's going to make good on his original intent and flee to Mexico.

But first things first.

Upstairs, Fuller fills up a pot with some water, puts it on the stove, and drops in the syringe.

As it boils, Fuller removes a heroin vial from his pocket and shakes out four big chunks. It doesn't look like the black tar he's been using—it's lighter in color, and crumbles easier. He sniffs it. There's no odor of vinegar, a telltale trait of smack.

What did that kid call it? Hydro? Maybe it's a hybrid—heroin and coke, or heroin and XTC.

Fuller doesn't care. It could be heroin and rat poison, and he'll inject it just the same. He needs a break from the pain.

There's a fat candle on the kitchen counter that smells like vanilla. Fuller lights it, dumps the boiling water into the sink, and puts the syringe back together.

Placing the granules in a metal tablespoon, he adds a squirt of water and holds the spoon over the candle flame.

With his free hand he removes a cotton ball from the open bag on the table and rolls it between his fingers until it's the size of a pea. When the drugs are fully dissolved, he puts the cotton on the spoon and watches it expand.

The needle goes into the center of the ball, the plunger is slowly pulled back, and all Fuller has to do is pick a vein and the good times will roll.

Not yet, though. First, he has a phone call to make.

Fuller takes out his cell phone and punches in Jack's number. Then he heads down the basement stairs, to wake up Herb.

CHAPTER 49

My cell phone rang. I ignored it.

Though Mom was nonresponsive to sound and touch, she still had brain activity, so I talked to her.

I talked about a lot of things.

Sometimes I talked about silly stuff, like the weather, or people we used to know. Other times I spilled my guts, apologizing for what happened, begging forgiveness she couldn't give.

Tonight I was in begging mode.

My cell rang, again. I couldn't handle any more condolences. Even from friends. Especially from friends. I finally had to tell Alan to back off, give me room to breathe, or I'd go crazy.

On the positive side, I hadn't taken any sleeping pills in days. I embraced my insomnia.

The phone rang once more. I finally picked it up and shut the damn thing off. I was crying, again, and I didn't want to talk to anybody.

Before I could begin another apology to Mom, the room phone rang.

I let it ring. And ring. And ring. It eventually stopped. Then it started again. Couldn't whoever it was take a hint?

"What?" I answered.

"Hi, Jack."

I almost dropped the phone in surprise. Fuller.

"I was beginning to think you weren't going to pick up. That wouldn't have been good for your friend here. Say hello, Herb."

A male voice screamed.

"Herb's not doing so well. And if you don't follow my directions, he's going to be doing even worse. Here's what I want you to do."

In the background Herb yelled, "It's a trap, Jack! Don't—"

Followed by another scream, even louder than before.

I tried to swallow, but my mouth was dry.

"What do you want, Fuller?"

"Turn your cell phone back on and call me on my cell. When you're ready, I'll give you the number."

I powered up my cell phone and punched in what he told me. It rang once, and he picked up.

"Good. Now hang up the hospital phone. Here's the deal. I want you to come over and join our party. We're having fun, right, Herb?"

Another scream.

"I'll be right over." I clenched the phone so tightly it shook. "Want me to stop for beer and pretzels?"

"Funny. What I want you to do is lose the police escort."

"How?"

"Tell them you got a call from me, and I'm in the parking lot. Be convincing. If you try to give them any signals . . ."

Benedict screamed again.

"Stop hurting him."

"Hurting him? You mean like this?"

I shut my eyes while poor Herb wailed in agony.

"I'll do what you say, Barry."

"Good girl. Remember—I'm listening. Ready . . . go!"

I went into the hallway and yelled at the two cops on duty.

"Fuller just called me! He's in the parking garage!"

They drew weapons and took off down the hall.

"Are they gone?"

"Yes."

"Who's nearby?"

"No one. A nurse."

"Give the nurse the phone."

"Why?"

Mistake. A part of me died inside when I heard Herb's scream.

"Nurse!" I hurried to her. "Someone wants to talk to you."

She gave me a quizzical look. "Who?"

"Just tell him whatever he wants to know."

The nurse took the phone. "No. . . . Nope. . . . Nobody." Then she handed it back. "He wanted to know if there were any men outside the door to room 514."

I growled into the cell. "Satisfied?"

"Not yet. But I will be. Get in your car and go north on Lasalle. I want to hear your voice the whole time."

"What if the cell signal goes out?"

Herb screamed again.

"You'd better make sure it doesn't, Jack. Now keep talking. Start with the ABC's."

I recited the alphabet while I hurried through the corridor. Elevator or stairs? Which was better for cell transmission? I picked the stairs, moving as fast as I could. When I made it down to the parking garage, I saw one of the cops ordered to guard me, his gun drawn, creeping around a corner. I threw my back against a wall so he didn't see me.

"Jack? You there?"

". . . Q . . . R . . . S . . . T . . . U . . ."

I paused for a moment, and then made a beeline for my car, stepping lightly so my footsteps didn't echo on the asphalt.

My cell reception became staticky.

"It sounds like I'm losing you, Jack. I hope not, for Herb's sake. Frankly, I don't know how much more he can take."

I made it to my car and fumbled with the keys, beginning the alphabet for the third time. When I opened the door, one of my cops saw me.

"Lieutenant! We can't find him!"

"Uh-oh, Jack," Fuller purred into the phone. "You'd better hurry."

I hopped in the driver's seat, my cell signal getting even weaker. I was yelling the alphabet now, hoping my louder voice got through. Both cops converged on my car. I jammed it into gear and hit the gas.

The exit was up a concrete ramp.

"Jack?" Barry was yelling. "I can't hear you, Jack. Jack—"

The phone went dead.

CHAPTER 50

Fuller scowls at the dial tone. He hits Redial. Daniels picks up immediately.

"I lost the signal on the exit ramp. I didn't do anything stupid." She sounds anxious, breathless.

"How can I believe you, Jack?"

"Don't hurt him again."

Fuller lifts his foot, ready to stomp on Benedict's dislocated elbow. Herb stares up at him, hate in his eyes.

"We had a deal, Jack."

"If I hear him scream once more, I swear to God, I'm hanging up and throwing my phone out the window."

"How do I know the cops aren't with you?"

"I'm alone. I ditched them in the parking garage."

"Maybe you called for backup, on your radio."

"I didn't have time. If my radio was on, you'd hear it."

Fuller walks away from Herb, takes the Sig out of his belt. He fires a round, up the stairs.

"What did you just do, Barry? Let me talk to Herb."

"That was a warning. If I think you're lying to me, if I think you're bringing more cops, I end Herb Benedict's life. Understand?"

"Let me talk to Herb."

Fuller rolls his eyes. He holds out the phone. "Herb, say something."

Benedict looks away, lips pressed shut.

"Hold on a second, Jack. He's being stoic."

Fuller plays pull'n' bend with Herb's swollen arm until the guy sings like a choir boy.

"Tell her you're okay."

"Jack!" Benedict screams. "Don't come!"

"There, Jack? Satisfied he's still with us?"

"When I get there, Barry . . ."

"Stop it, Jack. You're scaring me. Where are you?"

"Going north on Lasalle."

"When you get to Division Street, take a left. And let's hear that alphabet."

Jack begins the ABC's again, and Fuller goes back upstairs. His head thumps like someone's bouncing a bat off of it, and his eye does its best to compete for the gold medal in the Pain Olympics.

The syringe calls to him from the kitchen table.

One little shot, and the pain will go away.

But Daniels will be here soon. That will also make the pain go away.

The head pain. Not the eye pain. Take the shot.

She's coming armed. It's important to stay alert.

You can handle her. Take the shot.

Fuller lifts the needle. His arms are weight-lifter arms, the veins pushed to the surface by all the muscle. He doesn't need to tie off.

Good.

Fuller shoots up, waiting for the warm rush of heroin to flood through him.

The rush doesn't come.

"What the hell?"

"Barry? Did you say something?"

Fuller grits his teeth, staring at the empty syringe. That little Mexican bastard. What the hell did I just shoot up? Baking soda?

"Barry, I'm going west on Division. Barry?"

"Go right on Clybourn," Barry growls. He raises the syringe to throw it across the room. But then . . .

Something happens.

It's a subtle change at first. The kitchen seems to come into sharper focus. Barry stares at his hand, and his stare magnifies his fist until it's the size of a baked ham.

Barry looks at his feet, and they also seem to grow. He's ten, fifteen, twenty feet tall. How can he fit in this tiny room? A-ha! The kitchen is growing with him, walls getting longer, wider, stretching out and out.

And as he's growing, the pain in his head is shrinking. Until it's a tiny spot—a speck of minor irritation—in the middle of his swollen eye.

Fuller giggles, and the sound echoes through his head deep and slow. He hears someone talking, and notices he's holding a phone.

"Barry? Are you there, Barry? What's the address?"

Address? Oh, it's Jack. She's coming to the party.

"Twenty-one sixty," someone says. It's him. The words feel solid in his mouth, like they're made of clay and he's spitting them out rather than saying them.

This is fun.

He spins in a slow circle. The room moves with him, shifting and bending. When he stops, the room keeps moving, because he wills it to. He can control it. He can control everything.

"I'm a god."

Fuller touches his face, feels the bandage. Gods don't need bandages. He rips it off, and that causes a spark of pain in his eye.

"No more pain." His voice is thunder.

He glides over to the drawer, dumps the contents on the table.

A corkscrew.

It only hurts for a moment, and he cries a lot.

No, he's not crying.

It's blood.

He hears a car outside. A visitor.

All pain is gone now, replaced with something else.

Anger.

Jack Daniels is here. She's the one who put him in jail. She's the one who gave him these headaches.

She's trying to stop him from being a god.

He wipes some blood off of his cheek and balls his hands into fists.

"I'm in here, Jack."

CHAPTER 51

"Fuller? Fuller, dammit, are you there?"

There's no answer. Where was he? Was Benedict still alive? What happened?

I disconnected and dialed 911, giving them the Clybourn address. Then I spun the cylinder on my .38, counted six bullets, and set my jaw.

Fear, anxiety, and all of my other neuroses be damned; I was going to go save my best friend.

I was three steps up the porch stairs when the door swung open.

Fuller filled the doorway, arms stretching out as if offering me a hug. His face was awash with blood, a gaping hole where his left eye used to be.

Training took over. I brought up my gun and grouped three shots in the midsection.

Rather than fall back, Fuller did something unexpected.

He lunged.

I caught him in the shoulder with the fourth shot, and then he was on me, knocking me backward, onto the sidewalk, him on top.

I felt a rib or two crack under his weight, motes of light exploding in front of my eyes. My gun arm was over my head. I tried to bring it around, but Fuller grabbed it, his enormous hand swallowing mine and my weapon. I fired, and the bullet ripped through his palm, forcing out a collection of small bones. But he didn't let go.

Fuller's other hand moved up my body, and closed around my neck.

It rained blood, dripping from his face onto mine. I squeezed my eyes shut and brought up my free hand, digging at his empty socket.

Fuller howled, rolled off me.

I aimed my last bullet at his head, but he shifted and I missed.

Breathing hurt. I pressed my hand to my ribs, and it helped a little. I managed to get to my knees, then my feet.

So did Fuller. He faced me, gushing blood from too many places to count. But he didn't seem bothered by that fact, as evidenced by the wide grin on his face.

I found my center, reared back, and aimed a reverse kick at the holes in his chest.

It was like kicking a tree. He didn't budge an inch.

I spun around, using the gun as a bludgeon, and cracked him across the cheek.

The blow snapped his head back, but he didn't stagger.

He swung at me, slow, and I got under it and drove a fist into his ribs, pulling away before he could grab me.

Another swing, and he didn't come close to connecting. I kicked upward, between his legs, and missed, bouncing harmlessly off his massive thigh.

Fuller lashed out again, faster this time. I pulled back, but his knuckles caught my cheek. I rolled with the blow, hitting the frozen grass, yelping when my ribs bumped the ground.

A gunshot. Then another.

Herb.

He was at the top of the porch, his right arm hanging at his side, twisted in a funny way, handcuffs on his wrist attached to a piece of metal pipe.

In his left hand he held a semiautomatic.

Benedict couldn't hit an elephant from five paces with his left hand.

Luckily, Fuller was damn near as big as an elephant.

Herb's third shot connected with Fuller's chest. The fourth went wide, but the fifth buried itself into his right leg.

I heard sirens in the distance. Just a little longer.

Fuller rushed at Herb, incredibly fast. Benedict's next shot missed, and then he got buried under three hundred and fifty pounds of snarling, screaming, bleeding muscle.

I staggered to my feet, forced myself up the stairs. Out of bullets, I began to hammer at Fuller's skull with my .38, putting my whole body into it, trying to get him off Herb. Herb's face went from red to blue.

On the fourth hit, Fuller backhanded me, then climbed off of Herb and went stumbling into the house.

Benedict choked for breath. I felt his throat; there didn't seem to be anything broken.

Herb mumbled something.

"What, Herb?"

"Get out of here. He's got a . . ."

The slug flew over my head close enough that I felt the wind. I dropped down on the porch, on top of Herb, and peered into the house.

Fuller, impossibly, stood in the hallway in a quickly spreading puddle of his own blood. The Colt in his hand was pointing at me.

Herb raised up his left hand. He still gripped the Sig, but wasn't pointing it anywhere near Fuller.

I grabbed Benedict's wrist, lifted it up, trying to aim.

"I'm a god," Barry Fuller said.

Herb answered, "Bullshit," and he squeezed the trigger and the gun fired, catching Fuller right in the middle of his face and blowing his brains out the back of his diseased head.

CHAPTER 52

Alan located me in the ER, while they were taping my ribs. His face glistened with tears.

He didn't rush to embrace me.

"I can't take this, Jack. I can't live like this. First your mother, and now you."

I thought about telling him that I quit, that I was no longer a cop.

But love doesn't have conditions.

"Good-bye, Alan."

He left his brown bomber jacket on the cot.

A nurse came in, tried to give me a shot of Demerol for the pain.

I declined.

"Is Detective Benedict out of surgery yet?"

"Not yet."

I lay back on my cot and stared at the ceiling.

Cops came, wanting to debrief me. I told them all to go to hell. Captain Bains stopped by. He told me there would always be a spot on the force for me, if I decided to come back.

I laughed in his face.

Five hours later, Benedict was wheeled into recovery. I sat in his room with him until he woke up.

"Hi, Jack." His voice was hoarse, a symptom of a bruised larynx.

"Hi, Herb. They told me your surgery went well. You'll get full use of your arm back."

"Are we okay?"

My eyes teared up.

"We're okay, buddy."

"You're my partner, Jack. You're supposed to tell me when I'm acting like an idiot."

"Maybe we were both acting like idiots."

He nodded. "Can you do me a favor?"

"Sure, Herb."

"Can you call my wife, tell her I'm done being an idiot?"

I smiled through the tears. "I think I can do that."

"Tell her to bring doughnuts."

"I will."

"Two boxes."

"I will."

CHAPTER 53

I spent my days in the hospital, keeping vigil over Mom. Nights I spent at home, alone, staring at the ceiling.

Christmas came. New Year's Eve. Valentine's Day.

Bains refused to accept my resignation, and I got a modest biweekly pension check. I had very few needs. I made do.

Herb was promoted to sergeant, and when he visited, he made me call him Sarge. He traded the Camaro for a Chrysler, and he and Bernice took a two-week vacation in Napa Valley, visiting old friends.

My mother's condition showed some signs of improving. She wasn't coming out of the coma yet, but her Glasgow Scales were getting better, if only slightly. I talked to her, every day. Even when I didn't feel like talking.

"You remember what you told me, Mom? That there are no medals for the completion of a good life? I've been thinking about that. About how no one wins. Like you said, it's impossible to win, because the finish line is death."

I stroked my mother's hand.

"So what's the point? What's the meaning? Why do we all struggle if we're in a race we can never, ever win? You said we should still run the best that we can. The answer isn't in the winning. The answer is in the running. And you know something, Mom? I think you may be right."

The next day, I got off early retirement and went back to work for the Chicago Police Department.

And I ran on.